Geometrical Conics

Including Anharmonic Ratio and Projection, with numerous examples

SALZWASSER VERLAG

Charles Taylor

Geometrical Conics

Including Anharmonic Ratio and Projection, with numerous examples

Reprint of the original, first published in 1863.

1st Edition 2022 | ISBN: 978-3-37500-694-5

Verlag (Publisher): Salzwasser Verlag GmbH, Zeilweg 44, 60439 Frankfurt, Deutschland
Vertretungsberechtigt (Authorized to represent): E. Roepke, Zeilweg 44, 60439 Frankfurt, Deutschland
Druck (Print): Books on Demand GmbH, In de Tarpen 42, 22848 Norderstedt, Deutschland

GEOMETRICAL CONICS.

GEOMETRICAL CONICS;

INCLUDING

ANHARMONIC RATIO AND PROJECTION,

WITH NUMEROUS EXAMPLES.

BY

C. TAYLOR. B.A.

London.

1863.

PREFACE.

THIS work contains elementary proofs of the principal properties of Conic Sections, together with Chapters on Projection and Anharmonic Ratio. The term Conic, elsewhere frequently employed as an abbreviation, is here formally adopted, with reference to the fact that it is no longer usual to define the curves in question as *sections* of a surface. The term Conic Section is introduced in Chapter XI.

In Chapter II., some fundamental propositions are proved by methods applicable to all Conics, a Conic being considered as the locus of a point whose distance from a fixed point bears a constant ratio to its perpendicular distance from a fixed straight line. The propositions of this Chapter have been selected as either important in themselves or useful in their application. To the latter class belong Props. VII., VIII. which are useful in proving the Anharmonic Properties of Conics. Prop. XII., in which the fundamental property of diameters is established, leads to important simplifications. Prop. XIII., which follows immediately from it, has been applied to prove that, in the ellipse, $CV.CT=CP^2$, (p. 81). The Lemma is shown, in the Appendix, to be closely connected with some important properties of central Conics.

It is also shown that Props. IX., X. are geometrically equivalent to the ordinary polar equation of a Conic; whilst Props. III., IV. lead to those of the tangent and chord respectively. The first of these results was pointed out by Professor Adams, to whom I am indebted for notes that have formed the basis of several proofs in the Chapter now under consideration. The above propositions are also useful in establishing theorems not usually proved by elementary geometrical processes (see Ex. 25, p. 22), whilst the interpretation of results is a manifest advantage to the student on his first introduction to analytical methods.

The proposition $QV^2 = 4SP.PV$, in the parabola, has been proved by assuming that $PV = PT$, and that the external angle between any two tangents is equal to that which either of them subtends at the focus; the latter being perhaps one of the most obvious deductions from the fundamental properties of tangents. Another proof has been given (p. 171), which depends upon the definition only.

Prop. II., Chapter IV., viz. that the sum of the focal distances of a point on the ellipse is constant, has been proved without assuming the no less difficult proposition that every ellipse has two directrices. The Lemma being assumed, these results follow as in Chapter II. It is proved conversely, in the Appendix, that an ellipse, defined by the constant sum of its focal distances, may be generated in two ways by means of a focus and directrix.

Prop. XIII., Chapter IV., is new, whilst Prop. VII. has been introduced as an important result admitting of a simple geometrical proof.

Prop. II., in the second Chapter upon the hyperbola, is also new, and has been applied to prove, amongst other theorems, that the portion of any tangent intercepted between the asymptotes is bisected at the point of contact.

I have in general made it an object to prove analogous properties by similar methods, the tendency of this arrangement being to diminish the labour of the student. Compare Props. XV., XVI., Chapter IV.; Props. XIII., XIV., Chapter VI.

In the Chapter on Corresponding Points, the results of Orthogonal Projection are obtained by a method not involving solid geometry. The connection between these methods is shown at the end of Chapter XV.

In Chapter XIII., the fundamental Anharmonic Properties of Conics are proved by general methods which were first exhibited, in the *Quarterly Journal of Pure and Applied Mathematics*, by Mr. B. W. Horne, Fellow of St. John's College.

The principal properties of Poles and Polars are proved, in Chapter XIV., by methods applicable to all Conics. They are also proved for the parabola in Chapter III., and for central Conics in Chapter V.

In the last Chapter, the method of Conical Projection has been explained and illustrated with the help of figures.

The treatment of the subject is elementary and geometrical, no allusion being made to the analytical conception of imaginary points.

The definitions are in a majority of instances placed at the beginnings of the various Chapters; some of the most general are given at the commencement of the work, whilst another class, in which especial explanation is required, may be found by referring to the Table of Contents.

In references, the number of the page has usually been given, except when the proposition referred to occurs in the same Chapter as the reference.

The symbol of equality has been used in stating proportions, as well adapted to express that equality or similarity of ratios by which proportion is defined, and as superior in distinctness to the symbol (::) more commonly employed. The term eccentricity has been defined, and used as a convenient abbreviation throughout the work.

Cambridge, *November*, 1863.

ELEMENTARY COURSE.

CHAPTER I.
" II. Props. 1—3, 5, 6, 9, 10, 12, 13.
" III. " 1—12, 15—17, 19.
" IV. " 1—16, 18—20.
" V. " 1—5, 7—9, 12—14, 16, 18.
" VI. " 1—16, 18.
" VII. " 1—18.
" VIII., X., XI.

CONTENTS.

CHAPTER IV.

CHAPTER V.

CHAPTER VI.

CHAPTER VII.

CHAPTER VIII.

CHAPTER IX.

CHAPTER X.

CHAPTER XI.

CHAPTER XII.

CHAPTER XIII.

CHAPTER XIV.

CHAPTER XV.

APPENDIX.

ERRATA.

Page 25, Figure, dele S. See p. 171.
" 102, After line 12, *insert*
Therefore the supplements HPG, PNH are equal.
" 127, line 4 from bottom, *for* part, *read* point.

GEOMETRICAL CONICS.

DEFINITIONS.

A CONIC is the curve traced out by a point which moves in such a way that its distance from a fixed point, called the *Focus*, bears always the same ratio to its perpendicular distance from a fixed straight line, called the *Directrix.*

Note. Let S be the focus, MX the directrix, P and P' any two points on a given conic. Draw SX, PM, $P'M'$ perpendicular to the directrix, and through P, P' draw any two parallel straight lines meeting the directrix in R, R'. Then by similar triangles PMR, $P'M'R'$,

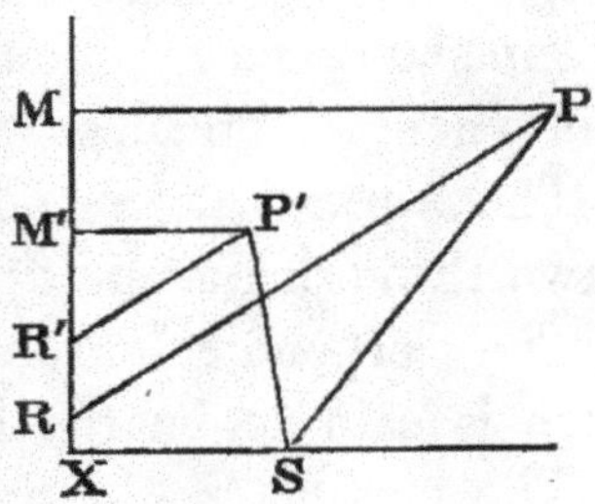

$$PM : PR = P'M' : P'R'.$$

But $\qquad SP : PM = SP' : P'M'$, [*Def.*

Therefore $\qquad SP : PR = SP' : P'R'$. [Euc. v., 22.

Now P' may be any point on the conic, but, whatever be the position of P', the ratio $SP' : P'R'$ is always equal to the ratio $SP : PR$. Hence a conic might have been defined as the curve traced out by a point which moves in such a way that its distance from the focus bears always the same ratio to its distance from the directrix, *measured parallel to any fixed straight line which meets the directrix.* The ordinary definition results from supposing this straight line perpendicular to the directrix.

The *Eccentricity* of a conic is the ratio which the distance from the focus, of any point on the curve, bears to its perpendicular distance from the directrix.

A conic is called a *Parabola*, *Ellipse*, or *Hyperbola*, according as its eccentricity is equal to, less or greater than unity.

The *Axis* is a straight line drawn from the focus perpendicular to the directrix, and the point in which it intersects the conic is called the *Vertex*.

The straight line joining any two points on a conic is said to be a *Chord* of the conic.

The *Latus Rectum* is the chord drawn through the focus at right angles to the axis.

Let P, Q be adjacent points on a conic, as in Prop. I., p. 6, and let Q move along the curve towards P, whilst P remains stationary. Then the chord PQ, in its limiting position, when Q coincides with P, becomes the *Tangent* at P.

The *Normal* at any point of the curve is the straight line drawn through that point at right angles to the tangent.

The perpendicular upon the axis from any point of the curve is said to be the *Ordinate* of the point.

The portion of the axis intercepted between the tangent and ordinate at any point on the curve is called the *Subtangent*.

The portion of the axis intercepted between the normal and ordinate at any point on the curve is called the *Subnormal*.

CHAPTER I.

TRACING THE CURVE.

1. *When the focus, directrix, and eccentricity of a conic are given, any number of points on the curve may be determined.*

For, let S be the focus, MM' the directrix.

Draw SX meeting the directrix at right angles in X, and in SX take a point A such that the ratio of SA to AX may be equal to the eccentricity. Then A is the vertex of the curve.

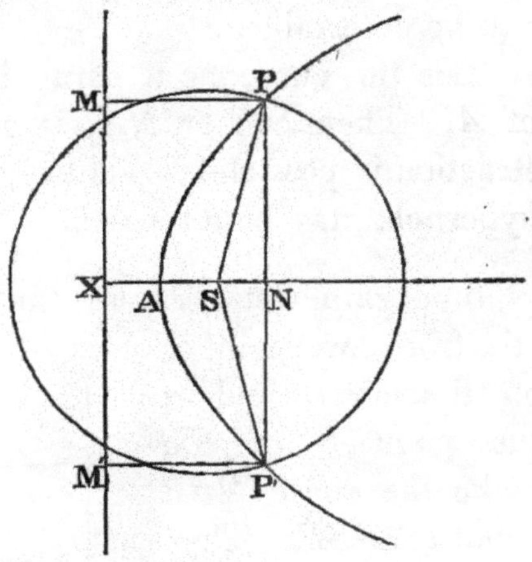

In AS, or AS produced, take any point N, and with centre S, radius SP, such that

$$SP : NX = SA : AX$$

describe a circle cutting in P, P', the straight line drawn through N parallel to the directrix.

Let PM, $P'M'$ be the perpendiculars from P, P' on the directrix. Then PM is equal to NX.

Therefore $$SP : PM = SA : AX,$$

or P is a point on the curve.

Similarly $$SP' : P'M' = SA : AX,$$

or P' is a point on the curve.

Thus any number of points on the curve may be determined corresponding to the various positions of N.

2. *The axis divides the curve into two equal and similar parts.* For, corresponding to any point P at a perpendicular distance PN from the axis, there is a point P' on the other side of the axis and at an equal distance $P'N$ from it.

3. If the point N be taken so as to coincide with A, then SP becomes equal to SN and the points P, P' coincide. In this case the chord PP' is a tangent to the conic. Hence *the tangent at the vertex is perpendicular to the axis.*

4. If the position of N be such that SP is less than SN, the straight line and circle, in the above construction, will not intersect. For such positions of N no points on the curve can be determined.

Let the curve be a parabola and let N lie to the right of A. Then SP, or NX, is greater than SN, and the construction is possible. Similarly, the cases of the ellipse and hyperbola may be discussed.

5. Again, let PM be the perpendicular on the directrix from any point P on the curve, and at the point S in SM make the angle MSR equal to MSP. Then the angle PSR is bisected by SM, and if RS, MP meet in Q,

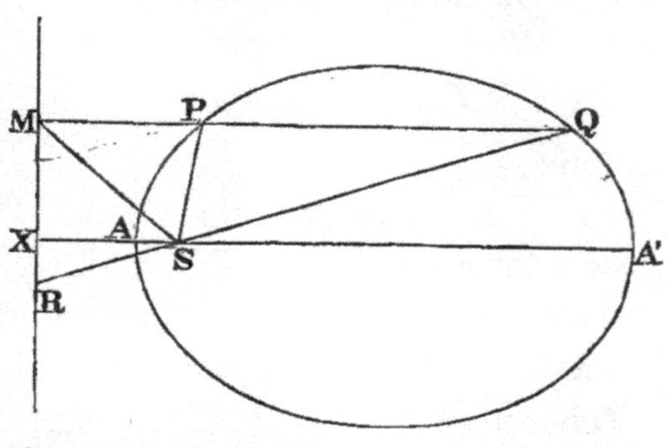

$$SQ : SP = QM : PM. \qquad \text{[Euc. VI., A. 3.}$$

Alternando $$SQ : QM = SP : PM,$$

or Q is a point on the curve. [*Def.*

Now the angle MSP is greater or less than SMP, according as SP is less or greater than PM (Euc. I., 18). Hence

MSR is greater or less than *SMP*, or than the alternate angle *MSX*, according as the eccentricity is less or greater than unity.

In the former case the straight line *RS* falls without the angle *MSX*, and the points *R*, *Q* lie on the same side of the directrix. Hence the curve consists of one oval branch as in the figure. When the eccentricity is greater than unity, the straight line *RS* falls within the angle *MSX*, and *P*, *Q* lie on opposite sides of the directrix. In this case the curve has two infinite branches with their convexities opposed. Compare the figures in the chapters upon the hyperbola.

If the eccentricity be equal to unity, the angles *MSR*, *MSX* will be equal. Hence *RS* coinciding with the axis will not meet *MP*, or a straight line *MP*, drawn parallel to the axis of a parabola, meets the curve in one point only. Hence the parabola consists of one infinite branch.

6. Let *MP* be *any* straight line which meets the directrix in *M* and the curve in *P*. Make the angle *MSR* equal to *MSP* and let *RS*, *MP* intersect in *Q*.

Then $$SQ : QM = SP : PM \text{ as above.}$$

Hence *Q* is a point on the curve. [*Def.*, *Note.*

It follows that a straight line, which meets a conic, will, in general, meet it in two points. Conversely, it may be shown that no straight line can meet a conic in more points than two.

From this property conics are termed *curves of the second order*.

CHAPTER II.

CONICS.

PROP. I. *The tangent to a conic, measured from the point of contact to the directrix, subtends a right angle at the focus.*

Let PQR be a straight line which meets the curve in P, Q, and the directrix in R. Produce PS to O.

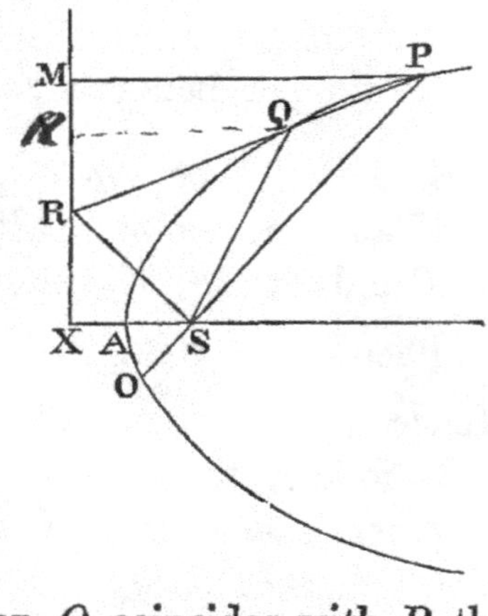

Then, since P, Q are points on the same conic,

$SP : PR = SQ : QR$. [*Def.*, *Note.*

Hence SR bisects the angle QSO (Euc. VI., A), or QSR is half the sum of the angles QSR, OSR.

Let the point Q move up to P. Then the chord PQ in its limiting position, when Q coincides with P, is the tangent at P. But, when Q coincides with P, the angles QSR, OSR are together equal to two right angles (Euc. I., 14). Therefore QSR, being half their sum, is a right angle, and it is equal to PSR, since Q coincides with P.

Hence the tangent PR subtends a right angle at S.

COR. To draw the tangent at a given point P on the curve. Let SR, drawn at right angles to SP, meet the directrix in R. Then PR is the tangent at P.

PROP. II. *Tangents at the extremities of a focal chord intersect upon the directrix, and the straight line joining their point of intersection to the focus is at right angles to the chord.*

Let OSP be any focal chord, SR a straight line at right angles to it, which meets the directrix in R; join R, P.

Then RP is the tangent at P. [Prop. I., Cor.

Similarly, RO is the tangent at O.

Hence the tangents at P, O, the extremities of a focal chord meet in a point R which lies upon the directrix, and the straight line RS is at right angles to OP.

PROP. III. *From any point T on the tangent at P, TL, TN are drawn meeting SP and the directrix at right angles in L, N. To prove that*

$$SL : TN = SA : AX.$$

Let M be the foot of the perpendicular from P on the

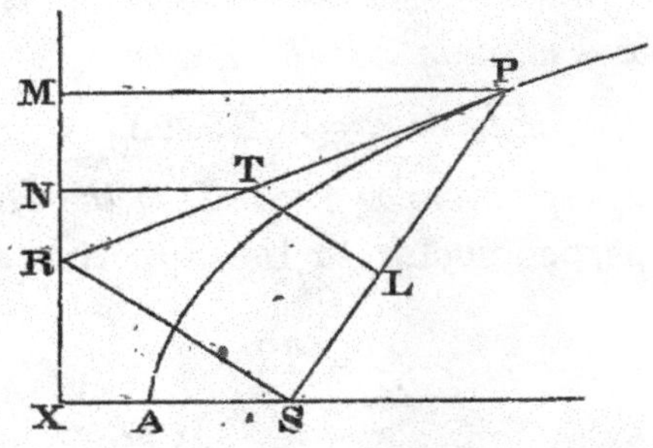

directrix, R the point in which the tangent at P meets the directrix.

Then TL is parallel to RS. [Prop. I.

Therefore $SL : SP = RT : RP$ [Euc. VI., 2.

$$= TN : PM,$$

by similar triangles RTN, RPM.

Alternando $SL : TN = SP : PM$

$$= SA : AX.$$

COR. Conversely, if TL, TN be perpendiculars, from any point T, on SP and the directrix, and if

$$SL : TN = SA : AX,$$

then TP will be the tangent at P.

Note. If PSR be a right angle, then, without assuming that PR touches the curve, we obtain, as above,

$$SL : TN = SA : AX.$$

But the hypotenuse ST is greater than SL. Hence, if T be taken anywhere on TR or TR produced, the ratio $ST : TN$ will be greater than $SA : AX$, except when L coincides with P. It follows that all points on PR, with the exception of P, lie on the convex side of the curve (Ex. 1, p. 19). Hence PR is the tangent at P.

PROP. IV. *If from any point T of a chord, which meets the curve in P and the directrix in R, a straight line be drawn parallel to RS and meeting SP in L, then*

$$SL : TN = SA : AX,$$

where TN is the perpendicular from T on the directrix.

Draw PM perpendicular to the directrix and meeting it in M. Then

$$SL : SP = TR : PR \qquad \text{[Euc. VI., 2.}$$

$$= TN : PM,$$

by similar triangles RTN, RPM.

Alternando $$SL : TN = SP : PM$$

$$= SA : AX.$$

PROP. V. *To draw tangents to a conic from an external point T.*

Let N be the foot of the perpendicular from T on the directrix: with centre S, radius SL, such that

$$SL : TN = SA : AX$$

describe a circle. Draw TL touching the circle, and let SL

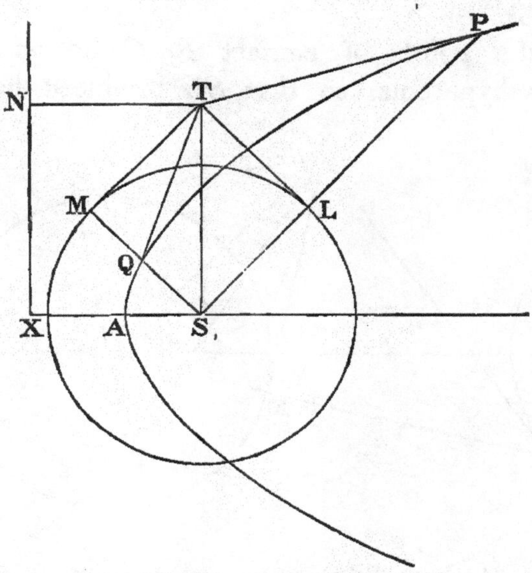

meet the conic in P. Then, SLT being a right angle, TP touches the conic. [Prop. III., Cor.

Similarly, if TM be the other tangent from T to the circle, and SM meet the conic in Q, then TQ will be the tangent at Q.

PROP. VI. *The tangents at P, Q intersect in T. To prove that TP, TQ subtend equal angles at S.*

Let TL, TM, TN be the perpendiculars from T on SP, SQ, and the directrix.

Then $$SL : TN = SA : AX$$ [Prop. III.

since T lies on the tangent at P.

So $$SM : TN = SA : AX$$

since T lies on the tangent at Q.

Hence, in the right-angled triangles SLT, SMT, the sides SL, SM are equal. But the hypotenuse ST is common.

Therefore the angles TSL, TSM are equal, or TP, TQ subtend equal angles at S.

Note. If the points of contact P, Q lie on opposite branches of a hyperbola, so that SL produced backwards

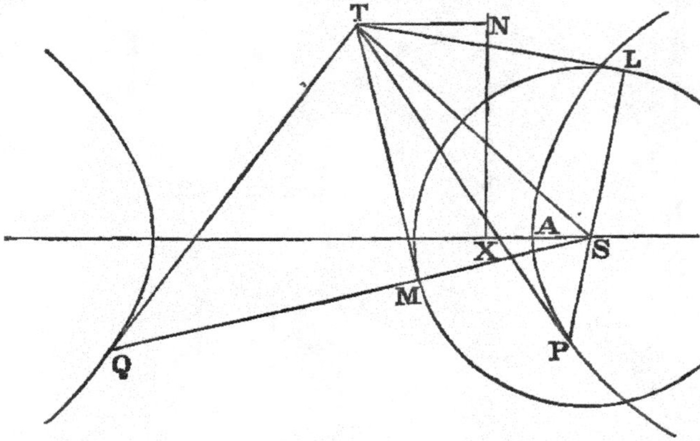

passes through P, then TSL is the supplement of the angle which TP subtends at S. In this case the tangents TP, TQ subtend *supplementary* angles at S.

PROP. VII. *The chords PR, QR meet the directrix in p, q, and the tangents at P, Q meet the tangent at R in p', q'. To prove that*

$$\angle pSq = \tfrac{1}{2}PSQ = p'Sq'.$$

Since P, R are points on the same conic,

$$SP : Pp = SR : Rp. \qquad [Def., Note.$$

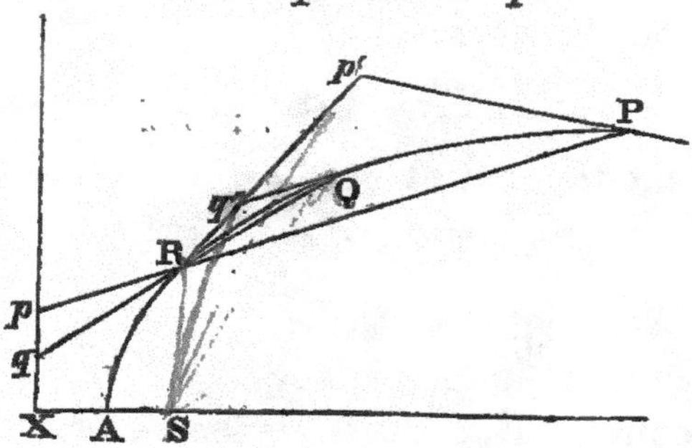

Therefore Sp bisects the angle between PS produced and RS, or

$$\angle pSR = \tfrac{1}{2} \text{ supplement of } RSP.$$

Similarly $\angle qSR = \tfrac{1}{2}$ supplement of RSQ.

By subtraction $\angle pSq = \tfrac{1}{2}PSQ$.

Again, $p'R$, $p'P$ subtend equal angles at S. [Prop. VI.

Therefore $\angle p'SR = \tfrac{1}{2}PSR$.

Similarly $\angle q'SR = \tfrac{1}{2}QSR$.

By subtraction $\angle p'Sq' = \tfrac{1}{2}PSQ = pSq$ from above.

Prop. VIII. *The chord of contact of tangents through T meets the directrix in R. To prove that TSR is a right angle.*

Since P, Q, the points of contact, lie on the same conic,

$$SP : PR = SQ : QR. \qquad \text{[}Def., Note.$$

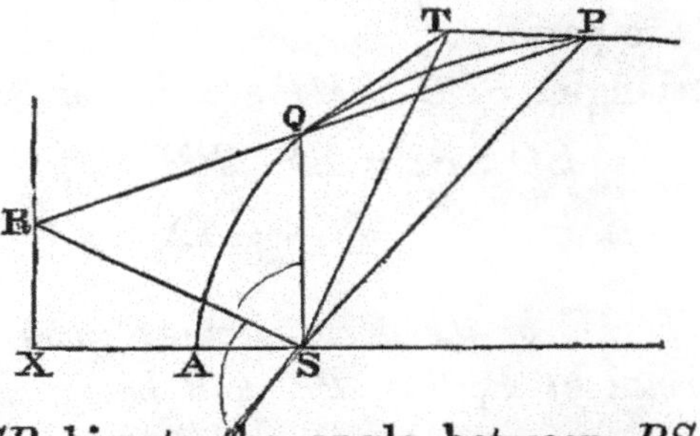

Therefore SR bisects the angle between PS produced and QS, or

$$\angle QSR = \tfrac{1}{2} \text{ supplement of } PSQ.$$

Also $\angle QST = \tfrac{1}{2}PSQ$. [Prop. VI.

By addition $\angle TSR =$ a right angle.

Cor. If a chord PQ, being produced, pass through a fixed point R on the directrix, the tangents at P, Q will meet on the fixed straight line ST, drawn at right angles to RS.

PROP. IX. *To prove that SGP, SPM are similar triangles, and that*

$$SG : SP = SA : AX,$$

PG being normal at P, and PM perpendicular to the directrix.

Let the tangent at P meet the directrix in R. Then the circle described on PR as diameter passes through S, since PSR is a right angle; and also through M, where PM is the perpendicular from P on the directrix. But PG, being at right angles to PR, touches the circle (Euc. III., 16, Cor.). Therefore

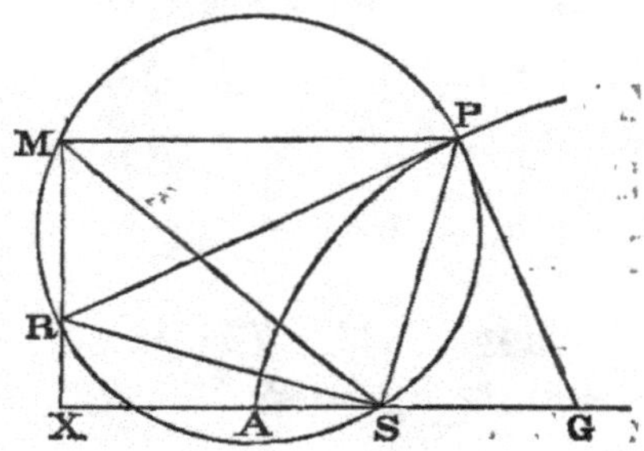

$$\angle SPG = SMP. \qquad \text{[Euc. III., 32.}$$

Also $$\angle PSG = SPM, \qquad \text{[Euc. I., 29.}$$

since SG, MP are parallel.

Hence the triangles SPG, SMP are similar, and

$$SG : SP = SP : PM$$
$$= SA : AX.$$

PROP. X. *If GK be the perpendicular upon SP from the foot of the normal at P, then PK will be equal to half the latus rectum.*

Let PN meet the axis at right angles in N. Then the

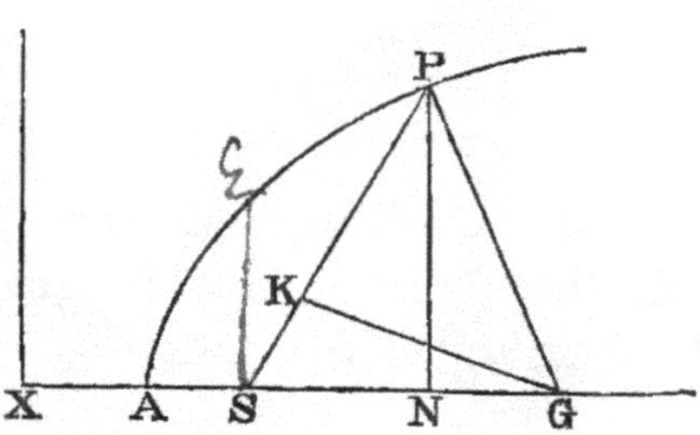

right-angled triangles SKG, SNP have the angle at S common and are similar.

Therefore $SK : SN = SG : SP$

$= SA : AX$. [Prop. IX.

Alternando $SK : SA = SN : AX$,

also $SP : SA = NX : AX$. [*Def.* and alternando.

Therefore $PK : SA = SX : AX$. [Euc. V., 24, Cor. 1.

But $SE : SA = SX : AX$, [*Def.* and alternando,

where SE is the ordinate through S.

Therefore $PK = SE = \frac{1}{2}$ latus rectum.

PROP. XI. *If PQ be any focal chord, then*

$$2SP.SQ = SE.PQ,$$

SE being half the latus rectum.

Let the normals at P, Q meet the axis in the points G, F,

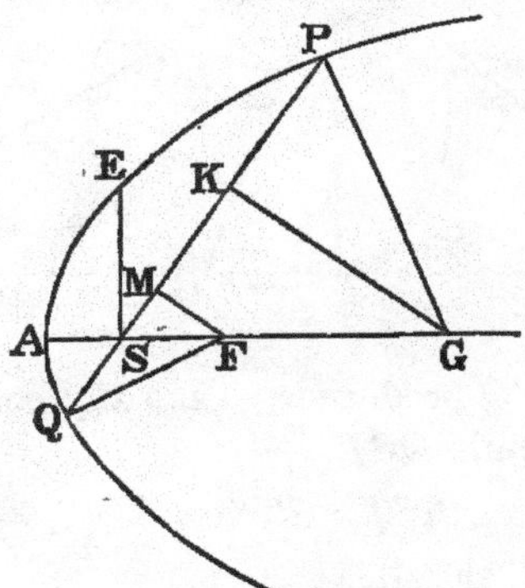

and let K, M be the feet of the perpendiculars drawn from those points to PQ. Then FM is parallel to GK.

Therefore $SK : SG = SM : SF$. [Euc. VI., 2.

Also $SG : SP = SA : AX$ [Prop. IX.

$= SF : SQ$ similarly.

Therefore $SK : SP = SM : SQ,$ [Euc. v., 22.

or $SK.SQ = SM.SP.$

But $SK = SP - PK = SP - SE$ [Prop. x.

Similarly $SM = QM - SQ = SE - SQ.$

Therefore $(SP - SE)\,SQ = (SE - SQ)\,SP$ from above,

or $2SP.SQ = SE(SP + SQ) = SE.PQ.$

LEMMA. *If S be the vertex of a triangle, O the middle point of the base PQ, and R a point in the base, such that SP : PR = SQ : QR, then*

$$OY : OR = SP^2 : PR^2,$$

Y being the foot of the perpendicular from S upon PQ.

On SQ as diameter describe a circle, and let it cut SR in M. This circle passes through Y, since SYQ is a right angle.

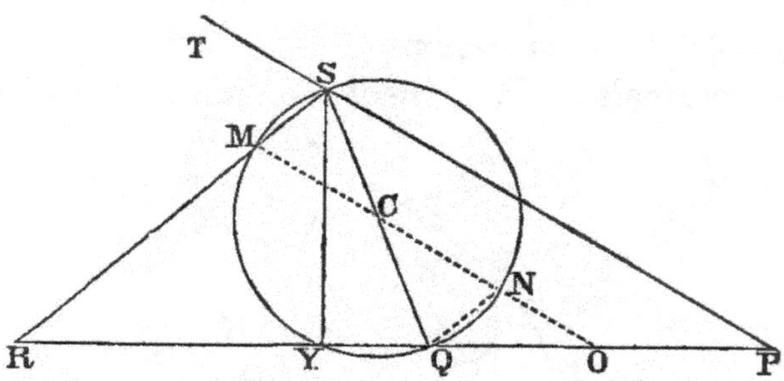

First, let R lie in PQ produced. Take any point T in PS produced. Then SR bisects the angle QST. [Euc. vi., A.

Therefore $\angle RST = RSQ = SMC,$ [Euc. i., 5.

where C is the centre of the circle.

Hence MC is parallel to SP, and since it bisects SQ it also passes through O, the middle point of PQ. [Euc. vi., 2.

Let MO meet the circle in N.

Then the angle CSM is equal to CMS (Euc. i., 5), or to CQN, in the same segment. Hence QN, RS are parallel.

But $ON.OM = OQ.OY.$ [Euc. iii., 6, Cor.

Hence $OY : OM = ON : OQ$

$= OM : OR.$ [Euc. vi., 2.

Therefore $OY : OR = OM^2 : OR^2$ [Euc. VI., 20, Cor. 2.

$= SP^2 : PR^2$ by similar triangles.

The proof is similar when R lies between P and Q.

PROP. XII. *The middle points of all parallel chords lie on a straight line, called a* DIAMETER.

Let O be the middle point of a chord PQ, which meets

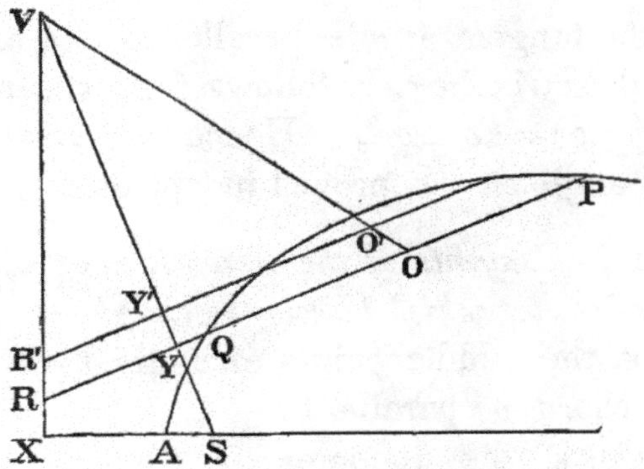

the directrix in R. Draw SY, meeting the chord at right angles in Y, and let V be the point in which SY meets the directrix.

Then $SP : PR = SQ : QR$. [*Def.*, *Note*.

Therefore $OY : OR = SP^2 : PR^2$. [Lemma.

Let any chord parallel to PQ meet SY and the directrix in Y', R'. Let O' be its middle point. Then, since $SP : PR$ is a constant ratio for all parallel chords (*Def.*, *Note*); therefore $OY : OR$ is a constant ratio.

Hence $OY : OR = O'Y' : O'R'$.

Therefore O' lies on the straight line VO, or the middle points of all chords parallel to PQ lie on the fixed straight line VO.

COR. 1. Let PQ move parallel to itself until its middle point lies on the curve. Then OP, OQ, being always equal, vanish together, and the chord becomes a tangent. Hence the tangent at a point in which any diameter VO meets the curve is parallel to the chords which that diameter bisects.

COR. 2. The following is a construction for the diameter bisecting a given chord. Join the middle point of the chord to the point in which the focal perpendicular upon the chord meets the directrix.

Note. If the tangent at o be parallel to PQ, and meet SY in y and the directrix in r, it follows from the above proposition that $oy : or = So^2 : or^2$. Hence $oy : oS = oS : or$ and oSr is a right angle as was proved independently in Prop. I.

PROP. XIII. *Tangents at the extremities of any chord intersect on the diameter which bisects the chord.*

Let O, o be the middle points of a given chord PQ and any adjacent chord pq parallel to PQ. Then Oo is the diameter bisecting PQ. [Prop. XII.

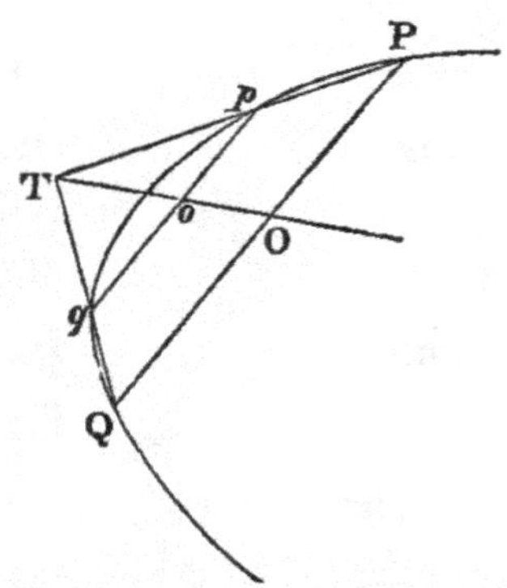

Let Pp meet Oo in T. Then, since PQ, pq are bisected in O, o; therefore

$$OQ : oq = OP : op$$
$$= OT : oT,$$

by similar triangles.

Therefore TqQ is a straight line, and, if the chord pq move parallel to itself up to PQ, the chords TP, TQ will become tangents at P, Q. Also T lies on the diameter which bisects PQ.

Conversely, if the tangents at P, Q intersect in T, the diameter through T bisects PQ.

Students reading this subject for the first time are recommended to omit the next two propositions. The results there obtained are investigated independently in subsequent articles.

PROP. XIV. *The middle points of all chords parallel to the axis of a conic, which is not a parabola, lie on a straight line perpendicular to the axis.*

Let O be the middle point of a chord PQ, which is parallel

Fig. 1.

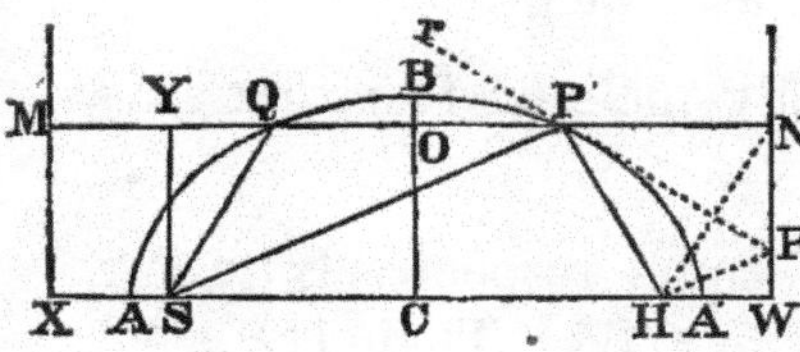

Fig. 2.

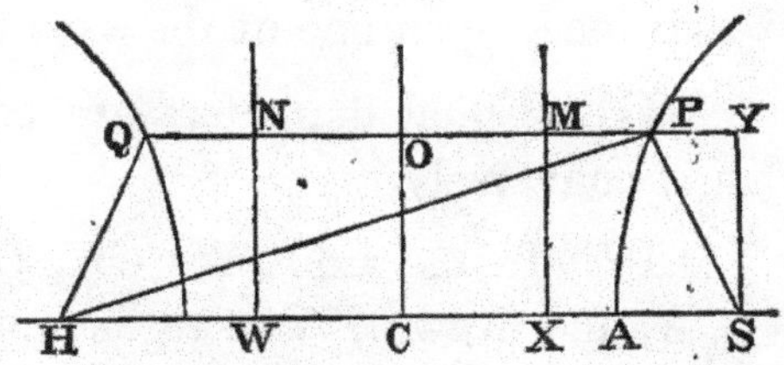

to the axis and meets the directrix in M. Draw SY perpendicular to PQ, and therefore parallel to the directrix. Then, in the triangle PSQ,

$$SP : PM = SQ : QM. \qquad \text{[Def}$$

Therefore $$OY : OM = SP^2 : PM^2. \qquad \text{[Lemma.}$$

Or the ratio $OY : OM$ is constant for all chords parallel to the axis. Hence $OY : YM$ is constant; but MY is always equal to SX; hence OY is constant, and O lies on a fixed straight line perpendicular to the axis.

Note. Let this fixed straight line meet the axis in C; then, corresponding to any point Q, on the curve, at a perpendicular distance QO from CO, there is another point situated upon the opposite side of CO and at an equal distance PO from it. Hence CO *divides the curve into two equal and similar parts.* So too does the axis. [§ II., p. 4.

Hence, from the symmetry of the curve it is evident that:

I. Any chord drawn through C is bisected at that point, and hence that all diameters pass through C, a diameter being defined as the straight line which bisects a system of parallel chords.

The point C is termed the *centre*, and conics which have a centre are called *central conics.*

II. Tangents drawn to a central conic from a point on either of the *axes* CX, CO, are equal and equally inclined to either axis. Conversely, tangents equally inclined to either axis meet upon one of the axes and are equal.

III. Equal diameters are equally inclined to either axis, and conversely.

IV. In *the* axis take CH, CW equal respectively to CS, CX, and draw WN at right angles to CW. Then $HP = SQ$ and $PN = QM$, where PN is perpendicular to NW.

Hence
$$HP : PN = SQ : QM$$
$$= SA : AX.$$

Or every central conic can be generated by means of a *second* focus (H) and directrix (WN).

V. All theorems which have been proved for one focus and directrix are true for the other. Thus, if RPr be the tangent at P (fig. 1), meeting the directrix WN in R, then, since it has been proved that Pr, produced to meet XM, subtends a right angle at S, it follows that PR subtends a right angle at H.

Again, PHR being a right angle, a circle goes round $PHRN$, and the angles HPR, HNW, in the same segment, are equal. This theorem, being true for one focus and directrix, is true for the other. Hence, the angles SPr, SMX are equal; which proves *at once*, since the triangles SMX, HNW are equal in all respects, that the angles SPr, HPR are equal, or *the tangent at P makes equal angles with PS, PH.*

So, in the hyperbola, the tangent at P bisects the angle SPH. [fig. 2.

In the ellipse, the tangent at the point B, in which CO meets the curve, is parallel to the chords which CO bisects, and therefore to the axis. In the hyperbola, CO does not meet the curve.

Prop. XV. *In a central conic the sum or difference of the focal distances of any point P is constant.*

For, $SP : PM = SA : AX$, in figs., Prop. xiv.

Alternando $SP : SA = PM : AX$.

Similarly $HP : SA = PN : AX$. [§ iv., p. 18.

Therefore $SP + HP : SA = MP + PN : AX$ [Euc. v., 24.

$= MN : AX$, [fig. 1,

and $HP - SP : SA = NP - PM : AX$ [Euc. v., 24, Cor.

$= MN : AX$. [fig. 2.

In the first case $SP + PH$, in the second $SP \sim PH$, is constant.

Several properties of central conics may now be proved, as in the Appendix, by means of the construction used in the Lemma.

EXAMPLES.

1. Any point, whose distance from the focus of a given conic bears to its perpendicular distance from the directrix a ratio greater than the eccentricity, lies on the convex side of the curve.

2. The ordinate NP meets a conic in P, and the tangent at an extremity of the latus rectum in Q. Prove that $SP = QN$.

3. Given the focus of a conic, the length of the latus rectum, a tangent, and its point of contact; show how to construct the curve.

4. A focal chord PSQ of a conic section is produced to meet the directrix in K, and KM, KN are drawn through the feet of the ordinates PM, QN. If KN produced meet PM produced in R, prove that $PR = PM$.

5. Straight lines drawn through the extremities of a focal chord pass through the vertex and intersect the directrix in M, N. Prove that MN subtends a right angle at the focus.

6. The opposite sides of a quadrilateral, described upon any two focal chords as diagonals, intersect on the directrix.

7. If the focus of a conic and two points on the curve be given, the directrix will pass through a fixed point.

8. Two points on a conic being given, and also the angle which the straight line joining them subtends at the focus; prove that the straight line drawn from the focus to the point of intersection of the tangents at the given points passes through a fixed point.

9. Given the directrix of a conic and two points on the curve; the locus of the focus is a circle.

10. Given the focus of a conic inscribed in a triangle; determine the points of contact.

11. The tangents at P, Q intersect in R. Prove that if PR be parallel to SQ, then $SP = PR$.

12. Tangents at the extremities of a focal chord meet the tangents parallel to the chord in the points R, R'. If SY be the focal perpendicular on RR', then $SY^2 = YR.YR'$.

13. The portion of the directrix intercepted by any two chords, and the straight line joining the points in which pairs of tangents at the extremities of those chords intersect, subtend equal angles at the focus.

14. Pairs of tangents intercept on a fixed tangent a straight line which subtends a right angle at the focus.

Determine the locus of the point in which the variable tangents intersect.

15. If PG be the normal at P to a conic, the ordinate of P varies as the perpendicular from G upon SP.

16. PSQ is any focal chord of a conic; the normals at P and Q intersect in K, and KN is drawn perpendicular to PQ; prove that PN is equal to SQ.

17. If the tangents and normals at P, Q intersect in T, N respectively, then

$$PN : QN = PT : QT.$$

18. If SY be the focal perpendicular on the tangent, and G the foot of the normal at P; prove that $PG.SY = SP.SE$, where SE is the semi-latus rectum.

19. A circle has its centre on the axis of a conic which it touches. Prove that the chord of the circle drawn through the focus and either point of contact is of constant length.

20. If the circle pass through the focus determine the focal radii to the points of contact.

21. If SE be the semi-latus rectum, QSQ' any focal chord, and PG the normal to which it is perpendicular, then

$$PG^2 = SQ.SQ' = QO.SE,$$

O being the middle point of the chord.

For, if SY, the focal perpendicular upon the tangent at P, meet the directrix in V, and the tangent at P meet the tangents at Q, Q' in R, R', then

$$\begin{aligned} QO^2 : SQ.SQ' &= RP^2 : YR.YR' \\ &= SP^2 : SY^2 \qquad \text{[Ex. 11, 12.} \\ &= PG^2 : SE^2. \qquad \text{[Ex. 18.} \end{aligned}$$

The required result readily follows by Prop. XI.

22. In the last example; if GU, drawn at right angles to PG, meet PS in U, then $PU = QO$.

23. Any two chords of a conic and the diameters which bisect them meet the directrix in L, L'; M, M' respectively; show that LL', MM' subtend equal angles at the focus.

24. The directrix of a conic meets in V the diameter through an external point T. A point R is taken in the directrix such that TSR is a right angle. From R a straight line is drawn perpendicular to SV and meeting the conic in P, Q. Prove that TP, TQ are tangents to the conic.

25. If a chord of a conic subtend a constant angle at the focus, the tangents at its extremities will intersect upon a conic having the same focus and directrix.

For, if the angle TSP be given (Prop. VI.), ST bears a constant ratio to SL, and therefore to TN. [Prop. III.

26. If a chord subtend a constant angle at the focus, its envelope will be a conic having the same focus and directrix.

27. If the base of a triangle described about a conic subtend a constant angle at the focus, its vertex will lie on a fixed conic.

28. If two sides of a triangle be given in position and the third subtend a constant angle at a fixed point, its envelope will be a conic touching the other two sides and having the fixed point for focus.

29. If O, P, Q, R be points on a conic, such that OP, QR subtend equal angles at S, the chords OP, RQ will intersect upon the straight line which bisects the angle PSQ.

30. If OP, PQ, QR subtend constant angles at S, the angles OSP, QSR being equal, then OP, RQ intersect upon a fixed conic.

31. In the parabola all diameters are parallel to the axis.

32. SY, the focal perpendicular upon the tangent at P to a conic, meets the directrix in V, and G is the foot of the normal at G. Prove that

$$PG : SY = SV : VY.$$

This result may be deduced from Ex. 21.

33. If the diameter bisecting a focal chord in O meet the directrix, the curve, and the axis in V, P, C, then

$$CP : CV = OP : PV.$$

34. What do the results of the last two examples become in the case of the parabola?

35. If SY be the perpendicular from the focus upon the tangent at any point P of a conic, the circle described on SP as diameter touches the locus of Y.

36. The normal at Y to the locus of Y bisects SP.

37. If a diameter of a conic meet the curve in two points, the tangents at those points are parallel.

38. Given a conic; determine the position of its axis.

39. Every diameter of a conic bisects the curve.

40. Parallel diameters of similar and similarly situated conics bisect the same systems of parallel chords.

CHAPTER III.

THE PARABOLA.

Def. A PARABOLA is the curve traced out by a point which moves in such a way that its distance from a fixed point, called the *Focus*, is always equal to its perpendicular distance from a fixed straight line, called the *Directrix*.

In Prop. XII., p. 15, a *Diameter* of a conic has been defined as the straight line which bisects a system of parallel chords.

In the parabola all diameters are parallel to the axis (Prop. I.), and therefore to one another.

A diameter of a parabola is sometimes *defined* as a straight line parallel to the axis. In this case it may be shown, conversely, that every diameter bisects a system of parallel chords.

The focal chord parallel to the tangent at any point is said to be the *Parameter* of the diameter passing through that point.

The term ordinate is not confined to straight lines measured perpendicular to the axis of the parabola; but, if QV be drawn from any point Q on the curve, parallel to the tangent at P and meeting the diameter through P in V, then QV is said to be the *Ordinate* of the point Q, with reference to the diameter through P.

Also PV is called the *Abscissa* of Q.

Note. The terms ordinate and abscissa *usually* have reference to the axis. The context will determine when they are to be understood in their more general sense.

Several propositions that have been proved generally for conics assume simpler forms in the case of the parabola.

Thus, in Prop. II., p. 7, since $SA = AX$, therefore $SL = TN$.

Similarly $SG = SP$. [Prop. IX., p. 12.

Also PK, or the semi-latus rectum, is equal to SX or $2SA$. [Prop. X., p. 12.

PROP. I. *The middle points of all parallel chords lie on a straight line parallel to the axis.*

Let a straight line through the focus S meet the directrix

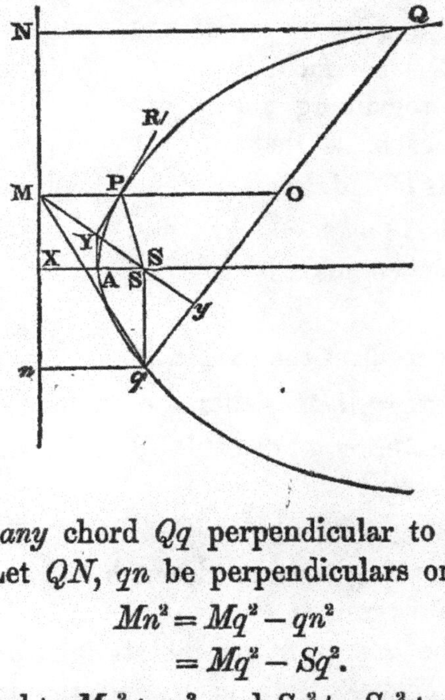

in M. Draw *any* chord Qq perpendicular to MS and meeting it in y. Let QN, qn be perpendiculars on the directrix.

Then $$Mn^2 = Mq^2 - qn^2 \qquad \text{[Euc. I., 47.}$$
$$= Mq^2 - Sq^2. \qquad \text{[Def.}$$

But Mq^2 is equal to $My^2 + qy^2$, and Sq^2 to $Sy^2 + qy^2$. [Euc. I., 47.

By subtraction $My^2 - Sy^2 = Mq^2 - Sq^2 = Mn^2$.

Similarly it may be shown that MN^2 is equal to $My^2 - Sy^2$, and therefore to Mn^2.

Hence M is the middle point of Nn.

Draw MO, parallel to the axis, to meet Qq in O.

Then O is the middle point of *any* chord Qq drawn perpendicular to SM. Therefore MO bisects all chords parallel to Qq.

PROP. II. *The tangent at P makes equal angles with SP, PM, where PM is perpendicular to the directrix. Also, if the tangent meet the axis in T, then*

$$\angle STP = SPT.$$

Let the tangent at P meet the directrix in R. Then PSR is a right angle. [Prop. I., p. 6.

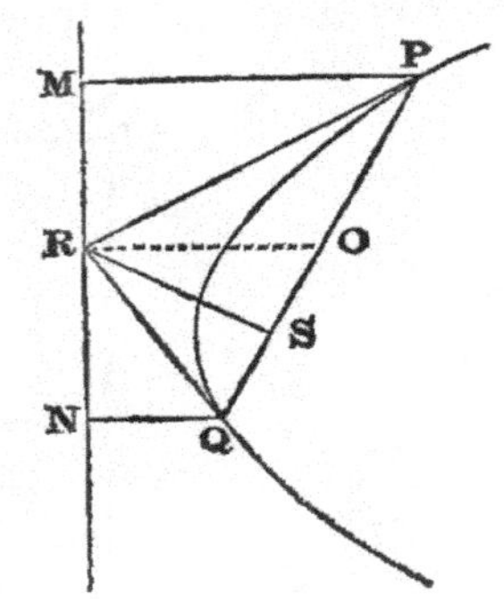

Also, in the right-angled triangles SPR, MPR, the sides SP, PM are equal, and PR is common.

Hence the remaining angles are equal, each to each, so that

$$\angle SPR = MPR.$$

Hence also the *supplementary* angles, which RP produced makes with SP, PM, are equal.

Produce PR to meet the axis in T.

Then $\angle SPT = MPT =$ alternate angle STP.

COR. The exterior angle PSO (fig., Prop. III.) is therefore equal to $2STP$. [Euc. I., 32.

Note. Conversely, if the straight line YPR be drawn (fig., Prop. I.) making equal angles with SP, PM, this straight line will be the tangent at P.

For, if R be *any* point on the straight line, then, since SP, $PR = MP$, PR, each to each, and the included angles are equal, by construction; therefore SP is equal to PR, and consequently greater than the perpendicular distance of R from the directrix.

Hence it may be shown that all points on the straight line PR, except P, lie on the convex side of the curve, or that PR is the tangent at P.

PROP. III. *The external angle between any two tangents is equal to the angle which either of them subtends at the focus.*

Let the tangents at P, Q, intersect in R, and meet

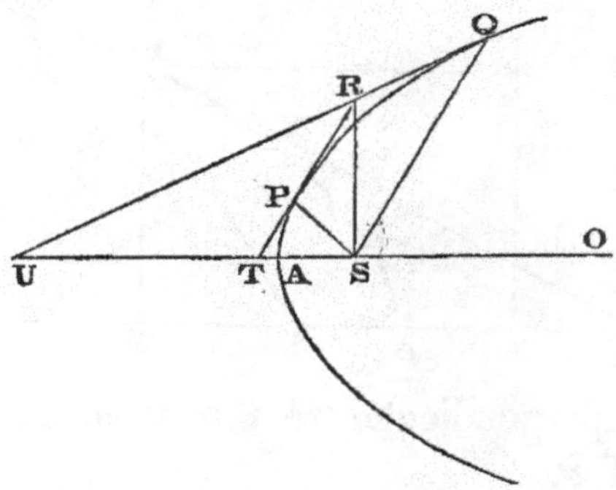

the axis in T, U, respectively. Take any point O in AS produced.

Then $\angle PSO = 2STP$. [Prop. II., Cor.

Similarly $\angle QSO = 2SUQ$.

By subtraction $\angle PSQ = 2TRU$. [Euc. I. 32.

Hence, the angles PSR, QSR being equal (Prop. VI., p. 9), either of them is equal to TRU.

PROP. IV. *The subnormal is equal to $2AS$ or half the latus rectum.*

Let the tangent and normal at P meet the axis in T, G, respectively. Let PM be perpendicular to the directrix, and PN the ordinate of P. [fig., Prop. V.

Then $\angle SPT = STP$. [Prop. II.

Hence the complements SPG, SGP are equal.

Therefore $SG = SP = PM = NX$,

or $SN + NG = SN + SX$.

Hence NG is equal to SX, that is, to $2SA$, or to the ordinate through S.

PROP. V. *The subtangent is equal to twice the abscissa.*

Let the tangent at P meet the axis in T.

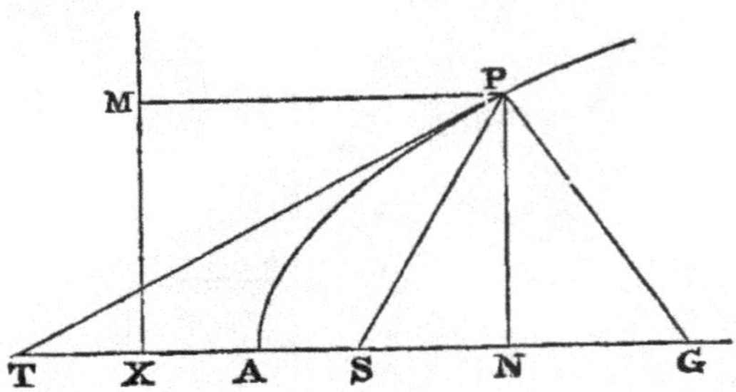

Draw PM perpendicular to the directrix and let PN be the ordinate of P.

Then $\angle SPT = STP$. [Prop. II.

Therefore $ST = SP = PM = NX$,

or $SA + AT = NA + AX$.

But $SA = AX$ (*Def.*). Therefore $AT = AN$, or $NT = 2AN$.

PROP. VI. *If PN be the ordinate of P, then*

$$PN^2 = 4AS.AN.$$

Draw the normal PG. Then TPG, PNG are right angles.

Therefore $PN^2 = NG.NT$ [Euc. VI., 8, Cor.

$= 2AS.2AN$. [Props. IV., V.

Therefore $PN^2 = 4AS.AN$.

Or thus: since S divides AN so that $AN + AS = XN$, therefore

$SN^2 + 4AS.AN = XN^2$. [Euc. II., 8.

Also $SN^2 + PN^2 = SP^2$, [Euc. I., 47.

and $SP^2 = XN^2$. [*Def.*

Therefore $PN^2 = 4AS.AN$.

PROP. VII. *The diameter through any point P, on the curve, meets the ordinate of Q in V, and the tangent at Q in T. To prove that*

$$PV = PT.$$

Let the tangent at P meet QT in R. Then RU, drawn

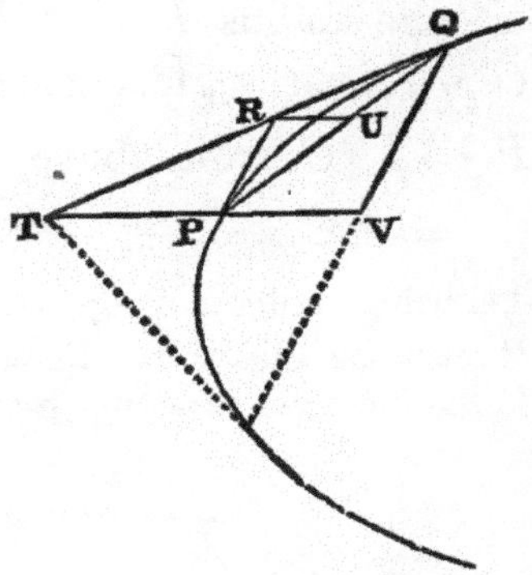

to the middle point of PQ, is a diameter (Prop. XIII., p. 16), and therefore parallel to TP.

But the ordinate QV is parallel to PR. [*Def.*, p. 24.

Hence $$PV : PT = RQ : RT$$ [Euc. VI., 2.

$$= UQ : UP \text{ similarly.}$$

But $UQ = UP$, by construction. Therefore $PV = PT$.

Cor. Since $VT = 2PT$, therefore $QV = 2RP$.

Prop. VIII. *To determine the length of any focal chord PSQ.*

Draw PM, QN perpendicular to the directrix, and SR, perpendicular to PQ, to meet the directrix. [fig., Prop. II.

Then, since $SP = PM$ and PR is common to the right-angled triangles SPR, MPR, therefore

$$RM = RS$$

$$= RN \text{ similarly.}$$

Draw RO parallel to the axis and meeting PQ in R. Then $PO = OQ$.

Hence $$PM + QN = 2RO.$$

But $$SP = PM \text{ and } SQ = QN.$$ [*Def.*

Therefore $$PQ = PM + QN = 2RO.$$

Again, if RO meet the curve in P', then the circle described with centre P' and radius $P'R$ or $P'S$ has RO for a diameter, since RSO is a right angle. Therefore $RO = 2SP'$.

Hence $$PQ = 2RO, \text{ from above,}$$ $$= 4SP'.$$

The result of Prop. IX. being assumed, Prop, VIII. follows thus:

Let the tangent at P meet the axis in T. Draw QR, the focal chord parallel to PT, and PV the diameter bisecting it.

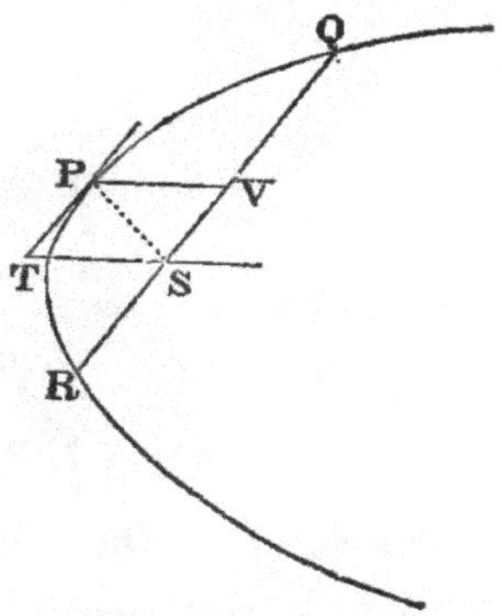

Then $PV = ST = SP$, since the angles SPT, STP are equal. [Prop. II.

Therefore $$QV^2 = 4SP.PV \quad \text{[Prop. IX.}$$ $$= 4SP^2.$$

Hence $$QR = 2QV = 4SP.$$

Note. Hence the parameter of the diameter through P is equal to $4SP$. [*Def.*, p. 24.

PROP. IX. *If QV be the ordinate and PV the abscissa of a point Q on the parabola, measured along the diameter through any point P, then*

$$QV^2 = 4SP.PV.$$

Let the tangents at P, Q intersect in R, and let PM, drawn perpendicular to the directrix, meet QR in T.

Then, in the triangles MPR, SPR, the side MP is equal to SP, and PR is common. Also $\angle MPR = SPR$. [Prop. II.

Therefore the remaining angles are equal, each to each, so that

$$\angle RMP = RSP = PRT. \qquad \text{[Prop. III.}$$

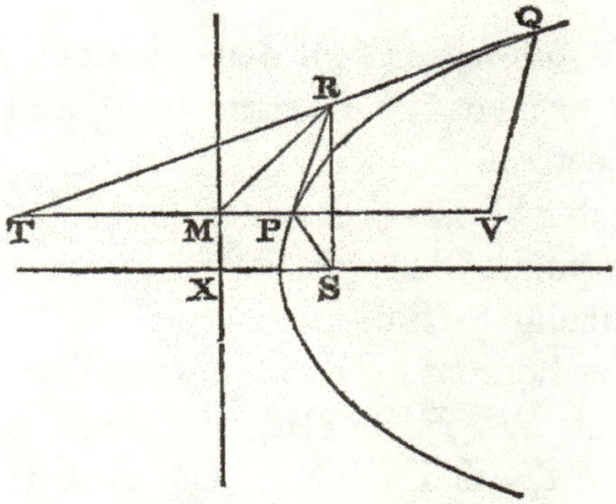

Hence the triangles PRT, PRM, having the angles PRT, RPT equal to RMP, RPT, each to each, are similar.

Therefore $\qquad PT : PR = PR : PM.$

Hence $\qquad PR^2 = PM.PT = SP.PV.$ [Prop. VII. and *Def.*

It follows that QV^2, being equal to $4PR^2$ (Prop. VII., Cor.), is equal to $4SP.PV$.

PROP. X. *The foot of the focal perpendicular upon the tangent at any point lies on the tangent at the vertex.*

From any point P on the curve (fig., Prop. I.) draw PM perpendicular to the directrix, and let PY meet SM at right angles in Y.

Then, in the triangles SPY, MPY, the side SP is equal to PM, and PY is common. Also the right angles at Y are equal. Therefore the remaining sides and angles are equal, each to each.

Hence $\qquad SY = MY$, and $\angle SPY = MPY$.

Now PY is the tangent at P, since it is equally inclined to SP, PM.

Also, since $SY = MY$ and $SA = AX$, therefore AY, being parallel to MX (Euc. VI., 2), or perpendicular to the axis, is the tangent at the vertex.

Note. The following proof depends upon Prop. I. only:

Draw SM to meet the directrix in M, and let the diameter through M meet the curve in P.

This diameter bisects chords perpendicular to SM (Prop. I.), and therefore passes through the point of contact of the tangent perpendicular to SM.

Hence the tangent PY is perpendicular to SM (fig., Prop. I.). But SP, $PY = PM$, PY, each to each. [*Def.*

Therefore $SY = MY$ (Euc. I., 47), as in the first proof, &c.

PROP. XI. *If SY be the focal perpendicular on the tangent at P, then*

$$SY^2 = SA.SP.$$

Since Y (fig., Prop. I.) lies on the tangent at A (Prop. XI,), and

$$YSA = \text{alternate angle } YMP$$
$$= YSP,$$

in the isosceles triangle PSM; therefore SAY, SPY are similar right-angled triangles.

Therefore $$SY : SA = SP : SY,$$

or $$SY^2 = SA.SP.$$

PROP. XII. *Tangents drawn from any point on the directrix are at right angles to one another.*

The tangent RP, drawn from a point R on the directrix, subtends a right angle at S. [Prop. I., p. 6.

Draw PM perpendicular to the directrix.

Then, in the right-angled triangled triangles SPR, MPR, the angles SPR, MPR are equal (Prop. II.). Hence

$$\angle SRP = MRP.$$

Draw the tangent RQ, and let QN be perpendicular to the directrix. Then it may be shown, similarly, that

$$\angle SRQ = NRQ.$$

Hence $\quad \angle SRP = \frac{1}{2}SRM,$

and $\quad \angle SRQ = \frac{1}{2}SRN.$

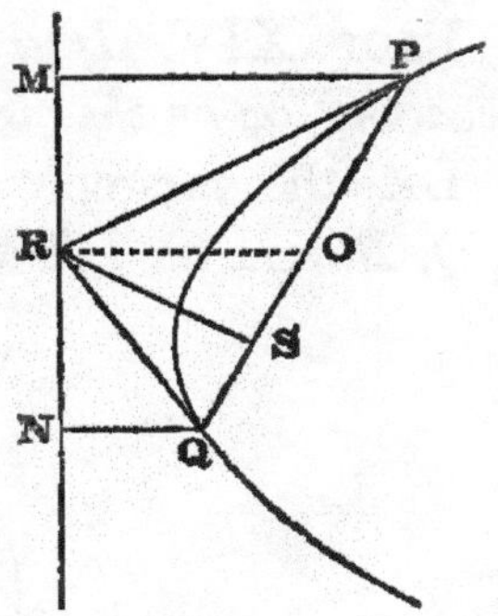

By addition

$$\angle PRQ = \tfrac{1}{2}SRM + \tfrac{1}{2}SRN$$

$$= \text{a right angle.}$$ [Euc. I., 14.

Prop. XIII. *If a pair of tangents intersect in R, the angle which either of them makes with SR is equal to that which the other makes with the axis.*

Let the tangents at P, Q intersect in R and meet the axis in T, U respectively.

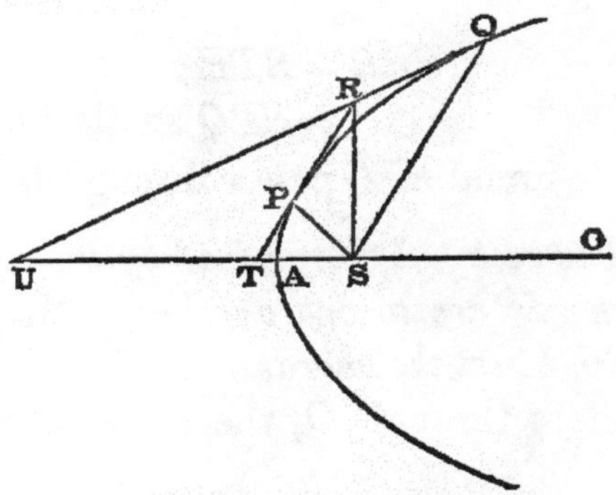

Then $\quad \angle SRU = RSQ + RQS.$ [Euc. I., 32.

Also $\quad \angle URT = RSQ.$ [Prop. III.

By subtraction $\quad \angle SRP = RQS$

$= SUR.$ [Prop. II.

Similarly $\quad \angle SRQ = STR.$

Cor. Since $\quad \angle RSQ = RSP,$ [Prop. VI., p. 9,

and $\quad \angle RQS = SRP$ from above,

the triangles RQS, RPS are similar.

PROP. XIV. *If a parabola be inscribed in a triangle, the focus will lie on the circle which circumscribes the triangle.*

Let the tangents which form the triangle intersect in P, Q, R, and let PR meet the axis in T. Let S be the focus.

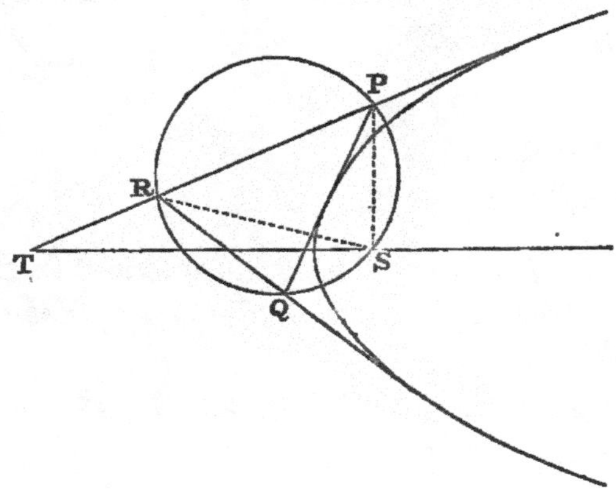

Then $\angle SRQ = STP$ [Prop. XIII.

$= SPQ$ similarly.

Therefore the circle round SPQ passes through R. [Euc. III., 21.

PROP. XV. *The rectangles contained by the segments of any two intersecting chords are to one another as the parameters of the diameters which bisect the chords.*

Let the diameters through O, the intersection of any two

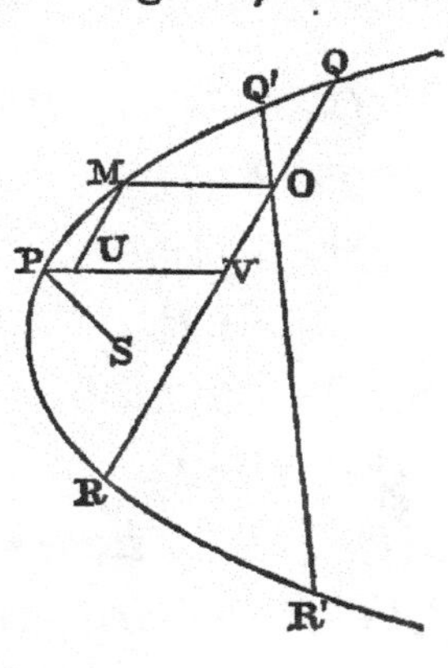

chords QR, $Q'R'$, and through V, the middle point of QR, meet the curve in M, P respectively. Draw MU parallel to QR and meeting PV in U. Join SP, S being the focus.

Then $$QO.OR = QV^2 - OV^2 \qquad \text{[Euc. II., 5, Cor.}$$
$$= QV^2 - MU^2$$
$$= 4SP.PV - 4SP.PU \qquad \text{[Prop. IX.}$$

But $PV - PU$ is equal to UV or MO.

Therefore $$QO.OR = 4SP.OM.$$

Similarly $Q'O.OR' = 4SP'.OM$, if P' be the point in which the diameter bisecting $Q'R'$ meets the curve.

Hence $$QO.OR : Q'O.OR' = 4SP : 4SP',$$

which proves the proposition. [*Note*, p. 30.

The proof is similar when O lies without the curve.

Let QR move parallel to itself until it becomes the tangent at P.

Then $$OP^2 : Q'O.OR' = 4SP : 4SP'.$$

Again, let $Q'R'$ become the tangent at P'.

Then $$OP^2 : OP'^2 = 4SP : 4SP'.$$

It is also evident that the ratio of $4SP$ to $4SP'$ is the same for any pair of chords parallel to QR, $Q'R'$, and does not depend on the position of O.

Hence the proposition may be stated in either of the following forms:

The rectangles contained by the segments of any two intersecting chords are to one another (i) as the parameters of the diameters which bisect the chords, that is, as the focal chords to which they are parallel; or (ii) as the squares of the tangents to which they are parallel; or (iii) as the rectangles contained by the segments of any other two chords parallel to the former.

Prop. XVI. *If a circle intersect a parabola, the common chords will be equally inclined to the axis of the parabola.*

Let QR, $Q'R'$, common chords of a circle and parabola, intersect in O.

Then $QO.OR$ and $Q'O.OR'$ are to one another as the focal chords parallel to QR, $Q'R'$. [Prop. XV.

But $QO.OR = Q'O.OR'$ in the circle. [Euc. III., 35.

Hence, the focal chords parallel to QR, $Q'R'$ are equal, and therefore equally inclined to the axis, since the curve is symmetrical with respect to its axis.

Hence QR, $Q'R'$ are equally inclined to the axis.

Similarly, the pairs of chords QQ', $R'R$, and QR', $Q'R$ are equally inclined to the axis.

PROP. XVII. *If a chord of a parabola pass through a fixed point, the tangents at its extremities will intersect on a fixed straight line.*

Let o be the middle point of a chord which passes through a fixed point O; op, OP, the diameters through o, O, meeting the curve in p, P. Draw the tangent at p and let it meet OP in V. Let the tangents at the extremities of the chord through O intersect in t. Through t, p draw straight lines parallel to the tangent at P and meeting OP in T, U respectively.

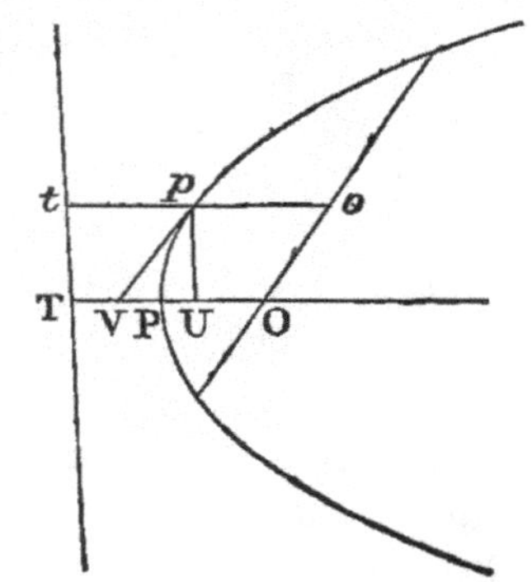

Then tU is a parallelogram, since all diameters are parallel.

Also Vo is a parallelogram. [Prop. XII., Cor. 1, p. 16.

Hence TU, $OV = tp$, po, each to each.

But $tp = po$. [Prop. VII.

Therefore $TU = OV$.

Also $UP = VP$. [Prop. VII.

By subtraction $TP = PO$, which is constant.

Hence T is a fixed point and tT a fixed straight line.

Conversely, if t lie on a fixed straight line, the chord of contact of tangents through t will pass through a fixed point.

Def. The fixed point O is said to be the *Pole* of the fixed straight line Tt, and Tt is called the *Polar* of O.

PROP. XVIII. *If Oo be the chord of contact of tangents to a parabola through any point t, and p'op any chord passing through t, then tpop' will be cut harmonically.*

Let tO be the diameter through t meeting the curve in P and QT, the tangent parallel to tp, in T.

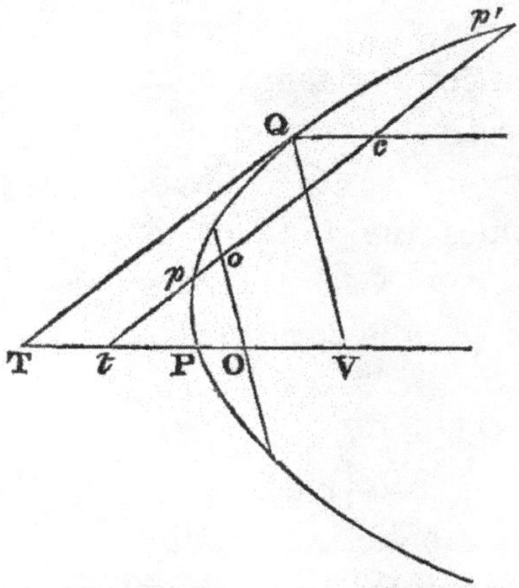

Draw QV, an ordinate of the diameter through P, and let Qc be the diameter through Q, bisecting pp' in c.

Then, it may be shown, as in Prop. XV., that $tp.tp'$ is equal to $4SQ.tP$, that is to $2SQ.tO$. [Prop. VII.

Similarly TQ^2 is equal to $2SQ.TV$.

Hence $$TQ^2 : tp.tp' = TV : tO$$
$$= TQ : to, \text{ by similar triangles,}$$
$$= TQ^2 : TQ.to.$$

Therefore $$tp.tp' = TQ.to = tc.to,$$

or $$2tp.tp' = to\,(tp + tp'),$$

since c is the middle point of pp'.

Note. The above proposition may be thus enunciated (*Def.*, p. 36):

A straight line, drawn through any point to meet a parabola, is cut harmonically by the point, the curve, and the polar of the point.

PROP. XIX. *Any ordinate, QV, and abscissa, PV, contain with the parabola an area equal to two-thirds of the parallelogram which has PV, QV for adjacent sides.*

Draw the adjacent ordinate RU; let RQ meet UP in T; complete the parallelogram $RUTL$; let RL and QO, which is drawn parallel to VP, meet the tangent at P in M, O respectively.

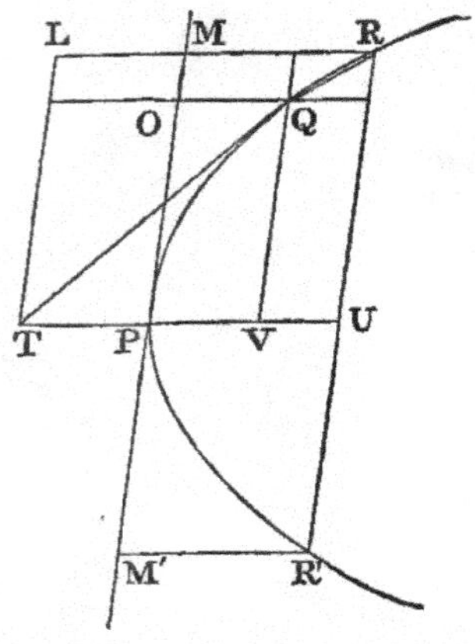

Let R move up to Q. Then, when QT becomes the tangent at Q, $PV = PT$ (Prop. VII.). Hence PM bisects the parallelogram QL. (Euc. I., 36).

Therefore $2QM = QL =$ complement QU. [Euc. I., 43.

Divide the parabolic arc PQ by any number of points, through which draw straight lines parallel to OP, VP, so as to form two series of parallelograms having their bases on VP and OP.

Let the number of the parallelograms be increased and their breadths diminished indefinitely.

Then, as above, each parallelogram in the first series is double of the corresponding one in the second. Hence the sum of the first series, which ultimately becomes the parabolic area QVP, is twice the sum of the second series, or of the area QOP.

Hence the area QVP is two-thirds of $QVP + QOP$, that is, of the parallelogram VO.

COR. Let RU produced meet the curve in R'. Complete the parallelogram $R'RMM'$.

Then area $PUR = \frac{2}{3}$ parallelogram MU,

and area $PUR' = \frac{2}{3}$ parallelogram $M'U$,

U being the middle point of RR'.

Hence the whole area cut off by the chord RR' is two-thirds of the parallelogram MR'.

EXAMPLES.

1. Any point whose distance from the focus of a given parabola is greater than its perpendicular distance from the directrix, lies on the convex side of the curve.

2. Prove that the perpendicular drawn, from the foot of the normal, to the focal distance of any point on the curve, is equal to the ordinate of the point.

3. If PG be the normal at P, and GK perpendicular to SP, prove that $PK = 2SA$, and hence show that the subnormal is constant.

4. In Prop. I. prove that the tangent PY is perpendicular to SM, and hence that it bisects the angle SPM.

5. If the tangents at P, Q, intersect in R, then the circle through P, which touches QR in R, passes through the focus.

6. If PG be any normal, and the triangle SPG be equilateral, then $SP =$ latus rectum.

7. If PP' be a chord meeting the axis at right angles in N, the diameter of the circle through P, P', and the vertex A, is equal to $4AS + AN$.

If PP' be the latus rectum, the diameter is equal to $5AS$.

8. The tangent at any point of a parabola meets the directrix and the latus rectum produced in points equidistant from the focus.

9. The tangent at a point P, whose ordinate is PN, meets the axis in T, and the tangent at the vertex in Y. Prove that $NY = TY$, and that $TP.TY = TS.TN$.

10. If QSQ' be a focal chord and QM, $Q'M'$ perpendiculars on the directrix, then will MSM' be a right angle.

11. If QSQ' be any focal chord and PG the normal to which it is perpendicular, then $PG^2 = SQ.SQ'$.

12. A circle has its centre at the vertex A of a parabola whose focus is S, and the diameter of the circle is $3AS$; show that the common chord bisects AS.

13. A point moves so that its shortest distance from a given circle is equal to its distance from a given fixed diameter of that circle; find the locus of the point.

14. If a circle touch a given circle and a given straight line, the locus of its centre will be a parabola.

15. PM is the ordinate of a point P in a parabola; a line is drawn parallel to the axis, bisecting PM and cutting the curve in Q; MQ cuts the tangent at the vertex in T; show that $AT = \frac{2}{3}PM$.

16. If PY be produced to meet the directrix in Z, then $PY.PZ = SP^2$, and $PY.YZ = AS.SP$.

17. The circle described on any focal chord touches the directrix.

18. The tangent from the vertex to the circle round SPN is equal to $\frac{1}{2}PN$, where PN is the ordinate of P.

19. Normals at the extremities of a focal chord intersect on the diameter which bisects the chord.

20. If PK, drawn at right angles to AP, meet the axis in K, then $2KG = 4AS = NK$, where PN is the ordinate of P.

21. If PQ be a common tangent to a parabola and the circle described on the latus rectum as diameter, then SP, SQ are equally inclined to the latus rectum.

22. If the ordinate of a point P bisect the subnormal of P', the ordinate of P is equal to the normal of P'.

23. The focus and a tangent being given, the locus of the vertex will be a circle.

24. The circle described on any focal radius as diameter touches the tangent at the vertex.

25. Given the focus and two points on the curve; show how to determine the tangent at the vertex.

26. Given the focus and one point on the curve; determine the envelope of the directrix.

27. Given the focus; describe a parabola passing through two given points.

28. Prove that two tangents can be drawn to a parabola from any external point.

29. Tangents and normals at the extremities of a focal chord intersect in T, N respectively. Prove that TN is parallel to the axis.

30. Given, in a parabola, two tangents and one of their points of contact. Prove that the locus of the focus is a circle.

31. Two tangents and their points of contact being given, determine the focus and directrix.

32. The locus of the centre of a circle, passing through a fixed point and touching a fixed straight line, is a parabola of which the given point is a focus.

33. If, from a fixed point O, OP be drawn to a given right line, and the angle TPO be constant, the envelope of TP is a parabola, having O for its focus.

34. If, from the vertex of a parabola, a pair of chords be drawn at right angles to each other, and on them a rectangle be completed, prove that the locus of the farther angle is another parabola.

35. PG, pg are normals at the extremities of a focal chord. Prove that $SG.Sg = AS.Pp$.

36. If three parabolas be inscribed in a triangle, when will the area of the triangle formed by joining their foci be greatest?

37. From the focus S of a parabola, SK is drawn making a given angle with the tangent at P. Determine the locus of K.

38. If a parabola roll upon another equal parabola, the focus traces out the directrix. What limitation is necessary?

39. To two parabolas, which have a common focus and axis, two tangents are drawn at right angles. Prove that the locus of their intersection is a straight line, and that this straight line is parallel to the directrices.

40. A chord of a parabola is drawn parallel to a given straight line, and on this chord as diameter a circle is described; prove that the distance between the middle points of this chord and of the chord joining the other two points of intersection of the circle and parabola will be of constant length.

41. A circle, which passes through S, touches the parabola in the points P, Q. Prove that

$$SP = 4AS = SQ.$$

42. Two circles, which have their centres on the axis of a parabola, touch the parabola and one another. Prove that the difference of their radii is equal to the latus rectum.

43. The squares of the normals at the extremities of a focal chord are together equal to the square of twice the normal perpendicular to the chord.

44. All chords which subtend right angles at A pass through a fixed point in the axis.

45. If a diameter meet a focal chord (which it also bisects) in V, and the directrix in H, then

$$KH^2 = HS.HV.$$

46. If two equal parabolas have a common axis, a straight line touching the interior and terminated by the exterior, will be bisected by the point of contact.

47. If QD be drawn at right angles to the diameter PV, then $QD^2 = 4AS.PV$, where V is the foot of the ordinate of Q.

48. PSp is a focal chord, and upon PS, ps as diameters circles are described; prove that the length of either of their common tangents is a mean proportional between AS and Pp.

49. From the foot of the directrix a chord is drawn to a parabola. Prove that the ordinates of the points in which the chord meets the parabola contain a rectangle equal to the square of the latus rectum.

50. If from the middle point of a focal chord of a parabola two straight lines be drawn, one perpendicular to the chord and meeting the axis in G, the other perpendicular to the axis and meeting it in N; show that NG is constant.

51. PSp is a focal chord of a parabola; RDr the directrix, meeting the axis in D; Q any point on the curve. Prove that, if QP, Qp be produced to meet the directrix in R, r, half the latus rectum is a mean proportional between DR, Dr.

52. Describe a parabola touching four given straight lines.

53. If the diameter PV meet the directrix in O, and the focal chord, parallel to the tangent at P, in V, prove that $PV = PO$.

54. In the last example, prove that the locus of V is a parabola.

55. The locus of the foot of the focal perpendicular upon the normal is a parabola, whose latus rectum is equal to AS.

56. AK, BL are two parallel straight lines such that AB is perpendicular to both of them; take any point Q in BL and join AQ; in AQ, produced if necessary, take a point P, such that, if PN be drawn perpendicular to AK, $PN = BQ$. Prove that the locus of P is a parabola.

57. If, from the point of contact of a tangent to a parabola, a line be drawn parallel to the axis and meeting the chord, tangent, and curve, this line will be divided by them in the same ratio as it divides the curve.

58. If AQ be a chord of a parabola through the vertex A, and QR be drawn perpendicular to AQ to meet the axis in R, prove that AR will be equal to the chord through the focus parallel to AQ.

59. Chords of a parabola are tangents to an equal parabola, having the same axis and vertex, but turned in the opposite direction. Show that the locus of the middle points of the chords is a parabola whose latus rectum is one-third of that of the given parabolas.

60. Two equal parabolas, having the same focus and their axes in contrary directions, intersect at right angles.

61. Two parabolas, with a common axis and vertex, have their concavities in opposite directions; the latus rectum of one is eight times that of the other; prove that the portion of a tangent to the former intercepted between the common tangent and axis is bisected by the latter.

62. If APC be a sector of a circle of which the radius CA is fixed, and a circle be described touching the radii CA, CP and the arc AP, the locus of the centre of this circle is a parabola.

63. From the points where normals to a parabola meet the axis, lines are drawn perpendicular to the normals; show that these lines will be tangents to an equal parabola.

64. If a circle and parabola, having a common tangent at P, intersect in Q, R, and if QV, UR be drawn parallel to the axis of the parabola and meeting the circle in V, U, respectively, then VU is parallel to the tangent at P.

65. A parabola touches the sides AB, AC, of the triangle ABC, at the points B, C. Prove that the angle OSA is a right angle, where O is the centre of the circle described about the triangle.

66. If, from any point P of a parabola, two straight lines PF, PH, be drawn, making equal angles with the normal at P, then $SG^2 = SF.SH$.

67. If, from a point P of a circle, PC be drawn to the centre, and R be the middle point of the chord PQ, drawn parallel to a fixed diameter ACB, then the locus of the intersection of CP, AR is a parabola.

68. TP, TQ are two tangents to a parabola, and, on TQ produced, TQ' is taken equal to TQ.

Prove that $TS.PQ' = TP.TQ$.

69. If, through any point O on the axis of a parabola, a chord POQ be drawn, and PM, QN be the ordinates of P, Q, prove that $AM.AN = AO^2$.

70. If PAQ be a right angle, then $AO = 4AS$.

71. The normal at P is a mean proportional between SP and the latus rectum.

72. The tangents at P, Q meet in T and are intersected by any other tangent in O, R.

Prove that the triangles STP, STQ, OSR are similar and that $SP.SQ = ST^2$.

73. If two tangents to a parabola be cut by a third, the alternate segments will be proportional.

74. If two equal tangents be cut by a third tangent, their alternate segments are equal.

75. PSp is any focal chord of a parabola. Prove that AP, Ap will meet the latus rectum in two points Q, q, whose distances from the focus are equal to the ordinates of P and p.

76. If SY, SZ be perpendiculars on the tangent and normal at any point, then YZ is parallel to the diameter through that point.

77. OP, OQ touch a parabola at the points P, Q; another straight line touches the parabola in R and meets OP, OQ in S, T respectively; if V be the intersection of PT, SQ, then ORV is a straight line.

78. If BV be the diameter through any point B, PV a semi-ordinate, Q any other point on the curve; and if QB cut PV in R, then $VR.VR' = VP^2$, R' being the point in which the diameter through Q meets PV.

79. QSQ' is a focal chord parallel to AP; PN, QM, $Q'M'$ are the ordinates of P, Q, Q'. Prove that $SM^2 = AM.AN$, and that $MM' = AP$.

80. If the tangents at P, Q intersect in T and PQ be perpendicular to PT, then PT is bisected by the directrix.

81. PQ is a chord of a parabola, PT the tangent at P. A line parallel to the axis of the parabola cuts the tangent in T, the arc PQ in E, and the chord PQ in F. Show that

$$TE : EF = PF : FQ.$$

82. A system of parallel chords is drawn in a parabola; prove that the locus of the point which divides each chord into segments containing a constant rectangle is a parabola.

83. If a line be drawn from the foot of the directrix to cut the parabola, the rectangle of the intercepts made by the curve is equal to the rectangle of the parts into which the parallel focal chord is divided by the focus.

84. In a given parabola inscribe a triangle having its sides parallel to three given straight lines, none of which is parallel to the axis of the parabola.

85. The area of the triangle formed by three tangents to a parabola is equal to half the area of the triangle formed by joining the points of contact.

86. PQ is any chord of a parabola cutting the axis in L; R, R' are the two points in the parabola at which this chord subtend a right angle. If RR' be joined, meeting the axis in L', then LL' will be equal to the latus rectum.

87. The area included between any two focal radii SP, SQ is equal to one-half of that included between the curve, the directrix, and the perpendiculars upon it from P, Q.

88. If PQ be a chord of a parabola, normal at P, and T the point in which the tangents at P, Q intersect, then

$$PQ : PT = PN : AN,$$

where PN is the ordinate of P.

89. Prove also that $PQ . AN = 4SP . SY$.

90. If PQ, PK be chords of a parabola, PQ being normal at P, and PK equally inclined to the axis with PQ, the angle PKQ will be a right angle.

91. A parabola touches one side of a triangle in its middle point, and the other two sides produced. Prove that the perpendiculars drawn from the angles of the triangle upon any tangent to the parabola are in harmonical progression.

92. The triangle ABC circumscribes a parabola whose focus is S. Through A, B, C lines are drawn perpendicular respectively to SA, SB, SC. Show that these lines pass through one point.

93. If PQR be a triangle circumscribing a parabola, PB, QM perpendiculars on QR and the directrix respectively, then

$$QM : QB = SQ : PQ.$$

Draw QL perpendicular to the focal distance of the point of contact of RQ (fig., Prop. XIV.); then SLQ and PBQ are similar triangles (Prop. III.), and $SL = QM$. [Prop. III., p. 7.

94. In the last example, if QO, drawn perpendicular to PR, intersect the directrix in O, then

$$QM : QO = SQ : D,$$

D being the diameter of the circle PQR.

The angle SPQ is equal to that which PR makes with the axis (Prop. XIII.), or QO with the directrix. Draw SY perpendicular to PQ; the required result follows by similar triangles QOM, SPY and (Euc. VI., C).

95. If a parabola be inscribed in a triangle the directrix passes through the point of intersection of the perpendiculars drawn from the angular points of the triangle to the opposite sides.*

By examples 93, 94,

$$QO : D = QB : PQ,$$

whence it is readily shown (Euc. VI., C) that O is the point in which QO is intersected by the perpendicular from either of the vertices P, R upon the opposite side.

96. Apply properties of the parabola to prove that—

(i) In any triangle, the feet of the three perpendiculars from any point of the circumscribing circle to the sides of the triangle, lie on the same straight line.

(ii) If four intersecting straight lines be taken three together so as to form four triangles, the perpendiculars of these triangles intersect in four points which lie on a straight line.

---

* For another proof see *The Lady's and Gentleman's Diary* for the year 1863.

97. If two parabolas be described, each touching two sides of a given equilateral triangle at the points in which it meets the third side, prove that they have a common focus and that the tangent to either of them at their point of intersection is parallel to the axis of the other.

98. Two parabolas are described, each touching two sides of an equilateral triangle at the points in which it meets the third side; determine the area common to the two curves.

99. Three parabolas being described, as in the last example, determine the common area.

100. Tangents drawn to a pair of similarly situated parabolas at the extremities of any common diameter intersect upon the common chord.

CHAPTER IV.

THE ELLIPSE.

The definition on p. 1 applies to the ellipse, the ratio spoken of being in this case *a ratio of less inequality.*

Let the curve cut the axis in A, A'. Bisect AA' in C. Take a point H in the axis, such that $CH = CS$, where S is the given focus. Then, for a reason which will appear (Prop. III.), H is called a focus.

Thus S, H are the *Foci.* Also C is the *Centre*, and A, A' are the *Vertices.*

Let BCB' be the central chord perpendicular to AA'.

Then AA' is the *Major* and BB' the *Minor Axis.*

AA' is sometimes called the *Transverse* and BB' the *Conjugate* axis. Also, when THE axis is spoken of, AA' is always signified.

The *Auxiliary Circle* is the circle on AA' as diameter.

Note. An ellipse is sometimes defined as the locus of a point (P) the sum of whose distances from two fixed points (S, H), called foci, is constant. The property in question follows, as in Prop. II., from the definition employed in the present Chapter. The converse proposition is proved in the Appendix.

It is shown in the Appendix that all diameters pass through the centre.

A diameter is sometimes *defined* as a straight line drawn through the centre. In this case it may be shown, conversely, that every diameter bisects a system of parallel chords.

The term *Ordinate* being defined as for the parabola (p. 24), CV is the *Abscissa* of Q.

Divide any straight line SX externally and internally in the same ratio by the points A', A, so that

$$SA' : SA = A'X : AX.$$

Bisect AA' in C and take the point H in CA' such that $CH = CS$. Produce CH to W and let $CW = CX$.

LEMMA I. By construction, $SA' = HA$. Hence, from above, alternando,

$$HA : SA = A'X : AX.$$

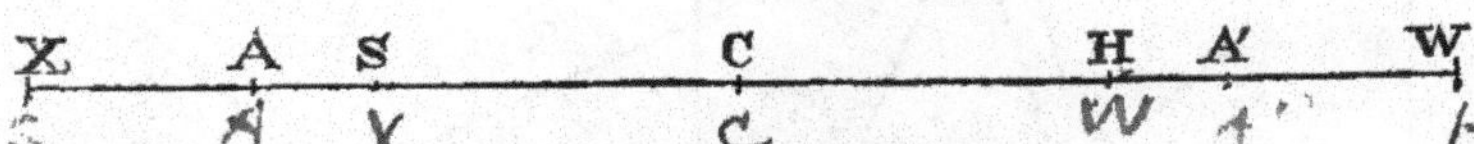

Dividendo $\quad HS : SA = A'A : AX,$

or $\quad SA : AX = HS : AA'$

$\quad = CS : CA.$ [Construction.

LEMMA II. By construction $A'X = WA$.

Hence $\quad SA' : SA = WA : AX.$ [Construction.

Componendo $\quad AA' : SA = WX : AX,$

or $\quad SA : AX = AA' : WX$

$\quad = CA : CX.$ [Construction.

LEMMA III. By Lemmas I., II.

$$CS : CA = CA : CX:$$

Therefore $\quad CS : CX = CS^2 : CA^2,$ [Euc. VI., 20, Cor. 2,

and $\quad CS.CX = CA^2.$ [Euc. VI., 17.

The proofs are similar when the points A, A' lie between S and H. [fig., Prop. II., Chap. VI.

Note. Let P be any point on an ellipse which has S for focus and MX for directrix. Let A be one vertex and PM perpendicular to MX.

Then $\quad SP : PM = SA : AX,$ [*Def.*

and $\quad SP : PM = CS : CA.$ [Lemma I.

Prop. I. *If PM be the perpendicular upon the directrix MX from any point P on an ellipse, then MS, drawn through the focus S, meets the normal at P on the minor axis.*

Let MS meet the minor axis Cg in g, and draw Pg cutting the major axis in G.

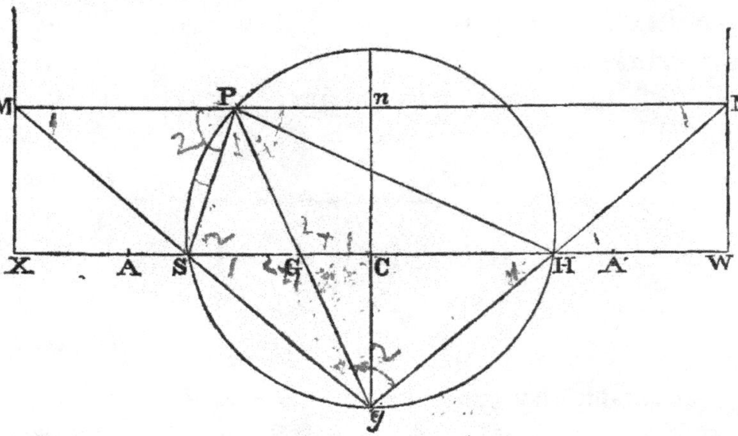

Then, by similar triangles SGg, MPg, the ratio $SG : PM$ is equal to $Sg : Mg$, which is equal, in like manner, to $CS : nM$. Also $nM = CX$.

Therefore $SG : PM = CS : CX$.

But $PM : SP = CA : CS$. [*Note*, p. 48.

Therefore $SG : SP = CA : CX$ [Euc. v., 22,

$= SA : AX$, [Lemma II.

which proves that PG is normal at P. [Prop. IX., p. 12.

Prop. II. *The sum of the focal distances of any point on the ellipse is equal to the major axis.*

Let A, A' be the vertices; S, H the foci; C the centre.

From any point P on the curve draw PM perpendicular to the directrix MX, and let MS meet the minor axis in g. Draw PGg cutting the major axis in G.

Then $SG : SP = SA : AX$, as in Prop. I.

$= SP : PM.$ [*Def.*

Hence the triangles SPG, SPM are similar, since the angles PSG, SPM are equal (Euc. I., 29), and the sides about them proportional.

Therefore $\angle SPG = SMP$ [Euc. VI., 6,

$= gSH$ [Euc. I., 29,

$= gHS$, [Euc. I., 4,

since $CH = CS$ and gC is common to the right-angled triangles gCH, gCS, which are therefore equal in all respects.

Hence a circle goes round $gSPH$. [Euc. III., 21.

Also the angles gPS, gPH stand upon equal circumferences and are equal. [Euc. III., 27, 28.

Therefore the ratio $HG : HP$ is equal to $SG : SP$ (Euc. VI., 3), that is, from above, to $SA : AX$, or to $CS : CA$. [Lemma I.

Alternando $HG : CS = HP : CA$,

and $SG : CS = SP : CA$.

Therefore $SG + HG : CS = SP + HP : CA$. [Euc. V., 24.

But $SG + GH$ is equal to SH or $2CS$.

Therefore $SP + HP$ is equal to $2CA$ or the major axis.

PROP. III. *Every ellipse has two directrices.*

The same construction being made as in the last proposition, it may be shown that

$$SG : SP = SA : AX,$$

and that a circle goes round $gSPH$.

Therefore $\angle gPH = gSH = gHS$. [Euc. III., 21, and I., 5.

Let MP meet the minor axis in n and gH in N. Draw NW to meet the major axis at right angles in W.

Then, since $CH = CS$, therefore (Euc. VI., 3) $nN = nM = CX$. Hence NW *is a fixed straight line.*

But $\angle gPH = gHS$, from above,

$= gNP$. [Euc. I., 29.

Also, the alternate angles GHP, HPG are equal.

Hence the triangles HPN, HPG are similar, and

$$HP : PN = HG : HP$$

$$= SG : SP,$$ [Euc. VI., 3,

since the angles gPS, gPH stand upon equal circumferences and are equal. [Euc. III., 27, 28.

Therefore, from above, HP bears to PN the *constant ratio* of SA to AX.

Hence NW has the same properties as the *directrix* MX.

Note. If the result of this proposition be assumed, it may be proved, as in Prop. XV., p. 19, that $SP + PH$ is constant.

PROP. IV. *The normal at any point bisects the angle between the focal distances of the point.*

Let the normal at P meet the axis in G.

Then $SG : SP = SA : AX$. [Prop. IX., p. 12.

Similarly $HG : HP = SA : AX$. [§ V., p. 18.

Therefore $SG : SP = HG : HP$, [Euc. V., 22,

or PG bisects the angle SPH. [Euc. VI., 3.

PROP. V. *The tangent at any point is equally inclined to the focal distances of the point.*

Let the tangent at P meet the directrix MX in R, PM being perpendicular to MX. Then the circle on PR as diameter passes through the focus S, since PSR is a right angle. [Prop. I., p. 6.

It also passes through M for a like reason. Hence the angles SPR, SMR, in the same segment, are equal, and, if

t be any point in RP produced, it may be shown, similarly, that the angles HPt, HNW are equal.

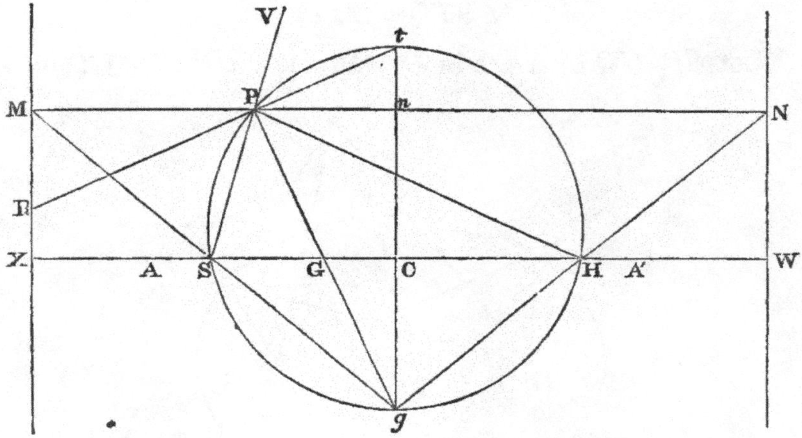

But $SX = HW$; $MX = NW$; and X, S are right angles.

Therefore $\angle SMX = HNW$.

Hence $\angle SPR = HPt$.

Also, if SP be produced to V,

$\angle HPt = SPR = VPt$. [Euc. I., 15.

Note. The method of Prop. VI., Chap. VI. may be here used.

PROP. VI. *The circle which passes through the foci and any point P on the ellipse passes also through the points in which the tangent and normal at P meet the minor axis.*

Describe the circle SPH, cutting the minor axis in g, t. Then the equal straight lines gS, gH cut off circumferences which subtend equal angles gPS, gPH. [Euc. III., 27, 28.

Hence Pg bisects the angle SPH, and is therefore the normal at P. [Prop. IV.

Again, gt bisects SH at right angles and is a diameter of the circle. Hence the angle tPg is a right angle, and Pt, being at right angles to the normal, is the tangent at P.

PROP. VII. *The tangents at P, Q intersect in T. To prove that*

$$\angle STQ = HTP.$$

Let SP, HQ intersect in O. Produce HP to any point V.

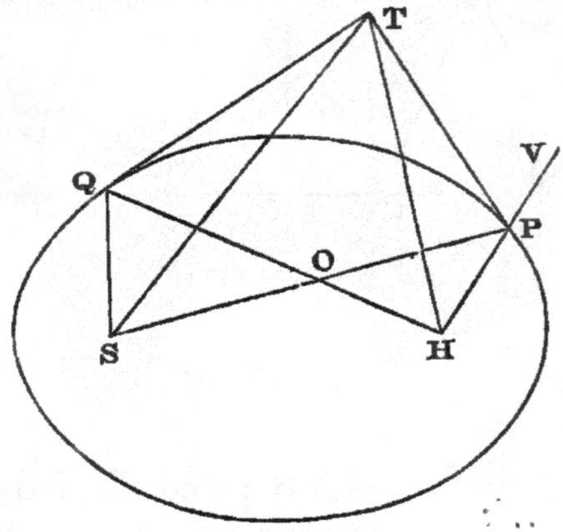

Then TP bisects the angle OPV. [Prop. v.

Also TH bisects the angle OHV. [Prop. VI., p. 9.

Hence $\angle HTP = TPV - THP$ [Euc. I., 32,

$= \frac{1}{2} OPV - \frac{1}{2} OHP$, from above,

$= \frac{1}{2} POH$. [Euc. I., 32.

Similarly $\angle STQ = \frac{1}{2} QOS$.

But the vertical angles at O are equal. [Euc. I., 15.

Therefore $\angle STQ = HTP$.

PROP. VIII. *To prove that*

$$CA^2 - CS^2 = CB^2 = AS \cdot SA',$$

where CB is the semi-minor axis and S either focus.

Since $CS = CH$, therefore

$$CS^2 + CB^2 = CH^2 + CB^2.$$

Therefore $SB^2 = HB^2$ (Euc. I. 47), or $SB = HB$.

Hence $SB = \frac{1}{2}(SB + HB) = CA$. [Prop. II.

Therefore $CB^2 = SB^2 - CS^2 = CA^2 - CS^2$.

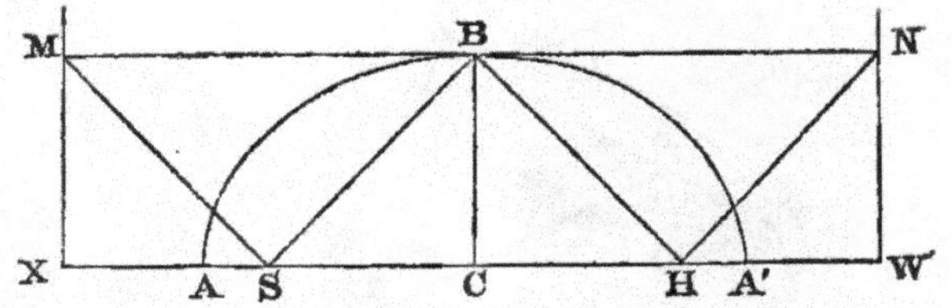

Again, the sum of CS, CA is equal to SA', and their difference to AS. Hence $CA^2 - CS^2 = AS.SA'$. [Euc. II., 5, Cor.

Therefore $CA^2 - CS^2 = CB^2 = AS.SA'$.

Note. BC bisects the angle SBH and is normal at B. [Prop. IV.

Also MBN, drawn parallel to the axis to meet the directrices in M, N, is at right angles to the normal BC and touches the curve at B.

Hence BSM is a right angle (Prop. I., p. 6); and since the angles SBC, SMB are equal, each of them being complementary to SBM, therefore the right-angled triangles SBC, SMB are similar.

Hence $CS : SB = SB : BM$.

Now $SB = CA$. Also (i) B is a point on the curve; and (ii) $BM = CX$.

Therefore $CS : CA = SA : AX$ .... (i),

and $CS : CA = CA : CX$ .... (ii),

compare the Lemmas, p. 48.

Prop. IX. *The foot of the perpendicular drawn from either focus to the tangent at any point lies on the auxiliary circle.*

Let CY, drawn parallel to HP, meet the tangent PY in Y and SP in O. Produce YP to Z.

Then, because CY is parallel to HP, and $CS = \frac{1}{2}HS$, therefore $CO = \frac{1}{2}HP$ (Euc. IV., 2), and $OS = \frac{1}{2}SP = OP$.

Again $\angle OPY = HPZ$ [Prop. V.

$= OYP$. [Euc. I., 29.

Hence $OY = OP = OS$, from above.

Therefore O is the centre of the circle round SPY and the angle SYP, in a semi-circle, is a right angle.

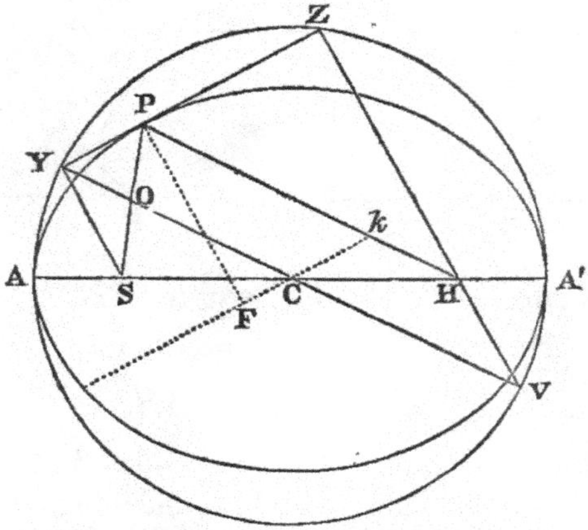

Also $$CO + OY = \tfrac{1}{2}HP + \tfrac{1}{2}SP, \text{ from above,}$$

or $$CY = CA.$$ [Prop. II.

Therefore Y lies on the auxiliary circle; and it has been shewn that SYP is a right angle.

Similarly, if HZ be drawn to meet the tangent YPZ at right angles, then Z lies on the auxiliary circle.

COR. Complete the parallelogram $PYCk$ by drawing the diameter parallel to the tangent at P or perpendicular to the normal PF.

Then $$Pk = CY = CA.$$

PROP. X. *To prove that*

$$SY.HZ = CB^2,$$

where SY, HZ are the focal perpendiculars upon the tangent at any point P.

Describe the auxiliary circle, passing through Y, Z (Prop. IX.), and let ZH meet YC in V.

Then YV is a diameter of the circle, since YZV is a right angle. [Construction.

Hence $CY = CV$ and $CS = CH$, in the triangles SCY, HCV. Also the vertical angles at C are equal.

Therefore $$SY = HV.$$ [Euc. I. 4.

Hence $$SY.HZ = HV.HZ$$
$$= AH.HA'$$ [Euc. III., 36, Cor.
$$= CB^2.$$

Since, in Prop. VIII., S may be *either* focus.

PROP. XI. *If the normal at P meet the major and minor axes in G, g, respectively, then*

$$PG : Pg = CB^2 : CA^2.$$

Draw PM perpendicular to the directrix (fig., Prop. I.) and let MS meet the minor axis in g. Then, as in Prop. I., Pg is the normal at P. Let it meet the major axis in G.

Then Pg is to Gg as Mg to Sg (Euc. VI., 3), or as nM to CS, by similar triangles PMg, GSg. Also $nM = CX$.

Therefore $$Pg : Gg = CX : CS$$
$$= CA^2 : CS^2.$$ [Lemma II.

Hence $$Pg : PG = CA^2 : CA^2 - CS^2$$
$$= CA^2 : CB^2.$$ [Prop. VIII.

PROP. XII. *If PN be the ordinate of P and PG the normal, then*

$$NG : CN = CB^2 : CA^2.$$

Let the normal meet the minor axis in g, and draw Pn perpendicular to CB.

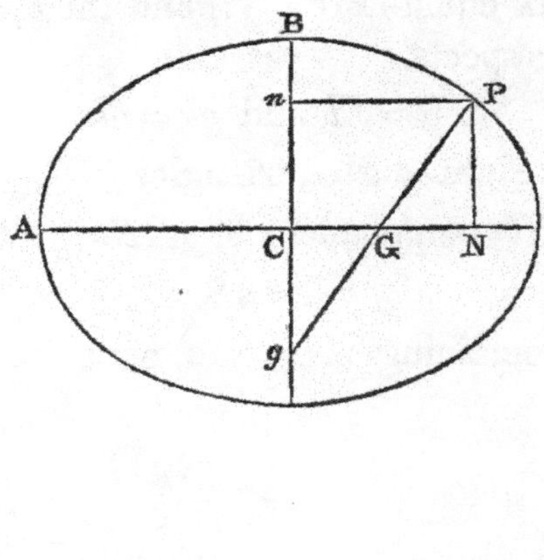

Then, by similar triangles PGN, Pgn,

$$NG : Pn = PG : Pg$$

$$= CB^2 : CA^2. \quad \text{[Prop. XI.}$$

Therefore $$NG : CN = CB^2 : CA^2.$$

Note. Similarly it may be shown that

$$ng : Cn = CA^2 : CB^2.$$

PROP. XIII. *The normal at P meets the minor axis in g, and gk meets SP at right angles in k. To prove that*

$$Pk = CA.$$

Let gl meet HP at right angles in l.

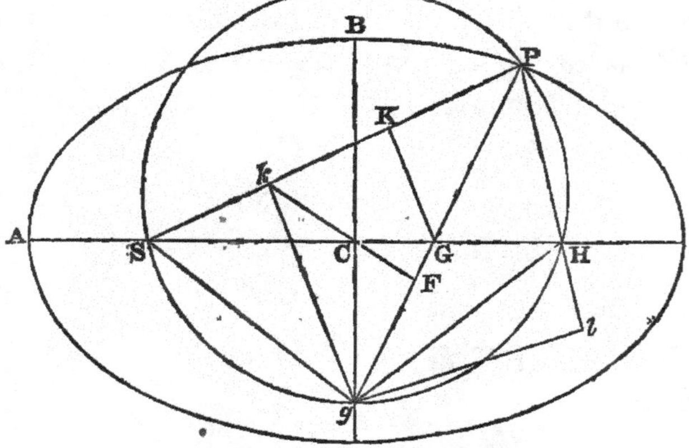

Then the right-angled triangles gPk, gPl, having the angles gPS, gPH equal (Prop. V.) and the side gP common, are equal in all respects.

Hence $$Pk = Pl \text{ and } gk = gl.$$

Again, in the right-angled triangles gHl, gSk,

$$\angle gHl = \text{supplement of } gHP = gSP, \quad \text{[Euc. III., 22.}$$

and $$gH = gS.$$

Hence the remaining sides are equal, each to each, so that $Hl = Sk$.

To each of these equals add $kP + PH$.

Then $$kP + Pl = SP + PH = 2CA.$$ [Prop. II.

But kP, Pl are equal, from above. Hence either of them is equal to CA.

COR. 1. By similar triangles PKG, Pkg, PK is to Pk as PG to Pg, or as $CB^2 : CA^2$. [Prop. XI.

But Pk is equal to CA. Hence

$$PK : CA = CB^2 : CA^2.$$

Therefore $$PK : CB = CB : CA.$$

Hence $PK.Pk$, that is $PK.CA$, is equal to CB^2.

COR. 2. Also, *CB is a mean proportional between CA and the semi-latus rectum*, since the semi-latus rectum is equal to PK. [Prop. X., p. 12.

PROP. XIV. *To prove that*

$$PF.PG = CB^2,$$

and $$PF.Pg = CA^2,$$

F being the point in which the normal meets the diameter parallel to the tangent at P, and G, g the points in which it meets the minor and major axes respectively.

Draw GK, gk perpendicular to SP.

Then FC meets SP in a point whose distance from P is equal to CA (Prop. IX., Cor.), and therefore passes through k. [Prop. XIII.

Hence, by similar right-angled triangles PFk, PKG,

$$PF : Pk = PK : PG,$$

or $$PF.PG = PK.Pk$$
$$= CB^2.$$ [Prop. XIII., Cor. 1.

Again, $$PF : Pk = Pk : Pg,$$

by similar right-angled triangles PFk, Pkg.

Therefore $$PF.Pg = Pk^2$$
$$= CA^2.$$ [Prop. XIII.

PROP. XV. *To prove that*

$$CN.CT = CA^2,$$

T being the point in which the tangent at any point P meets the major axis, and PN the ordinate of P.

Let the normal at P meet the minor axis in g, and the diameter parallel to the tangent at P in F.

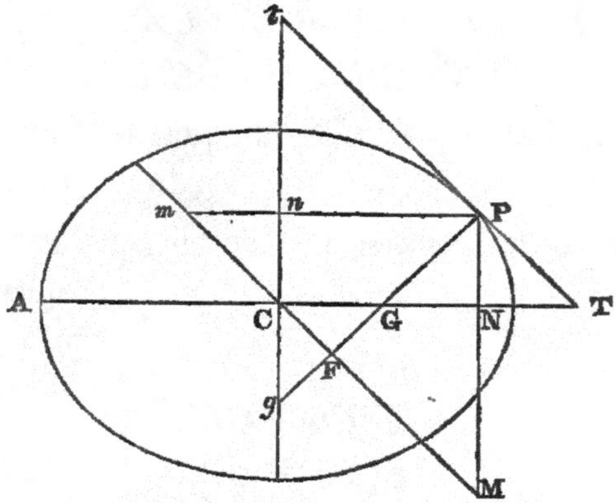

Draw Pn perpendicular to the minor axis and produce it to meet FC in m.

Then, the angles at n, F, being right angles, the circle on mg passes through n, F. [Euc. III., 31.

Therefore $Pn.Pm = PF.Pg$ [Euc. III., 36, Cor.

$= CA^2$. [Prop. XIV.

But $Pn = CN$ and $Pm = CT$.

Therefore $CN.CT = CA^2$.

PROP. XVI. *To prove that*

$$Cn.Ct = CB^2,$$

t being the point in which the tangent at any point P meets the minor axis, and Pn the perpendicular upon that axis.

Let the normal at P meet the major axis in G and the diameter parallel to the tangent at P in F.

Draw PN perpendicular to the major axis and produce it to meet CF in M.

Then, the angles at N, F, being right angles, the circle on MG passes through N, F. [Euc. III., 31.

Therefore $$PN.PM = PF.PG$$ [Euc. III., 36, Cor.
$$= CB^2.$$ [Prop. XIV.

But $$PN = Cn \text{ and } PM = Ct.$$

Therefore $$Cn.Ct = CB^2.$$

PROP. XVII. *Tangents to an ellipse which include a right angle intersect on a fixed circle.*

Let SY, HZ, and SY', HZ', be the focal perpendiculars

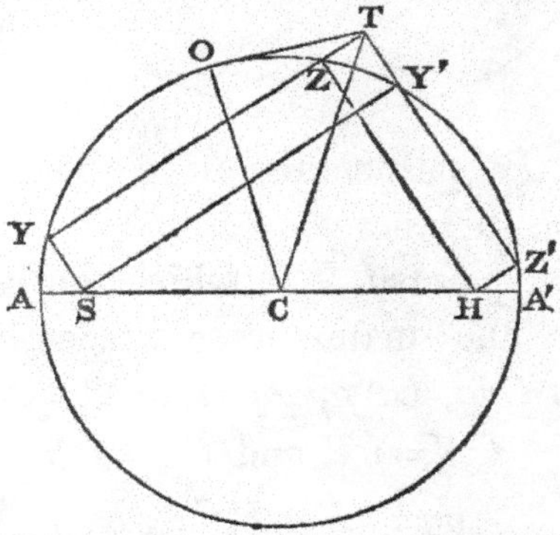

upon two tangents which intersect at right angles in T. Then the figures TH, TS are rectangles and their opposite sides are equal.

Hence $$TY.TZ = SY'.HZ' = CB^2.$$ [Prop. X.

Let TO be drawn touching the auxiliary circle in O. Then since Y, Z are points on the circle (Prop. IX.), therefore
$$TY.TZ = TO^2.$$ [Euc. III., 36.

But it has been shown that $TY.TZ = CB^2$. Hence $TO^2 = CB^2$. Also the radii CO, CA, are equal.

Therefore $CT^2 = CO^2 + TO^2 = CA^2 + CB^2$; which proves that T lies on a fixed circle, whose centre is C.

Prop. XVIII. *Ordinates drawn from the same point in the axis to the ellipse and auxiliary circle are to one another as CB to CA.*

Let the ordinate NP, of the ellipse, be produced to any

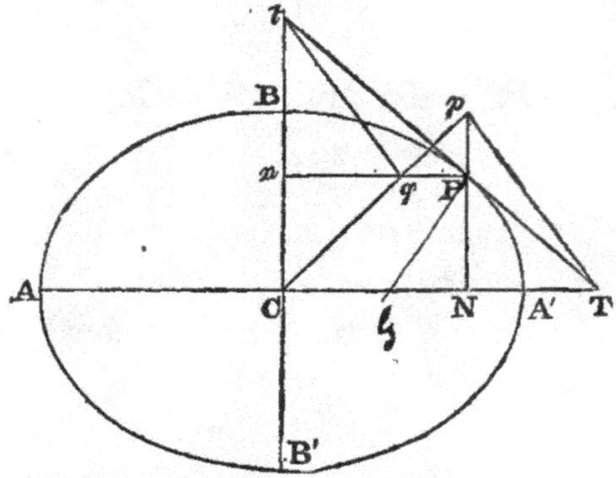

point p. Draw Pn perpendicular to the minor axis, and let Cp, Pn intersect in q.

Join q, p to the points t, T in which the tangent at P intersects the minor and major axes respectively. Then, by similar triangles Cnq, CNp, qn is to CN as Cn to pN.

But $\qquad CN = nP$ and $Cn = PN$.

Therefore $\qquad nq : nP = PN : pN$.

Also $\qquad nP : nt = NT : PN$, by similar triangles.

Therefore $\qquad nq : nt = NT : pN$. [Euc. v., 22.

Hence tq, pT are parallel and $\angle CpT = Cqt$.

Let these equal angles be right angles. Then

$$Cp^2 = CN.CT = CA^2,$$ [Prop. xv.

and $$Cq^2 = Cn.Ct = CB^2.$$ [Prop. xvi.

Hence p, q are points on the circles described upon the major and minor axes respectively.

Also $\qquad PN : pN = Cq : Cp$ [Euc. vi., 2.

$\qquad = CB : CA$, from above,

which proves the proposition.

Note. By the help of this property of the circle upon the major axis many propositions concerning the ellipse may be proved, as in the chapter on corresponding points. Hence the name *Auxiliary Circle.*

Since the circle on the minor axis possesses the analogous property

$$Pn : qn = CA : CB,$$

it may sometimes be convenient to speak of it as the *Minor Auxiliary Circle.*

PROP. XIX. *If PN be any ordinate,*

$$PN^2 : AN.NA' = CB^2 : CA^2.$$

Produce NP to meet the auxiliary circle in p.

Then $$PN^2 : pN^2 = CB^2 : CA^2.$$ [Prop. XVII.

But $$pN^2 = AN.NA',$$ [Euc. VI., 8, Cor.

since the angle ApA', in a semi-circle, is a right angle.

Therefore $$PN^2 : AN.NA' = CB^2 : CA^2.$$

Note. Similarly it may be proved that

$$Pn^2 : Bn.nB' = CA^2 : CB^2.$$

Also, since the radii CA, Cp are equal,

$$pN^2 = Cp^2 - CN^2 = CA^2 - CN^2.$$

Therefore $$PN^2 : CA^2 - CN^2 = CB^2 : CA^2;$$

a form of the proposition which is sometimes useful.

PROP. XX. *Tangents drawn to an ellipse and its auxiliary circle from extremities of a common ordinate intersect upon the axis.*

Let the tangent to the ellipse at P meet the axis in T. Produce the ordinate NP to meet the auxiliary circle in p.

Then $$Cp^2 = CA^2 = CN.CT.$$ [Prop. XV.

Hence CpT is a right angle, and Tp touches the circle. [Euc. III., 16, Cor.

EXAMPLES.

1. If S, H be the foci of an ellipse, P any external point, $SP+PH$ is greater than $2\,CA$.

2. The major axis is the longest straight line that can be drawn in an ellipse.

3. The tangent at B meets the latus rectum on the circumference of the circle described upon the major axis as diameter, and the tangent to the circle at the point where it meets the latus rectum passes through the foot of the directrix.

4. Hence prove that $CS.SX=CB^2$ and deduce that CB is a mean proportional between CA and the semi-latus rectum.

5. For what position of P, on the ellipse, is the angle SPH greatest?

6. If P be any point on the ellipse, T any point on the straight line which bisects the angle between SP produced and HP, then $ST+HT$ is greater than the major axis. Hence show that PT is the tangent at P.

7. Prove that

$$CG : CN = CS^2 : CA^2,$$

where CN is the abscissa of any point on the ellipse and G the point in which the normal meets the major axis.

8. A circle touches an ellipse in two points. Prove that the chord of the circle drawn through either focus and point contact has one of two constant values.

9. The middle point of Gg lies on a fixed circle; G, g being the points in which any normal meets the axes.

10. The minor axis is the least diameter in an ellipse.

11. If SY be perpendicular to the tangent at P, then

$$SY^2 : CB^2 = SP : 2CA - SP.$$

12. If the tangent and normal at P meet the axis in T, G respectively, $CG.CT = CS^2$.

13. If the tangent and normal at P meet the minor axis in t, g respectively, $Cg.Ct = CS^2$.

14. The circle inscribed in the triangle SPH touches SP in M, and SH in N; prove that $PM = AS$ and that $AM = SP$.

15. PG is the normal at P, and a circle passing through P, G meets SP, HP in Q, R. Prove that $PQ + SR$ is equal to the latus rectum.

16. From g, the point in which the normal at P meets the minor axis, straight lines are drawn meeting SP, HP in M, N so that the angles gMP, gNP are supplementary. Prove that $PM + PN$ is constant.

17. Straight lines drawn from the centre parallel to the tangent and normal at P, cut off from SP a straight line equal to HP.

18. SL is the semi-latus rectum, A the vertex; LA produced meets the directrix in Q, and QS intersects the tangent at the vertex in R; prove that $AR = AS$.

19. If the centre of an ellipse, a tangent, and the transverse axis, be given; prove that the directrices pass each through a fixed point.

20. In an ellipse, the tangent at any point makes a greater angle with the focal distance than with the perpendicular upon the directrix.

21. The circle PTG cuts the circle on SH at right angles, where PT, PG are the tangent and normal at P.

22. The greatest value of $SY^2 + HZ^2$ is $2CB^2$.

23. The circle on CG cuts at right angles the circle described with centre P and radius equal to CB.

24. Prove that the normal and the focal perpendiculars on the tangent at any point are in harmonical progression.

25. If SY, SZ be perpendiculars on the tangent at P, the circle round YNZ will pass through C.

26. Prove that $\angle YAZ = \frac{1}{2} SPH$.

27. Prove that CB is a mean proportional between PY and the normal at P.

28. The circle on the normal PG cuts SP, HP in K, L. Prove that PG bisects KL at right angles.

29. The circle described on any focal radius as diameter touches the auxiliary circle.

30. Two tangents can be drawn to an ellipse from any external point.

31. With a given focus describe an ellipse passing through three given points.

32. Circles are escribed to the triangle SPH, opposite to S, H respectively. Determine the rectangle contained by their radii.

33. The locus of the centre of the circle inscribed in the triangle SPH is an ellipse.

The centre of the circle which touches SP produced, HP, and the major axis, lies on the tangent at the vertex.

The locus of the centre of the circle which touches the major axis and PS, PH, both produced, is an ellipse.

34. The subnormal is a third proportional to CT and CB, where CB is the semi-minor axis and T the point in which the tangent intersects the major axis.

35. Given a focus and the length of the major axis; describe an ellipse touching two given straight lines.

36. Given a focus, a tangent, and the length of the major axis; prove that the loci of the centre and the other focus are circles.

37. Given a focus, a tangent, and the length of the minor axis; the locus of the centre is a straight line.

38. If the angle SBH be a right angle, then $CA^2 = 2CB^2$.

39. If SY, HZ be the focal perpendiculars on the tangent at P, then SZ, HY intersect on the normal at P.

40. Construct on the major axis as base, a rectangle which shall be to the triangle SLH (where SL is the semi-latus rectum) in the duplicate ratio of the major to the minor axis.

41. If a circle touch one fixed circle externally and another internally, the locus of its centre will be an ellipse, one of the fixed circles being within the other.

42. If a series of ellipses be described having the same major axes, the tangents at the ends of their latera recta will pass through one or other of two fixed points.

43. SY, HZ are perpendiculars on the tangent at P, and PN is the ordinate of P; prove that

$$PY.PZ : PN^2 = CS^2 : CB^2.$$

44. Prove also that

$$NY : NZ = PY : PZ.$$

45. In an ellipse, if a line be drawn through the focus making a constant angle with the tangent; prove that the locus of its point of intersection with the tangent is a circle.

46. A tangent to an ellipse at a point P intersects a fixed tangent in T; if through S a straight line be drawn, making a constant angle with ST and meeting the tangent at P in Q, show that the locus of Q is a straight line touching the ellipse.

47. The external and internal bisectors of the angles between pairs of tangents to an ellipse, drawn from points on any circle through the foci, intercept a constant length on the minor axis.

48. Tangents to an ellipse, whose foci are S, H, intersect in T, and from T straight lines are drawn equally inclined to ST, HT. Prove that these straight lines are tangents to an ellipse which has S, H for foci.

49. The external and internal bisectors of the angle between the tangents, in the last example, are the tangent and normal, at T, to a confocal ellipse.

50. The external and internal bisectors of the angles between pairs of tangents to a given ellipse meet the axis in M, N. Prove that $CM.CN$ is constant.

51. Given one focus of an ellipse, the length of the minor axis, and a point on the curve; the locus of the other focus is a parabola.

52. If the ordinate at P meet the auxiliary circle in Q, the perpendicular from S on the tangent at Q is equal to SP.

53. Lines from Y, Z, perpendicular to the major axis, cut the circles on SP, HP as diameters in I and J. Prove that IS, JH, CB meet in a point.

54. From any point P on an ellipse PK is drawn, to the major axis, at right angles to AP. Prove that $2GK$ is equal to the latus rectum, PG being the normal at P.

55. An ellipse described on the longer side of a rectangle as major axis passes through the intersection of the diagonals. If lines be drawn from any point of the ellipse exterior to the rectangle to the ends of the remote side, they will divide the major axis into segments, which are in geometrical progression.

56. An ellipse slides between two straight lines at right angles to each other; find the locus of its centre.

57. Two ellipses have their foci coincident; a tangent to one of them intersects, at right angles, a tangent to the other; show that the locus of the point of intersection is a circle having the same centre as the ellipses.

58. A circle described with the centre C, radius CS, cuts the minor axis in F, F'; prove that the sum of the squares of the perpendiculars from F, F' upon any tangent to the ellipse is equal to the square on the semi-minor axis.

59. The sum of the squares of two straight lines which are inversely proportional to diameters at right angles, in the ellipse, is constant.

60. CP, CD are at right angles, and CK perpendicular to PD. Prove that CK is constant, PD being any chord.

61. If a circle passing through Y, Z touch the major axis in Q, and that diameter of the circle which passes through Q meet the tangent in P, show that $PQ = CB$.

62. TP, TQ are tangents drawn to the ellipse and auxiliary circle respectively from a point T on the axis. Prove that

$$PN : QN = CB : CA,$$

where CN is the abscissa of P.

63. If a quadrilateral circumscribes an ellipse, its opposite sides subtend supplementary angles at either focus.

64. From the focus of an ellipse a straight line is drawn inclined at a constant angle to the tangent at any point of the curve. Prove that the locus of the point in which it meets the tangent is a circle.

65. The locus of the foot of the perpendicular drawn from either focus of an ellipse to a chord which subtends a constant angle at that focus, is a circle.

66. An ellipse is inscribed in a triangle. If one focus be at the intersection of the perpendiculars drawn from the angular points upon the opposite sides, the other will coincide with the centre of the circle which circumscribes the triangle.

67. Prove also that the axis of the ellipse is equal to the radius of the circle which circumscribes the triangle.

68. With the intersection of the perpendiculars from the angles of a triangle upon the opposite sides, as focus, two ellipses are described touching a side of the triangle and having the other two sides as directrices respectively; prove that their minor axes are equal.

69. Show that the conic section which touches the sides of a triangle and has its centre at the centre of the circle passing through the middle points of the sides, has one focus at the intersection of the perpendiculars from the angles on the opposite sides, and the other at the centre of the circle circumscribing the triangle.

70. If a focus of an ellipse inscribed in a triangle be the centre of the inscribed circle, the ellipse will be a circle.

71. An ellipse is described so as to touch the three sides of a triangle; prove that if one of its foci move along the

circumference of a circle passing through two of the angular points of the triangle, the other will move along the circumference of another circle, passing through the same two angular points.

72. If one of these circles pass through the centre of the circle inscribed in the triangle, the two circles will coincide.

73. Given, in an ellipse, a focus and two tangents; prove that the locus of the other focus is a straight line.

74. Tangents and normals, at the extremities of a chord through the focus S, intersect in T, N; prove that TN passes through H.

75. The external angle between any two tangents is half the sum of the angles which the chord of contact subtends at the foci.

It may be shown, in Prop. VII., that the angle between QT produced, and PT is equal to the supplement of

$$(POH + STH).$$

Again, $\angle TSP + STH =$ supplement of $(POH + QHT)$.

Hence external angle $= QHT + PST$

$$= \tfrac{1}{2}PHQ + \tfrac{1}{2}PSQ.$$

76. Prove also that

$$\angle SPT + HQT + STH = \text{two right angles.}$$

77. The angle between the tangents at the extremities of a chord which passes through either focus is half the supplement of the angle which the chord subtends at the other focus.

78. The acute angles, which the focal radii to any two points on an ellipse make with the tangents at those points, are complementary. What is the least value of the eccentricity for which this is possible?

79. A', B' are fixed points in a straight line whose extremity is P. If A', B' move along two fixed straight lines which intersect at right angles in C, then P will trace out an ellipse.

Draw $PA'B'$, parallel to pC, to meet the axes (fig., Prop. XVIII.)

Then PA', PB' are equal to CA, CB respectively.

80. Prove also that the normal at P passes through an angular point of the rectangle which has CA, CB for adjacent sides.

CHAPTER V.

THE ELLIPSE CONTINUED.

One diameter is said to be the *conjugate* to another when the first bisects chords parallel to the second.

This definition is evidently consistent (Prop. XII., Cor., p. 15) with the following, which is sometimes used.

One diameter is said to be conjugate to another when the first is parallel to the tangent at an extremity of the second.

Supplemental Chords meet on the curve and pass through opposite extremities of the same diameter.

PROP. I. *If one diameter be conjugate to a second, the second will be conjugate to the first.*

Draw the supplemental chords OP, OP', and bisect them by the diameters CR, CQ.

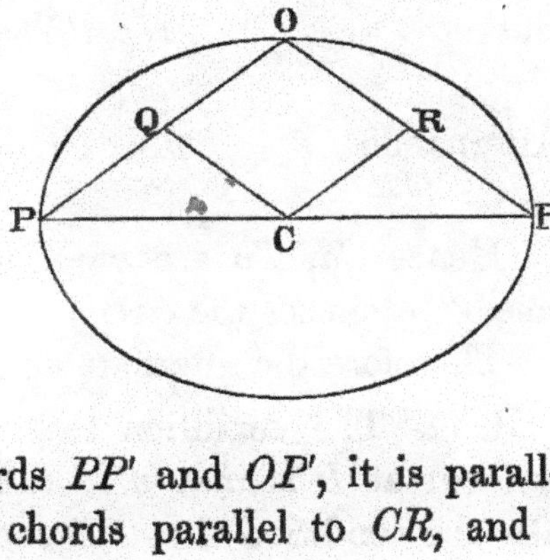

Then CQ, which bisects $P'P$, and OP is parallel to OP'. [Euc. VI., 2.

Hence CR bisects chords parallel to CQ and is therefore conjugate to CQ.

Also CQ will be conjugate to CR.

For, since CR bisects chords PP' and OP', it is parallel to PO. Hence, CQ bisects chords parallel to CR, and is therefore conjugate to CR.

COR. OP, OP' are parallel to CR, CQ, which are conjugate. Hence, supplemental chords are parallel to conjugate diameters.

PROP. II. *If the semi-diameters CP, CD be conjugate, and the ordinates NP, RD be produced to meet the auxiliary circle in p, d respectively, then pCd is a right angle.*

The tangent at P is parallel to CD, since CD is conjugate to CP.

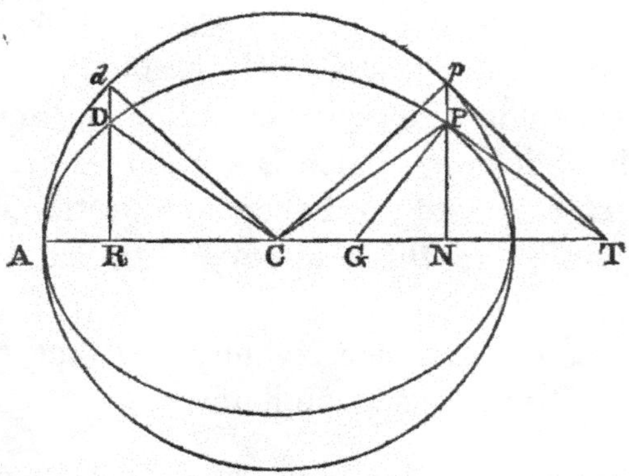

Let this tangent meet the axis in T. Draw Tp. Then by similar triangles PNT, DRC,

$$PN : DR = NT : RC.$$

But $pN : PN = CA : CB$ [Prop. XVIII., p. 64,

$= dR : DR$, similarly.

Alternando $pN : dR = PN : DR$

$= NT : RC$, from above.

Hence Cd, Tp are parallel. But TpC is a right angle since Tp touches the circle. [Prop. XX., p. 66.

Therefore the alternate angle pCd is a right angle.

COR. The condition that CD should be parallel to the tangent at P is that pCd should be a right angle. This is also the condition that CP should be parallel to the tangent at D, which proves Prop. I.

PROP. III. *If CN, CR be the abscissæ of P, D, the extremities of conjugate semi-diameters, then*

$$PN : CR = CB : CA,$$

and

$$DR : CN = CB : CA.$$

Let the ordinates of P, D meet the auxiliary circle in p, d respectively. Then pCd is a right angle. [Prop. II.

Hence $\angle pCN =$ complement of $dCR = CdR$,

and the triangles pCN, CdR are similar.

They are also equal, since $Cp = Cd$.

Therefore $pN = CR$ and $dR = CN$.

But $PN : pN = CB : CA$. [Prop. XVIII., p. 64.

Therefore $PN : CR = CB : CA$.

Similarly $DR : CN = CB : CA$,

COR. By Euc. I., 47, $Cd^2 = dR^2 + CR^2$.

But $dR = CN$, from above; and $Cd = CA$. Therefore

$$CA^2 = CN^2 + CR^2.$$

Similarly, by means of the circle on the minor axis, it may be proved that

$$CB^2 = PN^2 + DR^2.$$

PROP. IV. *To prove that*

$$PG : CD = CB : CA,$$

and

$$Pg : CD = CA : CB,$$

where CD is the semi-diameter conjugate to CP, and PGg the normal, meeting the axes in G, g.

Since CD, being conjugate to CP, is parallel to the tangent at P, it is therefore perpendicular to PG.

Draw the ordinates PN, DR.

Then the angles PGN, DCR are complementary and PGN, DCR are similar triangles.

Therefore $PG : CD = PN : CR$

$= CB : CA.$ [Prop. III.

Similarly it may be proved, by means of the minor auxiliary circle, that

$$Pg : CD = CA : CB.$$

Cor. Hence $PG . Pg = CD^2.$

Prop. V. *The parallelogram formed by drawing tangents at the extremities of a pair of conjugate diameters PP′, DD′ is of constant area.*

Let the normal at P meet DD' in F and the major axis in G.

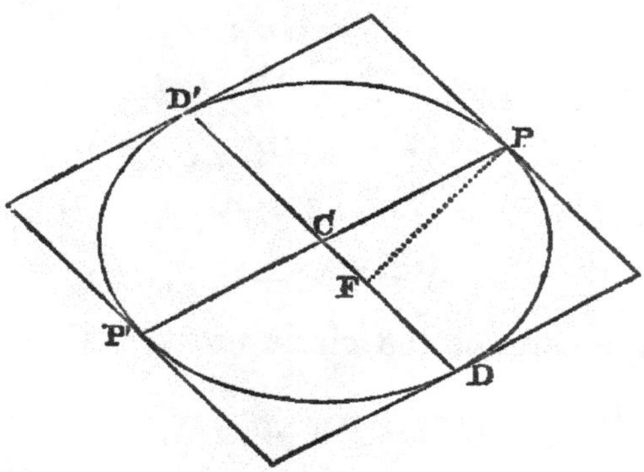

Then $PG : CD = CB : CA.$ [Prop. IV.

Alternando $PG : CB = CD : CA.$

But $PF . PG = CB^2.$ [Prop. XIV., p. 61.

Therefore $CB : PF = PG : CB$

$= CD : CA$, from above,

or $PF . CD = CA . CB.$

It is evident from the figure that the area of the circumscribing parallelogram is equal to $4PF . CD$, that is to $4CA . CB$ or $AA' . BB'$.

PROP. VI. *Tangents drawn to an ellipse from the same point are to one another as the parallel semi-diameters.*

In fig., p. 9, let the diameter parallel to the tangent at P meet SP in k and the normal in F. Then TPL, PkF are similar right-angled triangles.

Therefore $$TP : TL = Pk : PF$$
$$= CA : PF. \quad \text{[Prop. XIII., p. 60.}$$

Let CD be the semi-diameter parallel to TL.

Then $$PF.CD = CA.CB. \quad \text{[Prop. V.}$$

Therefore $$CD : CB = CA : PF$$
$$= TP : TL, \text{ from above.}$$

Similarly $$CD' : CB = TQ : TM,$$

where CD' is the semi-diameter parallel to TQ.

Hence $$TP : TQ = CD : CD',$$

TM, TL being equal, as in Prop. VI., p. 9.

PROP. VII. *To prove that*

$$SP.HP = CD^2,$$

where CP, CD are conjugate semi-diameters.

Draw the normal at P, meeting the major and minor

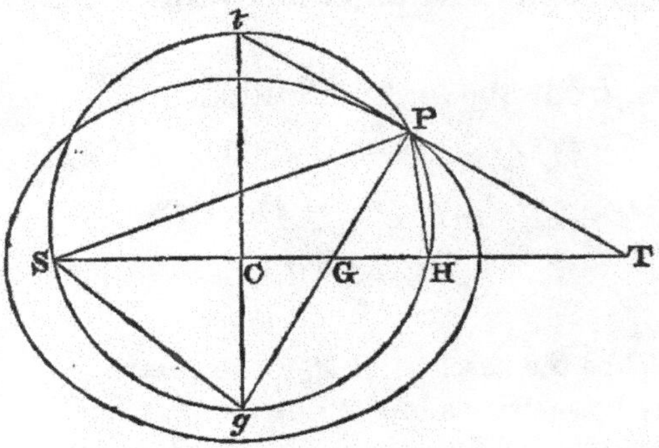

axes in G, g respectively. Then, since a circle goes round $SPHg$ (Prop. VI., p. 55), the angles PSg, PgH, in the same segment, are equal.

Also $\angle SPg = HPG$. [Prop. IV., p. 54.

Hence SPg, HPG are similar triangles, so that

$$SP : PG = Pg : PH.$$

Therefore $SP.HP = PG.Pg$

$$= CD^2.$$ [Prop. IV., Cor.

Note. Let the tangent at P meet the axes in T, t. Then by similar right-angled triangles PGT, Pgt,

$$PT : PG = Pg : Pt.$$

Therefore $PT.Pt = PG.Pg$

$$= CD^2.$$ [Prop. IV., Cor.

PROP. VIII. *To prove that*

$$CP^2 + CD^2 = CA^2 + CB^2,$$

where CP, CD *are conjugate semi-diameters.*

Since C is the middle point of SH (fig., Prop. VII.), therefore

$$SP^2 + PH^2 = 2\,CP^2 + 2\,CS^2.*$$

Also $2\,SP.PH = 2\,CD^2$. [Prop. VII.

But the square on $SP + PH$, or on $2\,CA$, is equal to the squares on SP, PH together with twice the rectangle $SP.PH$. [Euc. II. 4.

Therefore, from above, by addition,

$$4\,CA^2 = 2\,CP^2 + 2\,CD^2 + 2\,CS^2.$$

Hence $CP^2 + CD^2 = CA^2 + CA^2 - CS^2$

$$= CA^2 + CB^2.$$ [Prop. VIII., p. 57.

Or thus:

Let CN, CR be the abscissæ of P, D, respectively.

Then it may be shown, as in Prop. III., Cor., that

$$CN^2 + CR^2 = CA^2,$$

and $PN^2 + DR^2 = CB^2$.

---

* Todhunter's *Euclid*, Appendix.

By addition, since

$$CN^2 + PN^2 = CP^2 \text{ and } CR^2 + DR^2 = CD^2,$$

therefore $$CP^2 + CD^2 = CA^2 + CB^2.$$

PROP. IX. *To prove that*

$$CV.CT = CP^2,$$

where CV is the abscissa of any point Q on the ellipse, measured along a diameter which meets the curve in P, and T the point in which the tangent at Q meets CP.

Let the tangent at P, which is parallel to QV, meet QT in R. Complete the parallelogram $QRPO$.

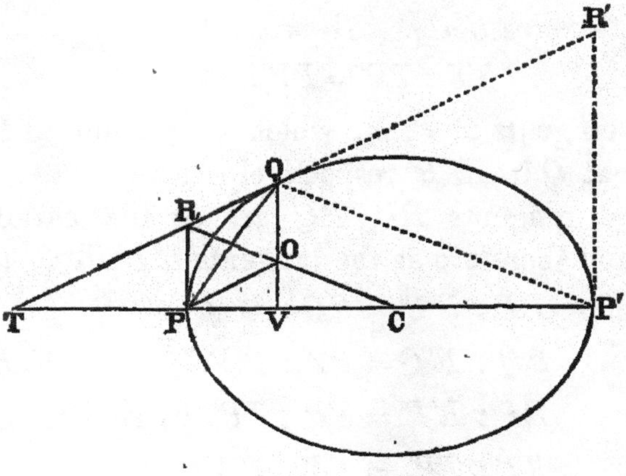

Then the diagonal RO bisects PQ and is therefore a diameter. [Prop. XIII., p. 16.

Let it be produced to the centre C.

Then, since QV, RP are parallel, and also QT, OP, by construction, therefore

$$CV : CP = CO : CR \qquad \text{[Euc. VI., 2,}$$

$$= CP : CT, \text{ similarly,}$$

or $$CV.CT = CP^2.$$

PROP. X. *If TPP' be any diameter and TQ the tangent at a point Q, whose abscissa is CV, then*

$$TC.TV = TP.TP'.$$

Let the tangents at P, Q meet in R. Draw PQ.

Then CR is parallel to $P'Q$, since it bisects PP' and also PQ. [Prop. XII., p. 16.

Also QV, RP are parallel.

Therefore $TC : TP' = TR : TQ$ [Euc. VI., 2,

$= TP : TV$, similarly.

Therefore $TC.TV = TP.TP'$.

PROP. XI. *The tangent and ordinate at Q meet the diameter PCP' in T, V respectively. To prove that*

$$TP : TP' = PV : P'V.$$

Let the tangents at P, P', which are parallel to QV, meet the tangent at Q in R, R' respectively.

Then the tangents RP, RQ are as the parallel semi-diameters, and therefore as the tangents $R'P'$, $R'Q$. [Prop. VI.

Alternando $RP : R'P' = RQ : R'Q$.

But $RQ : R'Q = PV : P'V$, [Euc. VI., 10,

and $RP : R'P' = TP : TP'$, by similar triangles.

Therefore $TP : TP' = PV : P'V$.

COR. The lines TP, TV, TP' are in harmonical progression, since the first is to the third as the difference between the first and second to the difference between the second and third.

Note. Any one of the last three propositions being assumed, the others follow by Euc. II.

For example, let Prop. X. be assumed.

Then $TC^2 - TC.CV = TC^2 - CP^2$,

or $CV.CT = CP^2$.

PROP. XII. *If CV, QV be the abscissa and ordinate of any point Q on the ellipse, then*

$$QV^2 : CP^2 - CV^2 = CD^2 : CP^2,$$

where CP is the semi-diameter on which CV is measured and CD that parallel to QV.

Draw Qv, an ordinate of CD, and let the tangent at Q meet CD, CP produced in t, T respectively.

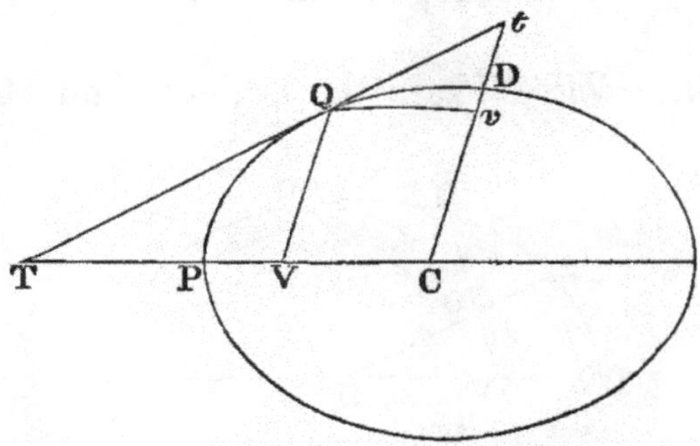

Then $\qquad QV : VT = Ct : CT$, by similar triangles,

and $\qquad QV : CV = Cv : CV$,

since QV, Cv are equal.

Therefore $QV^2 : CV.VT = Cv.Ct : CV.CT$

$$= CD^2 : CP^2. \qquad \text{[Prop. IX.}$$

But $\qquad CV.VT = CV.CT - CV^2 = CP^2 - CV^2$. [Prop. IX.

Therefore $QV^2 : CP^2 - CV^2 = CD^2 : CP^2$.

Note. Let PC meet the curve again in P'.

Then $\qquad CP^2 - CV^2 = PV.VP'$. [Euc. II., 5, Cor.

Therefore $\qquad QV^2 : PV.VP' = CD^2 : CP^2$ .... (i).

Again, Qv is an ordinate of the diameter CP, therefore

$$Qv^2 : CD^2 - Cv^2 = CP^2 : CD^2, \qquad \text{[Prop. XII.}$$

or $\qquad CV^2 : CD^2 - QV^2 = CP^2 : CD^2$.............. (ii),

(i) and (ii) are different forms of Prop. XII.

PROP. XIII. *The rectangle contained by the segments of a chord PQ which passes through a fixed point O bears a constant ratio to the square on the parallel semi-diameter CD.*

Also the rectangles contained by the segments of any two intersecting chords are to one another as the squares of the parallel semi-diameters.

Let the semi-diameter CP bisect the chord in V and let qv be the ordinate of the point in which CO produced meets the curve.

Then, since QV, CV are the ordinate and abscissa of Q,

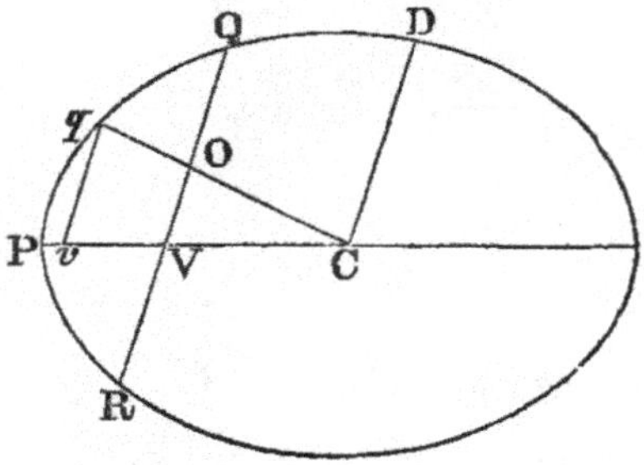

therefore $CD^2 - QV^2 : CV^2 = CD^2 : CP^2$ [Prop. XII., *Note*,

$= CD^2 - qv^2 : Cv^2$, similarly.

Also $OV^2 : CV^2 = qv^2 : Cv^2$, [Euc. VI., 2,

since the ordinates QV, qv are parallel.

Therefore $CD^2 - QV^2 + OV^2 : CV^2 = CD^2 : Cv^2$. [Euc. V., 24.

But $CV : Cv$ is equal to $CO : Cq$, which is a constant ratio since O, q are fixed points.

Hence $CD^2 - QV^2 + OV^2 : CD^2$ is a constant ratio.

Therefore $QO . OR$, being equal to $QV^2 - OV^2$ (Euc. II., 5, Cor.), bears a constant ratio to CD^2.

Again, take any other chord $Q'R'$, passing through O, and let CD' be the parallel semi-diameter.

Then, since $QO.OR : CD^2$ is constant for all chords through O, therefore

$$QO.OR : CD^2 = Q'O.OR' : CD'^2.$$

Cor. 1. Let the chords move parallel to themselves until they become tangents. Then the rectangles become the squares of tangents drawn from an external point. Hence tangents drawn from the same point are as the parallel semi-diameters.

Cor. 2. The ratio $CD : CD'$ is constant for all pairs of chords parallel to QR and $Q'R'$. Hence the rectangles contained by the segments of any two intersecting chords are as the rectangles contained by the segments of any other two chords parallel to the former.

One or more of these chords may be supposed to become tangents as in Cor. 1.

Cor. 3. In Cor. 2 let one pair of chords pass through the focus. Then, by Prop. XI., p. 13, the rectangles contained by the segments of any two intersecting chords are to one another as the lengths of the parallel focal chords.

Prop. XIV. *If a circle and an ellipse intersect in four points their common chords will be equally inclined to the axis of the ellipse.*

Let Q, R, Q', R' be the points of intersection and let QR cut $Q'R'$ in O.

Then the rectangles $QO.OR$, $Q'O.OR'$ are as the squares on parallel semi-diameters of the ellipse. [Prop. XIII.

But these rectangles are equal by a property of the circle. [Euc. III., 35.

Hence the diameters parallel to QR, $Q'R'$ are equal and therefore equally inclined to the axis.

It follows that QR, $Q'R'$ are equally inclined to the axis.

Similarly QR', $Q'R$ and QQ', RR' are equally inclined to the axis.

PROP. XV. *The tangent at P meets any diameter in T and the conjugate diameter in t. To prove that*

$$PT.Pt = CD^2,$$

where CD is the semi-diameter parallel to Pt.

Draw PV, Dv, ordinates of the diameter CT, and PM an ordinate of Ct.

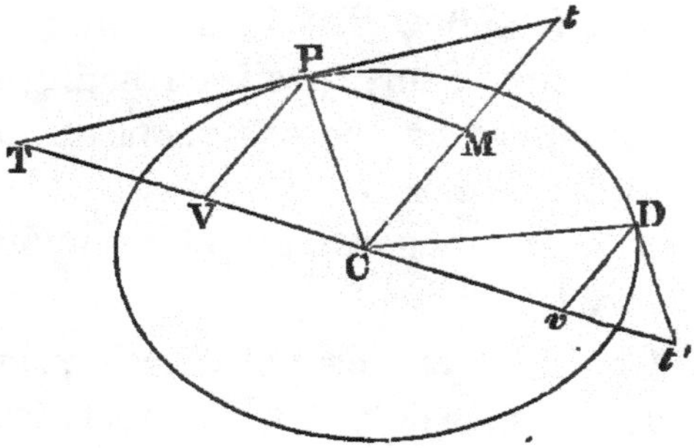

Let the tangent at D, which is parallel to CP, since CP, CD are conjugate, meet TC produced in t.

Then the rectangles $CV.CT$ and $Cv.Ct'$ are equal to one another, since they are both equal to the square on the same semi-diameter. [Prop. IX.

Therefore $$CV : Cv = Ct' : CT.$$

But the ratio $CV : Cv$, that is $PM : Cv$, is equal to $Pt : CD$, by similar triangles PtM, CDv.

Therefore $Pt : CD = Ct' : CT$, from above,

$$= CD : PT,$$

by similar triangles CDt', CPT.

Therefore $$PT.Pt = CD^2.$$

PROP. XVI. *If a chord pass through a fixed point, the tangents at its extremities will intersect on a fixed straight line.*

Draw CO, through the fixed point O, to meet the curve in P, and let T be the point of intersection of tangents at the extremity of the chord which is bisected in O.

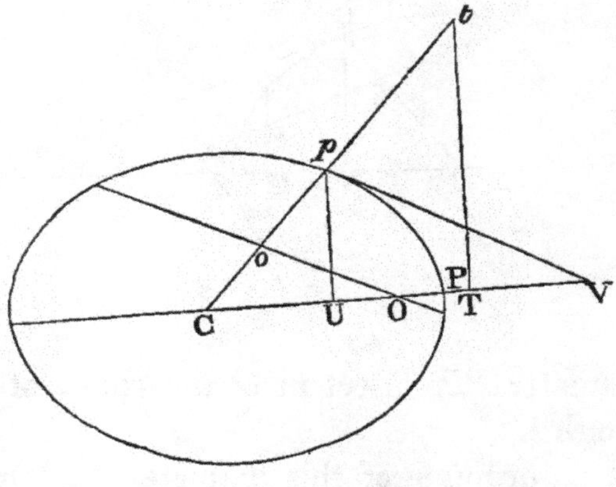

Draw Cop, bisecting in o any chord through O, and meeting the curve in p.

Draw pU an ordinate of the diameter through O, and let Tt, drawn through T parallel to Up, (and therefore *fixed*), meet Cp in t. Let CO produced meet the tangent at p in V.

Then $$CO.CT = CP^2 = CU.CV. \qquad \text{[Prop. IX.}$$

Therefore $$CO : CV = CU : CT.$$

But, by similar triangles, CO is to CV as Co to Cp, and CU to CT as Cp to Ct.

Therefore $$Co : Cp = Cp : Ct.$$

Hence $$Co.Ct = Cp^2,$$

and the tangents at the extremities of the chord Oo intersect in t. [Prop. IX.

Also Tt is a fixed straight line. [Construction.

Note. As in the case of the parabola, O is called the pole of Tt, and Tt the polar of O.

PROP. XVII. *If from any point t, tpp' be drawn to meet the ellipse in p, p', and the chord of contact of tangents through t in o, then $tpop'$ will be cut harmonically.*

Draw Cc to the middle point of pp' and produce it to meet the curve in Q.

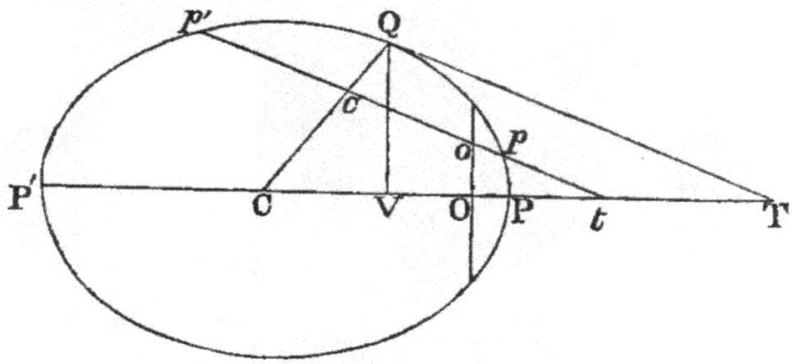

Let the diameter PP' bisect in O the chord of contact of tangents through t.

Draw QV, an ordinate of this diameter, and let the tangent at Q meet the diameter in T.

Then $$TQ : tc = TC : tC,$$
by similar triangles TQC, tcC;

and $$TQ : to = TV : tO,$$
by similar triangles TQV, toO.

Therefore $TQ^2 : tc.to = TC.TV : tC.tO$

$= TP.TP' : tP.tP'$ [Prop. x.

$= TQ^2 : tp.tp'$. [Prop. XIII., Cor. 2.

Hence $tc.to = tp.tp'$, or $2tp.tp' = to\,(tp + tp')$, since c is the middle point of pp'.

PROP. XVIII. *The areas of the ellipse and auxiliary circle are as CB to CA.*

Let P, Q be the adjacent points on the ellipse.

Produce the ordinates NP, MQ to meet the auxiliary circle in p, q respectively, and draw PQ, pq.

Then since PN and QM are to pN and qM respectively

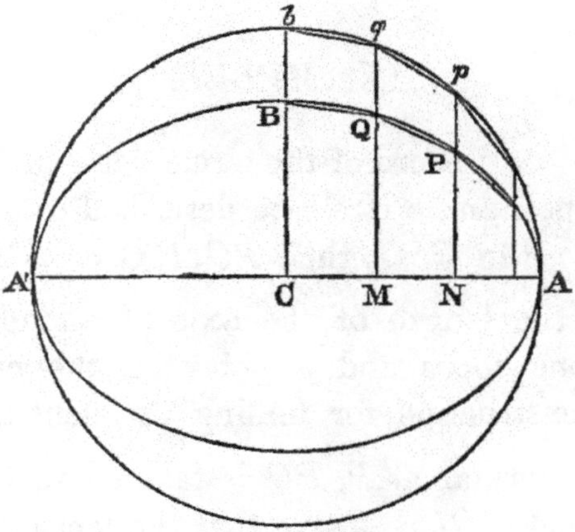

as CB to CA (Prop. XVIII., p. 64), therefore the rectilinear areas $PQMN$, $pqMN$ are as CB to CA.

Let a series of rectilinear figures CQ, MP, ... be inscribed, as above, in the elliptic quadrant ACB. Produce the ordinates of the points Q, P, ... to meet the auxiliary circle in p, q, ... respectively, and complete the figures Cq, Mp, ...

Then since each of the figures CQ, MP, ... is to the corresponding figure in the circle as CB to CA, the sum of the first series of figures is to that of the second in the same ratio. [Euc. V., 12.

This is true whatever be the number of the figures.

Let the number of the figures CQ, MP, ... be increased and the breadth of each diminished indefinitely, so that the sum of their areas becomes equal to the elliptic area ACB.

Then the sum of the rectilinear areas Cq, Mp, ... becomes equal to the circular area ACb.

Hence the areas ACB, ACb, and therefore those of the ellipse and circle, are as CB to CA.

EXAMPLES.

1. If PQP' be a chord of the circle described on the major axis of an ellipse, and a circle be described on the minor axis cutting the chord in Q, Q', then $PQ . P'Q = CS^2$.

2. Given, the length of the axis of an ellipse, and the positions of one focus and a point on the curve; give a geometrical construction for finding the centre.

3. On the normal at P, PQ is taken equal to the semi-conjugate diameter CD. Prove that the locus of Q is a circle whose radius is equal to half the difference of the axes.

4. A circle can be described passing through the foci and the points in which any tangent meets the tangents at the vertices.

5. The sum of the squares of normals at the extremities of conjugate diameters is constant.

6. The tangent and normal at P and a perpendicular from that point meet the minor axis in t, g, n. Prove that $Pn . gt = CD^2$.

7. The tangent at P meets any two conjugate diameters in T, t, and TS, tH intersect in Q. Prove that SPT, HPt, TQt are similar triangles.

8. If CP be conjugate to the normal at Q, CQ will be conjugate to the normal at P.

9. Given two conjugate diameters; determine the directions of the axes.

10. Tangents are drawn to confocal ellipses from a given point in the axis; prove that the normals at the points of contact pass through a fixed point.

11. CP, CD are conjugate semi-diameters, and the tangents at P, D meet in T. Prove that ST, HT meet CP, CD in four points which lie on a circle.

12. If AQ be drawn from one of the vertices perpendicular to the tangent at any point P, the locus of the point of intersection of PS, QA will be a circle.

13. If the tangent and normal at P meet the axis in T, G, and TQ touch the circle on AA' in Q, then

$$TQ : TP = CB : PG.$$

14. TP, TQ are tangents to an ellipse and PQ meets the directrices in R, R'; prove that

$$RP.R'P : RQ.R'Q = TP^2 : TQ^2.$$

15. The points in which the tangents at the extremities of the transverse axis of an ellipse are cut by the tangent at any point of the curve, are joined one with each focus; prove that the point of intersection of the joining lines lies in the normal at the point.

16. Two conjugate diameters of an ellipse are cut by the tangent at any point P in M, N; prove that the area of the triangle CPM varies inversely as that of the triangle CPN.

17. P is any point on the ellipse. To any point Q on the curve AQ, $A'Q$ are drawn meeting NP in R, S; prove that $NR.NS = NP^2$.

18. When is the sum of two conjugate diameters least?

19. The tangent at the vertex cuts any two conjugate diameters in T, T'; prove that $AT.AT' = CB^2$.

20. If any two chords AB, CD, which are not parallel, make equal angles with the axis, the lines AC, BD will make equal angles with the axis.

21. If PT be a tangent to an ellipse, meeting the axis in T, and AP, $A'P$ produced meet the straight line drawn through T, perpendicular to the major axis, in Q, R, then $QT = RT$.

22. Show that in every ellipse there are two equal conjugate diameters, coinciding in direction with the diagonals of the rectangle which touches the ellipse at the extremities of the axes.

23. The normal at P cuts the axes in G, g; prove that the length of the tangent from P to any circle which passes through the points G and g is equal to CD.

24. Prove that $CD^2 = PG^2 + SG.GH$.

25. Prove that $(SP - CA)^2 + (SD - CA^2) = CS^2$.

26. If PQ be the focal chord which is parallel to CD, then $PQ.CA = 2CD^2$.

27. If from the extremities of any diameter chords be drawn to any point in the ellipse, the diameter parallel to these chords will be conjugate.

28. Normals are drawn to an ellipse at the extremities of a chord parallel to one of the equi-conjugate diameters. Show that the locus of their intersection is a line through the centre perpendicular to the other equi-conjugate diameter.

29. The tangents TP, TQ meet the diameters QC, PC in P', Q'; prove that the triangles TQP', TPQ' are equal.

30. If PSp be a focal chord of an ellipse, and along SP there be set off SQ a mean proportional between SP and Sp, the locus of Q will be an ellipse having the same eccentricity as the original ellipse.

31. A tangent to an ellipse, whose foci are S, H, meets two given conjugate diameters in T, t; TS, tH meet in P, show that the locus of P is a circle.

32. From any point P of an ellipse PQ is drawn at right angles to SP meeting the diameter conjugate to CP in Q; prove that PQ varies inversely as the perpendicular from P on the major axis.

33. The loci of the middle points of PG, Pg are ellipses, where PGg is normal at P.

34. A series of ellipses have their equal conjugate diameters of the same magnitude, one of them being fixed and common, while the other varies. The tangents drawn from any point in the fixed diameter produced will touch the ellipses in points situated on a circle.

35. If two ellipses having the same major axes be inscribed in a parallelogram, the foci will be on the corners of an equiangular parallelogram.

36. A straight line is drawn from the centre of an ellipse meeting the ellipse in P, the circle on the major axis in Q, and the tangent at the vertex in T. Prove that as CT approaches and ultimately coincides with the semi-major axis, PT and QT are ultimately in the duplicate ratio of the axes.

37. Tangents to an ellipse are drawn from any point on a circle through the foci; prove that the lines bisecting the angles between the tangents all pass through a fixed point.

38. P, Q are points on two confocal ellipses at which the line joining the common foci subtends equal angles; prove that the tangents at P, Q contain an angle equal to that subtended by PQ at either focus.

39. If QQ' be any chord parallel to the tangent at a given point P of an ellipse, the circle round QPQ' will meet the curve in a fixed point.

40. If the tangents at P, Q, R intersect in R', Q', P', then

$$PR'.P'Q : PQ'.R'Q = P'R : Q'R.$$

41. An ellipse is inscribed in a triangle A, B, C; prove that if a, b, c be the points of contact, the straight lines Aa, Bb, Cc will pass through the same point.

42. Two ellipses, whose major axes are equal, have a common focus; prove that they intersect in two points only.

43. In an ellipse Pp, Dd are conjugate diameters; E is taken in Pp so that $PE : Ep = CD^2 : CP^2$; EF is drawn parallel to Dd, meeting the normal PF; GFH being any chord of the ellipse, prove that GPH is a right angle.

44. A parallelogram is inscribed in an ellipse, and from any point on the ellipse two straight lines are drawn parallel to the sides of the parallelogram; prove that the rectangles under the segments of these straight lines, made by the sides of the parallelogram, will be to one another in a constant ratio.

45. Normals at P and D, the extremities of semi-conjugate diameters meet in K; show that KC is perpendicular to PD.

46. The tangent at a point P of an ellipse meets the auxiliary circle in a point Q', to which corresponds Q on the ellipse. Prove that the tangent at Q cuts the auxiliary circle in the point corresponding to P.

47. The locus of a point which cuts parallel chords of a circle in a given ratio, is an ellipse having double contact with the circle.

48. YSZ is drawn through a fixed point S, meeting two fixed straight lines in Y, Z. Prove that the envelope of the circle on YZ is an ellipse having S for focus.

49. If a chord parallel to the axis meet the ellipse in P, P', and if $P'Q$, $P'Q'$ be chords equally inclined to the axis, then QQ' is parallel to the tangent at P.

50. PSp, QCq are any two parallel chords through the focus and centre of an ellipse, prove that

$$SP.Sp : CQ.Cq = CB^2 : CA^2.$$

51. If the diameter conjugate to CP meet SP, HP in E, F; then $SE = HF$ and the circles described about SCE, HCF are equal.

52. The common diameters of two equal, similar, and concentric ellipses are at right angles to one another.

53. If CM, MP be the abscissa and ordinate of any point P on a circle whose centre is C, and if MQ be taken equal to MP and inclined to it at a constant angle, the locus of Q is an ellipse.

54. The tangent at a point P of an ellipse meets the tangents at the vertices in V, V'; on VV' as diameter a circle is described, which intersects the ellipse in Q, Q'; show that the ordinate of Q is to the ordinate of P as CB to $CB + CD$.

55. From the extremity P of the diameter PQ, in an ellipse, the tangent TPT' is drawn meeting two conjugate diameters in T, T'. From P, Q the lines PR, QR are drawn parallel to the same conjugate diameters. Prove that the triangle PQR is to $CA.CB$ as $CA.CB$ to the triangle CTT'.

56. PCP' is any diameter of an ellipse. The tangents at any two points D and E intersect in F. PE, $P'D$ intersect in G. Show that FG is parallel to the diameter conjugate to PCP'.

57. SQ, HQ are drawn perpendicular to a pair of conjugate diameters. The locus of Q is a concentric ellipse.

58. A parabola of given latus rectum is described touching symmetrically two conjugate diameters of an ellipse; find the locus of the focus.

59. If AQ be drawn from one of the vertices of an ellipse perpendicular to the tangent at any point P, prove that the locus of the intersection of PS, QA will be a circle.

60. TP, TQ are tangents to an ellipse at the points P, Q. Prove that SP, HP, SQ, HQ are tangents to a circle described with T as centre.

61. Supplemental chords PL, PL' are equally inclined to a chord PQ, normal at P. Prove that LL' bisects PQ.

62. A, B, C are three points in a straight line; with A, B as foci an ellipse is, described passing through C, and with B and C as foci another ellipse is described passing through A and intersecting the former in P. If PN be drawn perpendicular to CA, prove that $AP+CP=PN+CA$.

63. If the normal at P in an ellipse meet the axis minor in G, and if the tangent at P meet the tangent at the vertex A in V; show that

$$SG : SC = PV : VA.$$

64. ABC is an isosceles triangle of which the side AB is equal to the side AC. BD, BE, drawn on opposite sides of BC and equally inclined to it, meet CA in D, E. If an ellipse is described round BDE having its axis minor parallel to CB, then AB will be a tangent to the ellipse.

65. Show that, if the distance between the foci of an ellipse be greater than the length of its axis minor, there will be four positions of the tangent for which the area of the triangle included between it and the straight lines drawn from the centre of the curve to the feet of the focal perpendiculars upon the tangent, will be the greatest possible.

66. Prove that the distance between the two points on the circumference of an ellipse at which a given chord, not passing through the centre, subtends the greatest and least angles, is equal to the diameter which bisects the chord.

67. In Ex. 61, prove that $LP+PL'$ is constant.

68. The rectangle contained by the radii of the inscribed and circumscribing circles of the triangle SPH varies as the square of the conjugate diameter.

69. The ordinates of all points on an ellipse being produced in the same ratio, determine the locus of their extremities.

70. The central radii of an ellipse being produced in a constant ratio, the locus of their extremities is an ellipse.

CHAPTER VI.

THE HYPERBOLA.

The definition on p. 1 applies to the hyperbola, the ratio spoken of being in this case *a ratio of greater inequality.*

Let the curve cut the axis in A, A'. Bisect AA' in C. Take a point H in the axis such that $CH=CS$, where S is the given focus. Then, for a reason which will appear (Prop. IV.), H is called a focus.

Thus S, H are the *Foci.* Also C is the *Centre*, and A, A' are the *Vertices.*

It has been shown, on p. 5, that a straight line drawn parallel to the axis of a hyperbola meets the curve in two points which are situated on opposite sides of the directrix, so that the hyperbola consists of two branches having their convexities in opposite directions.

Compare the first figure on p. 10.

It is hence evident that no straight line drawn perpendicular to the axis and intersecting it between the vertices will meet the curve.

It will however appear that, in the case of the hyperbola, the points B, B', determined as follows, correspond to the extremities of the minor axis in the ellipse.

Through C draw a straight line perpendicular to the axis, and on it take points B, B', equidistant from C, such that $CB^2 = CS^2 - CA^2$.

Then AA' is called the *Major* and BB' the *Minor Axis.*

These terms are employed as being analogous to those used in the case of the ellipse. In the case of the hyperbola AA' is not necessarily greater than BB'.

AA' is sometimes called the *Transverse* and BB' the *Conjugate* axis. Also, when THE axis is spoken of, AA' is always signified.

Note. A hyperbola is sometimes defined as the locus of a point (P), the difference of whose distances from two fixed points (S, H), called foci, is constant. The property in question follows, as in Prop. III., from the definition employed in the present Chapter. The converse proposition is proved in the Appendix.

It is shown in the Appendix that all diameters pass through the centre.

A diameter is sometimes *defined* as a straight line drawn through the centre. In this case it may be shown, conversely, that every diameter bisects a system of parallel chords.

The term *Ordinate* being defined as for the parabola (p. 24), CV is the *Abscissa* of Q.

Note. Let P be any point on a hyperbola which has S for focus and MX for directrix. Let A be one vertex and PM perpendicular to MX.

Then $\quad SP : PM = SA : AX,$ [*Def.*

and $\quad SP : PM = CS : CA.$ [Lemma I., p. 51.

PROP. I. *If PM be the perpendicular upon the directrix MX from any point P on a hyperbola, then SM, drawn from the focus S, meets the normal at P on the minor axis.*

Let SM meet the minor axis Cg in g, and produce gP to meet the major axis in G. [fig., p. 101.

Then, by similar triangles SGg, MPg, the ratio $SG : PM$ is equal to $Sg : Mg$, which is equal, in like manner to $CS : nM$. Also $nM = CX$.

Therefore $SG : PM = CS : CX.$

But $PM : SP = CA : CS.$ [*Note*, p. 99.

Therefore $SG : SP = CA : CX$ [Euc. v., 22.

$= SA : AX,$ [Lemma II., p. 51.

which proves that PG is normal at P. [Prop. IX., p. 12.

PROP. II. *If the normal at P meet the major and minor axis in G, g respectively, then*

$$PG : Pg = CB^2 : CA^2.$$

Draw PM perpendicular to the directrix MX, and let SM meet the minor axis in g. Then, as in Prop. I., Pg is the normal at P. Let it meet the major axis in G.

Then Gg is to Pg as Sg to Mg (Euc. VI. 3), or as CS to nM, by similar triangles GSg, PMg. Also $nM = CX$.

Therefore $Gg : Pg = CS : CX$

$= CS^2 : CA^2.$ [Lemma III., p. 51.

Dividendo $PG : Pg = CS^2 - CA^2 : CA^2$

$= CB^2 : CA^2.$

PROP. III. *The difference of the focal distances of any point on the hyperbola is equal to the major axis.*

Let A, A' be the vertices; S, H the foci; C the centre.

From any point P on the curve draw PM perpendicular to the directrix MX, and let MS meet the minor axis in g. Draw gPG cutting the major axis in G.

Then $SG : SP = SA : AX$, as in Prop. I.,

$= SP : PM.$ [*Def.*

Hence the triangles SPG, SPM are similar, since the angles PSG, SPM are equal (Euc. I. 29), and the sides about them proportional.

Therefore $\angle SPG = SMP$ [Euc. VI., 6.

$= gSH$ [Euc. I., 29.

$= gHS,$ [Euc. I., 4.

since $CH = CS$ and gC is common to the right-angled triangles gCH, gCS, which are therefore equal in all respects.

Therefore $\angle gHS + SPg = SPG + SPg =$ two right angles.

Hence, a circle goes round $gPSH$. [Euc. III., 22.

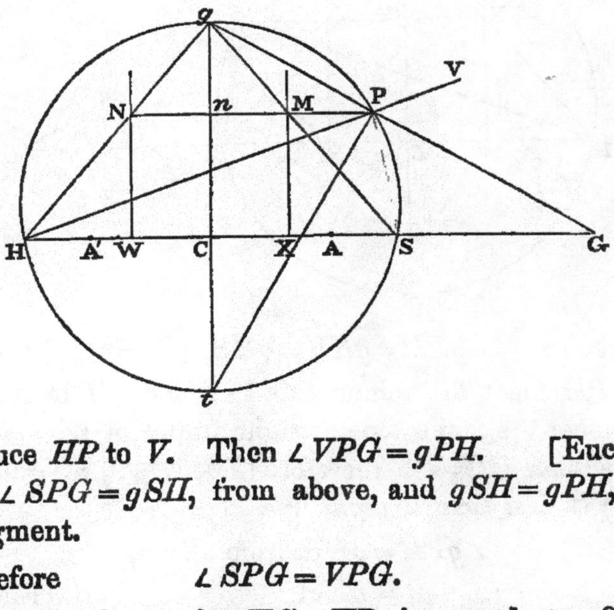

Produce HP to V. Then $\angle VPG = gPH$. [Euc. I., 15.

Also $\angle SPG = gSH$, from above, and $gSH = gPH$, in the same segment.

Therefore $\angle SPG = VPG$.

Therefore the ratio $HG : HP$ is equal to $SG : SP$ (Euc. VI., A), that is, from above, to $SA : AX$, or to $CS : CA$. [Lemma I., p. 51.

Alternando $HG : CS = HP : CA$,

and $SG : CS = SP : CA$.

Therefore $HG - SG : CS = HP - SP : CA$. [Euc. V., 24, Cor.

But $HG - SG$ is equal to SH or $2CS$.

Therefore $HP \sim SP$ is equal to $2CA$ or the major axis.

Prop. IV. *Every hyperbola has two directrices.*

The same construction being made as in the last proposition, it may be shown that

$$SG : SP = SA : AX,$$

and that a circle goes round $gSPH$.

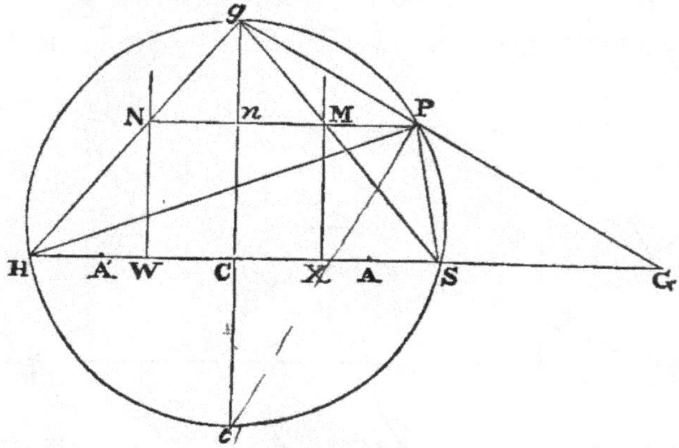

Therefore $\angle gPH = gSH = gHS$. [Euc. III., 21, and I., 5.

Let PM meet the minor axis in n and gH in N. Draw NW to meet the major axis at right angles in W.

Then, since $CH = CS$, therefore (Euc. VI., 3) $nN = nM = CX$. Hence NW *is a fixed straight line.*

But $\angle gPH = gHS$, from above,

$= gNP$. [Euc. I., 29.

Also, the alternate angles GHP, HPN are equal.

Hence the triangles HPN, HPG are similar, and

$$HP : PN = HG : HP$$

$$= SG : SP, \text{ as in Prop. III.}$$

Therefore, from above, HP bears to PN the *constant ratio* of SA to AX.

Hence NW has the same properties as the *directrix* MX.

Note. If the result of this proposition be assumed, it may be proved, as in Prop. XV., p. 19, that $SP \sim PH$ is constant.

PROP. V. *The normal at any point is equally inclined to the focal distances of the point.*

Let the normal meet the axis in G.

Then $SG : SP = SA : AX$. [Prop. IX., p. 12.

Similarly $HG : HP = SA : AX$. [§ V., p. 18.

Therefore $SG : SP = HG : HP$. [Euc. V., 22.

Hence PG bisects SPV, the exterior angle at P. [fig., p. 101.

Hence also $\angle SPG = GPV = HPg$.

PROP. VI. *The tangent at P bisects the angle SPH.*

Draw Pt bisecting the angle SPH, and let the normal at P meet the axes in G, g.

Then $\angle SPG = HPg$, as in Prop. V.

Also $\angle SPt = HPt$. [Construction.

By addition $\angle GPt = gPt =$ a right angle.

Therefore Pt, being at right angles to the normal is the tangent at P.

Note. The method of Prop. V., p. 54 is here applicable.

PROP. VII. *The circle which passes through the foci and any point P on the hyperbola passes also through the points in which the tangent and normal at P meet the minor axis.*

Describe the circle SPH, cutting the minor axis in g, t. Then the equal straight lines tS, tH cut off circumferences which subtend equal angles tPS, tPH. [Euc. III., 27, 28.

Hence Pt bisects the angle SPH, and is therefore the tangent at P. Prop. VI.

Again, gt bisects SH at right angles and is a diameter of the circle. Hence the angle tPg is a right angle, and Pg, being at right angles to the tangent, is the normal at P.

PROP. VIII. *If TP, TQ be tangents to opposite branches of the same hyperbola, then*

$$\angle STP = HTQ.$$

Let SQ, HP intersect in O. Produce PS to V.

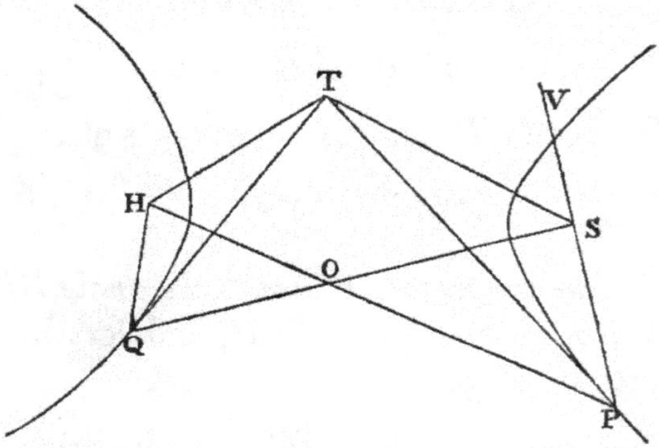

Then $\angle TSV =$ supplement of $TSP = TSQ$, [*Note*, p. 10.

therefore $\angle TSV = \frac{1}{2} QSV$. Also $\angle TPS = \frac{1}{2} HPS$. [Prop. VI.

Therefore $\angle STP = TSV - TPV$ [Euc. I., 32.

$$= \frac{1}{2} QSV - \frac{1}{2} HPS$$

$$= \frac{1}{2} POS.$$ [Euc. I., 32.

Similarly $\angle HTQ = \frac{1}{2} QOH = \frac{1}{2} POS.$

Therefore $STP = \angle HTQ.$

PROP. IX. *The foot of the perpendicular drawn from either focus to the tangent at any point lies on the circumference of the circle described upon the major axis as diameter.*

Let CY, drawn parallel to HP, meet the tangent PY in Y and SP in O.

Then, because CO is parallel to HP, and $CS = \frac{1}{2} HS$, therefore $CO = \frac{1}{2} HP$ (Euc. VI., 2), and $OS = \frac{1}{2} SP = OP$.

Again $\angle OPY = HPY$ [Prop. VI.

$$= OYP.$$ [Euc. I., 29.

Hence $OY = OP = OS$, from above.

Therefore O is the centre of the circle round SPY, and the angle SYP, in a semi-circle, is a right angle.

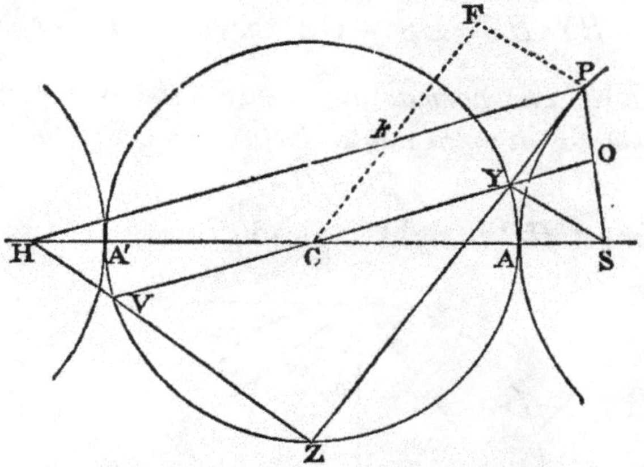

Also $$CO - OY = \tfrac{1}{2}HP - \tfrac{1}{2}SP, \text{ from above,}$$

or $$CY = CA.$$ [Prop. III.

Therefore Y lies on the circle described upon AA', and it has been shown that SYP is a right angle.

Similarly, if HZ be drawn to meet the tangent YP produced at right angles, then Z lies on the circle described upon AA'.

COR. Complete the parallelogram $PYCk$ by drawing the diameter parallel to the tangent at P or perpendicular to the normal PF. Then $Pk = CY = CA$.

PROP. X. *To prove that*

$$SY.HZ = CB^2,$$

where SY, HZ are the focal perpendiculars upon the tangent at any point P.

Describe the circle on AA', passing through Y, Z (Prop. IX.), and let ZH meet YC in V. Then YV is a diameter of the circle, since YZV is a right angle. [Construction.

Hence $CY = CV$, and $CS = CH$, in the triangles SCY, HCV. Also the vertical angles at C are equal.

Therefore $SY = HV$. [Euc. I., 4.

Hence $SY.HZ = HV.HZ = AH.HA'$ [Euc. III., 36, Cor.

Therefore $SY.HZ = CS^2 - CA^2$ (Euc. II., 5, Cor.) $= CB^2$.

PROP. XI. *The normal at P meets the minor axis in g, and gk meets SP at right angles in k. To prove that*

$$Pk = CA.$$

Let gl meet HP at right angles in l.

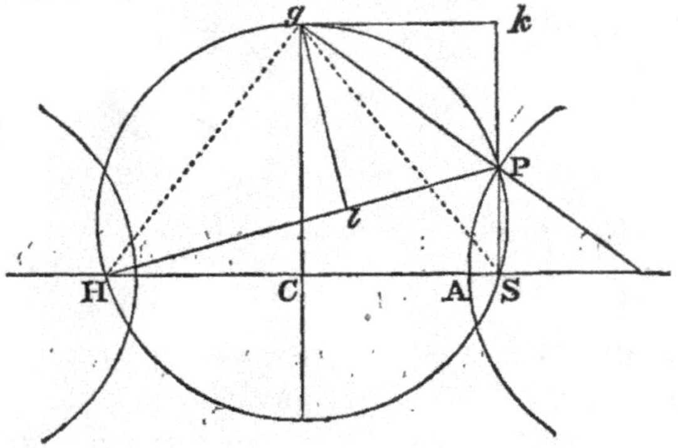

Then the right-angled triangles gPk, gPl, having the angles gPk, gPl equal (Prop. V.) and the side gP common, are equal in all respects.

Hence $Pk = Pl$ and $gk = gl$.

Again, in the right-angled triangles gHl, gSk, the sides gH, gS are equal and $\angle gHl = gSk$, in the same segment, since a circle goes round $gHSP$. [Prop. VII.

Hence the remaining sides are equal, each to each, so that $Hl = Sk$.

Therefore $SP + Pk = HP - Pl$.

Therefore $Pk + Pl = HP - SP = 2CA$. [Prop. III.

But Pk, Pl are equal, from above. Hence either of them is equal to CA.

COR. 1. By similar triangles PKG, Pkg (fig., Prop. XII.), PK is to Pk as PG to Pg, or as CB^2 to CA^2 (Prop. II.). But Pk is equal to CA.

Hence $$PK : CA = CB^2 : CA^2.$$

Therefore $$PK : CB = CB : CA.$$

Hence $PK.Pk$, that is $PK.CA$, is equal to CB^2.

COR. 2. Also CB *is a mean proportional between* CA *and the semi-latus rectum*, since the semi-latus rectum is equal to PK. [Prop. X., p. 12.

PROP. XII. *To prove that*

$$PF.PG = CB^2,$$

and $$PF.Pg = CA^2,$$

F being the point in which the normal meets the diameter parallel to the tangent at P, and G, g the points in which it meets the minor and major axes respectively.

Draw GK, gk perpendicular to SP.

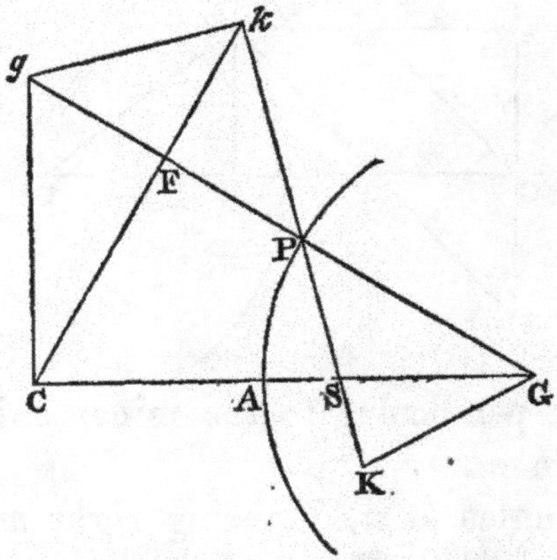

Then CF meets SP in a point whose distance from P is equal to CA (Prop. IX., Cor.), and therefore passes through k. [Prop. XI.

Hence, by similar right-angled triangles, PFk, PKG,

$$PF : Pk = PK : PG,$$

or $$PF.PG = PK.Pk$$
$$= CB^2. \qquad \text{[Prop. XI., Cor. 1.}$$

Again, $PF : Pk = Pk : Pg$, by similar triangles.

Therefore $$PF.Pg = Pk^2$$
$$= CA^2. \qquad \text{[Prop. XI.}$$

PROP. XIII. *To prove that*

$$CN.CT = CA^2,$$

T being the point in which the tangent at any point P meets the major axis, and PN the ordinate of P.

Let the normal at P meet the minor axis in g, and the diameter parallel to the tangent at P in F.

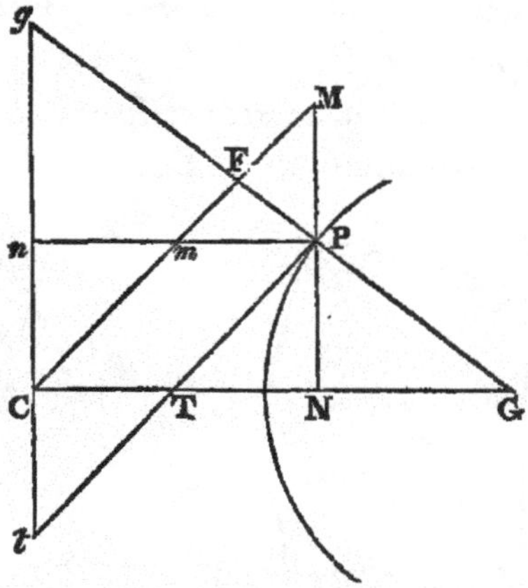

Draw Pn perpendicular to the minor axis and produce; let it cut FC in m.

Then, the angles at n, F, being right angles, the circle on mg passes through n, F. [Euc. III., 31.

Therefore $$Pn.Pm = PF.Pg \qquad \text{[Euc. III., 36, Cor.}$$
$$= CA^2. \qquad \text{[Prop. XII.}$$

But $Pn = CN$ and $Pm = CT$.

Therefore $$CN.CT = CA^2.$$

PROP. XIV. *To prove that*

$$Cn.Ct = CB^2,$$

t being the point in which the tangent at any point P meets the minor axis, and Pn the perpendicular from P upon that axis.

Let the normal at P meet the major axis in G and the diameter parallel to the tangent at P in F.

Draw PN perpendicular to the major axis and produce NP to meet CF in M.

Then, the angles at N, F, being right angles, the circle on MG passes through N, F. [Euc. III., 31.

Therefore $PN.PM = PF.PG$ [Euc. III., 36, Cor.
$= CB^2$. [Prop. XII.

But $PN = Cn$ and $PM = Ct$.

Therefore $Cn.Ct = CB^2$.

PROP. XVI. *If CN be the abscissa of any point P on the hyperbola, then*

$$PN^2 : CN^2 - CA^2 = CB^2 : CA^2,$$

and $$PN^2 : AN.NA' = CB^2 : CA^2,$$

where A, A' are the vertices.

Let the tangent at P meet the axes in T, t. Draw Pn perpendicular to the minor axis.

Then, by similar triangles PNT, tCT,

$$PN : NT = Ct : CT.$$

Also $PN : CN = Cn : CN$,

since $PN = Cn$.

Therefore $PN^2 : CN.NT = Cn.Ct : CN.CT$
$= CB^2 : CA^2$. [Props. XIII., XIV.

But $CN.NT = CN^2 - CN.CT = CN^2 - CA^2$. [Prop. XIII.

Therefore $PN^2 : CN^2 - CA^2 = CB^2 : CA^2$.

Therefore $PN^2 : AN.NA' = CB^2 : CA^2$,

since $CN^2 - CA^2 = AN.NA'$. [Euc. II., 5, Cor.

PROP. XVII. *Tangents to a hyperbola which include a right angle intersect on a fixed circle.*

Let any tangent intersect the circle upon AA' in the

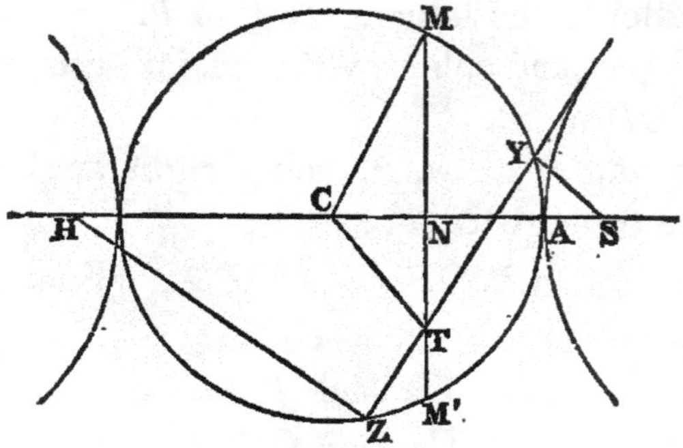

points Y, Z, and let a second tangent intersect the first at right angles in T.

Let MTM', a chord of the circle, cut the axis in N.

Then $$MN^2 - TN^2 = TM.TM' \quad \text{[Euc. II., 5, Cor.}$$
$$= TY.TZ. \quad \text{[Euc. III., 35.}$$

But it may be shown, as in Prop. XVII. p. 63, that

$$TY.TZ = CB^2.$$

Hence $$MN^2 = TN^2 + CB^2.$$

To each of these equals add CN^2.

Then $$CM^2 = CT^2 + CB^2. \quad \text{[Euc. I., 47.}$$

Therefore $$CT^2 = CM^2 - CB^2,$$
$$= CA^2 - CB^2,$$

which proves that T lies on a fixed circle whose centre is C.

PROP. XVIII. *If PN be the ordinate of P and PG the normal, then*

$$NG : CN = CB^2 : CA^2.$$

Let the normal meet the minor axis in g, and draw Pn perpendicular to CB.

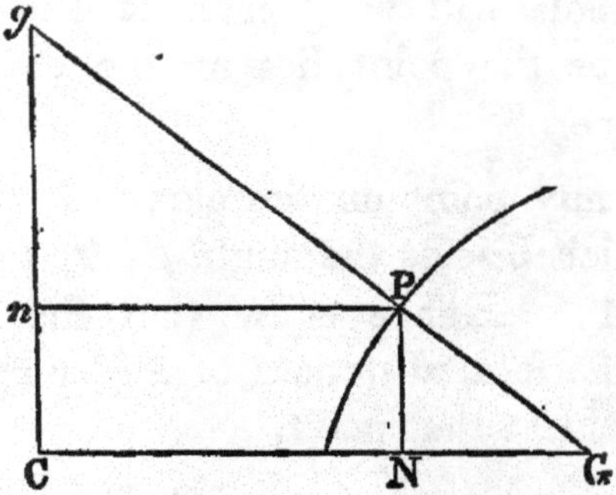

Then, by similar triangles PGN, Pgn,

$$NG : Pn = PG : Pg$$

$$= CB^2 : CA^2. \qquad \text{[Prop. II.}$$

Therefore $$NG : CN = CB^2 : CA^2.$$

Note. Similarly it may be shown that

$$ng : Cn = CA^2 : CB^2.$$

EXAMPLES.

1. The difference of the distances of any point from the foci of a hyperbola will be greater or less than the major axis according as the point lies on the concave or convex side of the curve.

2. If P be any point on the curve, T any point on the straight line which bisects the angle SPH, then $HT \sim ST$ is lesser than AA'. Hence show that the bisector of the angle between the focal distances of any point in the hyperbola is the tangent at that point.

3. PN is the ordinate of a point P on the curve, NQ a tangent to the circle on AA'; prove that

$$PN : CB = QN : CQ.$$

4. Hence show that

$$PN^2 : CN^2 - CA^2 = CB^2 : CA^2.$$

5. If SY be perpendicular to the tangent at P,

$$SY^2 : CB^2 = SP : 2CA + SP.$$

6. The tangent from the foot of the normal at any point to the circle on AA' varies as the normal.

7. Prove that $CS . SX = CB^2$ and deduce the length of the latus rectum.

8. Circles described through any point P of the curve and the point in which the normal at P meets either axis intersect the focal radii of P in H, K. Prove that $PH + PK$ is constant.

9. A circle touches SP, SH produced in L, M, and also touches HP; prove that $HM = AS$ and $SM = A'S$.

10. The locus of the centre of a circle touching two fixed circles is an ellipse or a hyperbola.

11. If the ordinate MP of a hyperbola be produced to Q, so that $MQ = SP$, find the locus of Q.

12. If an ellipse and a hyperbola have the same foci they will cut one another at right angles.

13. If on the portion of any tangent intercepted between the tangents at the vertices a circle be described it will pass through the vertices.

14. If PM be an ordinate drawn from a point P on the hyperbola, MQ a tangent to the circle on the major axis, and PN parallel to QC, then $MN = CB$.

15. If any chord AP, through the vertex of a hyperbola, be divided in Q so that $AQ : QP = CA^2 : CB^2$, and QM be drawn to the foot of the ordinate MP, show that QO, drawn at right angles to QM, cuts the transverse axis in the same ratio.

16. If the tangent and normal at any point of the hyperbola meet the transverse axis in T, G respectively, then $CG.CT = CS^2$.

17. Hence prove that $CN.CT = CA^2$, where CN is the abscissa of the point of contact.

18. The circle on any focal radius touches the circle on the axis.

19. Given, in an ellipse, a focus and two points; the locus of the other focus is a hyperbola.

20. Describe a hyperbola passing through three given points and having a given focus.

21. A parabola passes through two given points and has its axis parallel to a given line. Prove that the locus of the focus is a hyperbola.

22. If a circle be inscribed in the triangle formed by joining any point on a hyperbola to the foci, the locus of its centre is the tangent at the vertex.

23. If P be any point on a hyperbola whose foci are S, H, and a circle be described touching HP produced, SP, and the transverse axis, the locus of its centre will be a hyperbola.

24. CN being the abscissa of a point P, NQ is drawn parallel to AP and meeting CP in Q. Prove that AQ is parallel to the tangent at P.

25. If tangents at P, Q cut off AR, $A'R'$, AL, $A'L'$ from the tangents at the vertices A, A', then $AR.A'R' = AL.A'L'$.

26. The curve which trisects the arcs of all segments of a circle described on a given base is a hyperbola whose eccentricity is 2.

27. A chord which subtends a right angle at the vertex meets the axis in a fixed point.

28. Draw a normal to a conic from a given point on the axis minor.

29. P is a fixed point on a conic, and from Q, any point in the ordinate of P produced, QYG is drawn, cutting the polar of Q at right angles in Y and meeting the axis in G. Prove that G is a fixed point, and that $QG.GY$ is equal to the square of the normal at P.

30. The chord of contact of tangents to a central conic through an external point P meets the axis in T; PXG is drawn meeting the axis in G and cutting the chord at right angles in X. Prove that $CG.GT = ST.HT$.

31. Prove also that, if CM, SY, HZ be perpendiculars upon the chord, then $CM.PG = CB^2$ and $SY.HZ = CM.YG$. What do these theorems become when the point P lies on the curve?

32. If a pair of the chords of intersection of a circle and a conic be produced to meet a similarly situated conic, the four points of intersection will lie on another circle; and, if the two conics be similar and concentric, the circles will be concentric.

33. The normals to the circle on AA', in a central conic, at the points where the tangent at P meets it, bisect the focal radii to P.

34. If a circle be described through any point P of a given hyperbola and the extremities of the transverse axis, then the ordinate of P, being produced, meets the circle again on a fixed hyperbola. Also the axes of the first hyperbola and the conjugate axis of the second are proportionals.

35. An ellipse and a hyperbola are described so that the foci of each are at the extremities of the transverse axis of the other; prove that the tangents at their points of intersection meet the conjugate axis in points equidistant from the centre.

36. The points of trisection of a series of conterminous circular arcs lie on branches of two hyperbolas; determine the distance between their centres.

37. Given a focus, a tangent, and one point on a hyperbola; determine the locus of the other focus.

38. If, from a fixed point O, OP be drawn to a given circle, and the angle TPO be constant, the envelope of TP is a conic having O for focus.

39. If from the focus of a conic a line be drawn making a given angle with any tangent, find the locus of the point in which it intersects the tangent.

40. Tangents from any point to a system of confocal conics make equal angles with two fixed lines.

41. The locus of the intersection of tangents to a parabola which cut at a given angle, is a hyperbola.

42. A straight line drawn from the focus of a conic so as to make a constant angle with a chord subtending a constant angle at the focus, meets the chord, in general, upon the circumference of a fixed circle.

43. If an ellipse and hyperbola have the same foci and tangents be drawn to the one to intersect at right angles those drawn to the other, the locus of the points of intersection is a circle.

44. P, P' are points on a hyperbola and its conjugate, S, S' the interior foci of the branches on which P, P' lie. Prove that the difference of SP, $S'P'$ is equal to difference of CA, CB.

45. A, P and B, Q are points taken respectively in two parallel straight lines, A, B being fixed and P, Q variable. Prove that if the rectangle $AP.BQ$ be constant, the line PQ will always touch a fixed ellipse or a fixed hyperbola according as P, Q are on the same or opposite sides of AB.

46. Through a fixed point S a straight line SYY' is drawn to meet fixed parallel straight lines in Y, Y'. Prove that the envelope of the circle on YY' is a hyperbola, S being a focus and the fixed lines directrices.

47. PQ is a chord of an ellipse at right angles to the major axis AA'; PA, QA' are produced to meet in R; show that the locus of R is a hyperbola having the same axes as the ellipse.

48. If a hyperbola be described touching the four sides of a quadrilateral inscribed in a circle and one focus lie on the circle, the other focus will also lie on the circle.

49. If TP, TQ be tangents to an ellipse or hyperbola, S, H being the foci; then

$$ST^2 : HT^2 = SP.SQ : HP.HQ.$$

50. A point D is taken on the axis of a hyperbola, whose eccentricity is 2, such that its distance from the focus S is equal to the distance of S from the further vertex A'; P being any point on the curve, $A'P$ meets the latus rectum in K. Prove that DK and SP intersect on a certain fixed circle.

CHAPTER VII.

THE HYPERBOLA CONTINUED.

Take any point E (fig., Prop. II.,) on a fixed straight line drawn through the centre C, and let EN meet the axis at right angles in N. Then the ratio of EN to CN is the same whatever be the position of E on the fixed straight line.

If the ratio of EN to CN be equal to the ratio of the semi-axes CB, CA, the straight line CE is called an *Asymptote*, for a reason which will appear in Prop. I., Cor. 2.

Make the angle NCM equal to NCE. Then CM is the other asymptote.

It follows from the definition given above that, when N coincides with the vertex A, EN becomes equal to the semi-minor axis CB.

In this case $CE^2 = CB^2 + CA^2 = CS^2$.

Two hyperbolas are said to be *conjugate* when the transverse axis of each is the conjugate axis of the other.

Thus, in fig., Prop. VIII., the hyperbola which has CB, CA for semi-axes is conjugate to that which has CA, CB for semi-axes.

It is evident that any two conjugate hyperbolas have the same asymptotes.

Conjugate Diameters and *Supplemental Chords* may be defined as on p. 75.

Let PP' (fig., Prop. VIII.) be any diameter of a hyperbola, *terminated by the curve.* Then the conjugate diameter will not meet the curve, but its *extremities* are defined as the points D, D', in which it meets the conjugate hyperbola.

PROP. I. *If CN be the abscissa of any point P on the hyperbola, and NP produced meet one of the asymptotes in Q, then*

$$QN^2 - PN^2 = CB^2.$$ [fig., p. 123.

Since $PN^2 : CB^2 = CN^2 - CA^2 : CA^2$, [Prop. XVI., p. 109.

componendo $PN^2 + CB^2 : CB^2 = CN^2 : CA^2$.

But, since Q is a point on an asymptote, QN is to CN as CB to CA.

Therefore $QN^2 : CB^2 = CN^2 : CA^2$.

Hence $PN^2 + CB^2 = QN^2$,

or $QN^2 - PN^2 = CB^2$.

COR. 1. Hence $PQ\,(QN + PN) = CB^2$. [Euc. II., 5, Cor.

Therefore $PQ . PQ' = CB^2$, if QN produced meet the other asymptote in Q'.

COR. 2. Let CN, and consequently $QN + PN$, be increased indefinitely. Then, since $PQ\,(QN + PN)$ is always equal to CB^2, PQ is diminished indefinitely, but can never actually vanish. Hence the curve continually approaches the asymptote, but never meets it.

Note. The above proposition is a particular case of Prop. XVIII., which is proved similarly.

PROP. II. *The tangent and normal at any point of a hyperbola meet the asymptotes and axes respectively in four points lying upon a circle which also passes through the centre of the hyperbola.*

The circle described on Gg, the portion of any normal intercepted by the axes, passes through the centre C, since gCG is a right angle.

Let this circle meet the asymptotes in L, M, and let LM, Gg intersect in P. From any point E in CL draw EN perpendicular to CG and therefore parallel to gC.

Then $\angle ECN = GCM = GLP$, in the same segment.

Also $\angle CEN = ECg = LGP$, in the same segment.

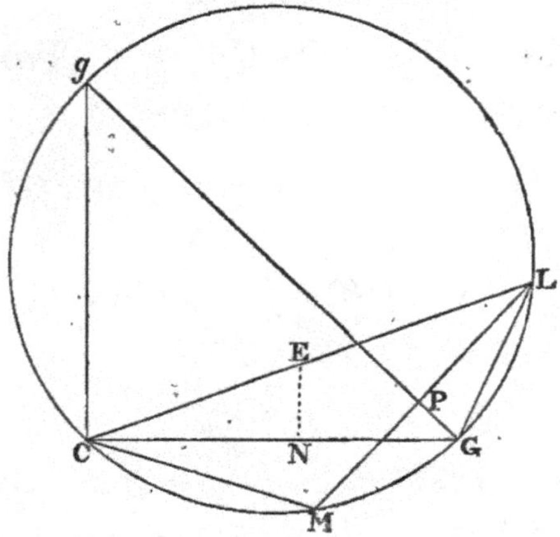

Hence, the triangles ECN, LPG being similar, the angle LPG *is a right angle*, and

$$PG : PL = EN : CN$$

$$= CB : CA. \qquad [\textit{Def.}, \text{p. } 119.$$

Similarly $\qquad PL : Pg = CB : CA.$

Hence $\qquad PG : Pg = CB^2 : CA^2,$

or P is the point at which Gg is normal to the curve. (Prop. II., p. 100).

Also, LPG being a right angle, LM is the tangent at P.

PROP. III. *The portion of any tangent intercepted between the asymptotes is bisected at the point of contact.*

Let the tangent and normal at P meet the asymptotes and axes respectively in the points L, M; G, g.

Then a circle goes round $LgCMG$. [Prop. II.

But Gg passes through the centre of the circle, since gCG is a right angle, and also cuts LM at right angles.

Hence LM is bisected in P. [Euc. III., 3.

COR. Any straight line Rr (fig., p. 128) terminated by the asymptotes, is bisected by the diameter CV to whose ordinates it is parallel.

PROP. IV. *If the tangent at P meet the asymptotes in L, M, then*

$$\triangle LCM = CA.CB.$$

Let the diameter parallel to the tangent at P meet the normal in F. Then PF is equal to the perpendicular from C to the base of the triangle LCM.

Therefore $\triangle LCM = \frac{1}{2}PF.LM = PF.PL.$ [Prop. III.

But $PF.PG = CB^2.$ [Prop. XII., p. 107.

Therefore $PF : CB = CB : PG$

$= CA : PL$, as in Prop. II.

Therefore $CA.CB = PF.PL = \triangle LCM.$

PROP. V. *If tangents be drawn to a hyperbola and its conjugate from a point on either asymptote, the points of contact will lie at the extremities of conjugate diameters.*

From the point L on the asymptote CL (fig., Prop. VI.) draw LP, LD, touching the hyperbola and its conjugate respectively in P, D. Produce LP, LD to meet the other asymptote in M, M'.

Then $\triangle LCM = CA.CB$ [Prop. IV.

$= \triangle LCM'$, similarly.

Therefore $CM = CM'$ (Euc. I., 38). But $PM = PL$. [Prop. II.

Therefore, by Euc. VI. 2, CP is parallel to $M'L$, the tangent at D. Similarly, CD is parallel to ML.

Hence CP, CD are conjugate.

COR. Conversely, if CP, CD be conjugate, the tangents at P, D intersect in a point L which lies on one of the asymptotes.

Also, $CPLD$ being a parallelogram,

$$CD = PL = PM. \qquad \text{[Prop. II.}$$

PROP. VI. *If the normal at P meet the major and minor axes in G, g, respectively, then*

$$PG.Pg = CD^2,$$

where CD is the semi-diameter conjugate to CP.

Let the tangent at P meet the asymptotes in L, M. Then a circle goes round $LGMg$. [Prop. II.

Therefore $$PG.Pg = PL.PM$$
$$= CD^2. \qquad \text{[Prop. V., Cor.}$$

PROP. VII. *If the normal at P meet the major and minor axes in G, g respectively, and CD be the semi-diameter conjugate to CP, then*

$$PG : CD = CB : CA,$$

and $$Pg : CD = CA : CB.$$

It may be shown, as in Prop. II., that

$$PG : PL = CB : CA,$$

where PL is the tangent, terminated by the asymptote CL.

But PL is equal to CD. [Prop. V., Cor.

Therefore $$PG : CD = CB : CA.$$

Similarly $$Pg : CD = CA : CB.$$

PROP. VIII. *The parallelogram formed by drawing tangents at the extremities of a pair of conjugate diameters PP', DD' is of constant area.*

Let the normal at P meet DD' in F and the major axis in G.

Then $PG : CD = CB : CA.$ [Prop. VII.

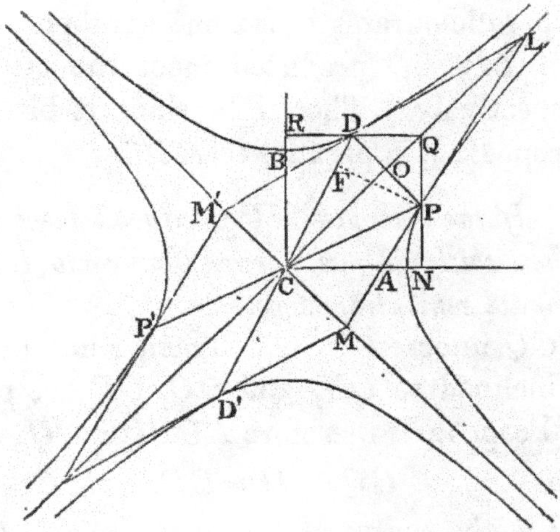

Alternando $PG : CB = CD : CA.$

But $PF.PG = CB^2.$ [Prop. XII., p. 107.

Therefore $CB : PF = PG : CB$

$= CD : CA$, from above,

or $PF.CD = CA.CB.$

It is evident from the figure that the area of the circumscribing parallelogram is equal to $4PF.CD$, that is to $4CA.CB$ or $AA'.BB'$.

Note. This proposition is another form of Prop. IV., since he parallelogram MM' is equal to four times the triangle LCM.

PROP. IX. *The straight line which joins the extremities of conjugate semi-diameters is parallel to one asymptote and bisected by the other.*

From the point L on the asymptote CL draw LP touching the hyperbola in P, and LD touching the conjugate hyperbola in D. Then the semi-diameters CP, CD are conjugate (Prop. V.,) and $CPLD$ is a parallelogram. [Prop. V., Cor.

Let PD, CL intersect in O. Then $OP=OD$, since the diagonals of parallelograms bisect one another.

Again, let LP, LD produced meet the other asymptote in M, M' respectively. Then PD, since it bisects both LM and LM' (Prop. III.), is parallel to MM'.

Prop. X. *If the ordinate NP produced meet the asymptote CQ in Q, then will QD be perpendicular to CB, where CP, CD are conjugate semi-diameters.*

Let PD, CQ intersect in O. Then, since the asymptotes are equally inclined to QN, and OQ, OP are parallel to the asymptotes (Prop. IX.), therefore $\angle OPQ = OQP$.

Therefore $\qquad OQ = OP = OD. \qquad$ [Prop. IX.

Hence, O is the centre of the circle round DQP and the angle PQD in a semi-circle is a right angle. Therefore QD is perpendicular to CB.

Prop. XI. *If the tangent at any point meet the asymptotes in L, M, then $CL.CM$ is constant and equal to CS^2.*

Let any other tangent meet the asymptotes in l, m, as in the figure.

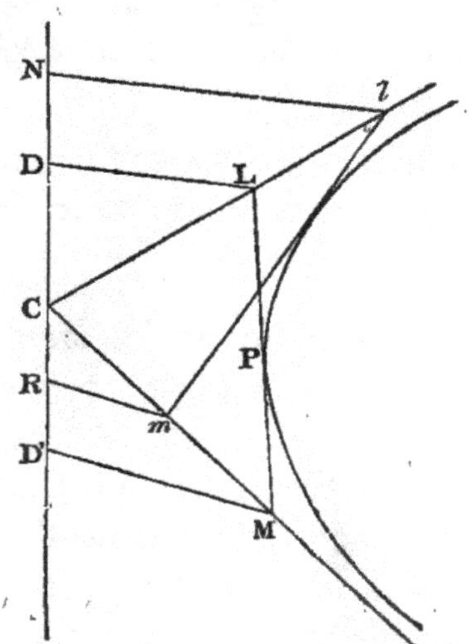

Then the triangles LCM, lCm are equal (Prop. IV.) and have the angle at C common.

Therefore $$CL : Cl = Cm : CM,$$ [Euc. VI., 15.

or $$CL.CM = Cl.Cm.$$

Let lm coincide with the tangent at the vertex, so that

$$Cl = CS = Cm.$$

Therefore $$CL.CM = CS^2, \text{ which is constant.}$$

Cor. From L, M, l, m draw straight lines parallel to PC, and let them meet the conjugate diameter in D, D', N, R respectively.

Then $$CD : CN = CL : Cl$$ [Euc. VI., 2.

$$= Cm : CM, \text{ from above,}$$

$$= CR : CD'.$$ [Euc. VI., 2.

Therefore $$CN.CR = CD.CD' = CD^2.$$

Prop. XII. *If from any point P on the curve PO be drawn, parallel to one of the asymptotes and meeting the other in O, then*

$$PO.CO = \tfrac{1}{4}CS^2.$$

Let the tangent at P meet the asymptotes in L, M, (fig., Prop. VIII.), and let PO be parallel to CM.

Then, since P is the middle point of LM (Prop. III.), $PO = \tfrac{1}{2}CM$ and $CO = \tfrac{1}{2}CL$. [Euc. VI., 2.

Therefore $$PO.CO = \tfrac{1}{4}CL.CM = \tfrac{1}{4}CS^2.$$ [Prop. XII.

Cor. Straight lines drawn from any point on the curve parallel to and terminated by the asymptotes contain a constant rectangle.

It may also be deduced (Euc. VI., 14) that they form with the asymptotes a parallelogram of constant area.

PROP. XIII. *If the tangent and ordinate at Q meet any diameter in T, V respectively, then*

$$CV.CT = CD^2,$$

where D is an extremity of the diameter.

Let the tangent at Q meet the asymptotes in l, m.

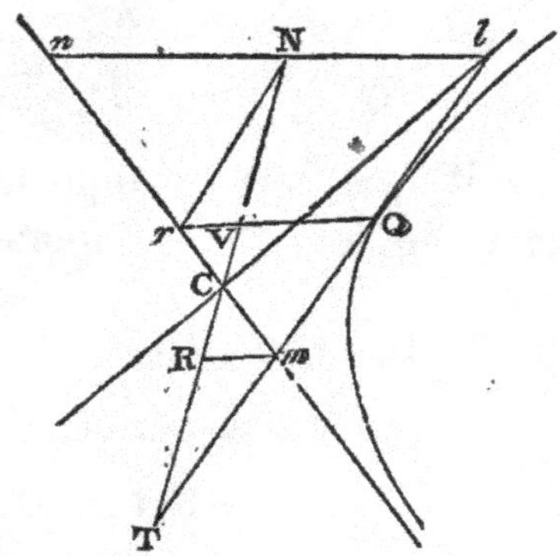

Draw lN, mR parallel to QV and meeting the diameter of which QV is an ordinate in N, R. Produce lN, QV to meet the asymptote mC in n, r. Join Nr.

Now ln, being parallel to the ordinates of CN, is bisected in N (Prop. III., Cor.). Also, Qr bisects lm (Prop. III.) and is parallel to ln. [Construction.

Therefore Nr, which bisects both ln and mn, is parallel to lm. [Euc. VI., 2.

Hence $CT : CN = Cm : Cr$ [Euc. VI., 2,

$= CR : CV$, similarly.

Therefore $CV.CT = CN.CR = CD^2$. [Prop. XI., Cor.

PROP. XIV. *If CP, CD be conjugate semi-diameters, then*

$$SP.PH = CD^2.$$

Let the normal at P meet the major and minor axes in G, g respectively. Then a circle goes round $SPgH$. [Prop. VII., p. 103.

Then $\angle PgH =$ supplement of PSH [Euc. III., 22,
$= PSG$.

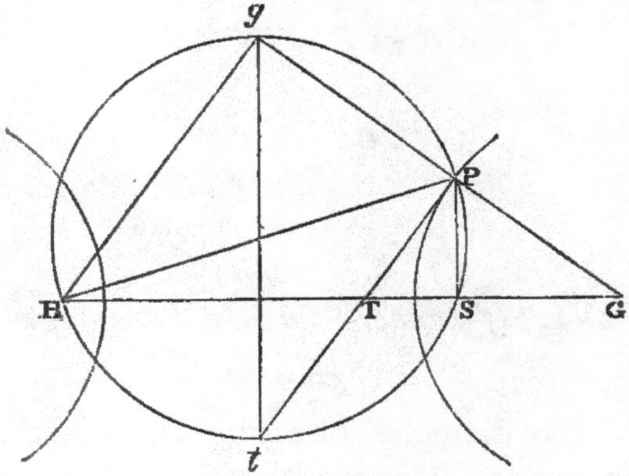

Also $\angle gPH = SPG$. [Prop. V., p. 103.

Therefore the triangles HPg, SPG are similar, so that

$$SP : PG = Pg : PH,$$

Therefore $SP.PH = PG.Pg = CD^2$. [Prop. VI.

PROP. XV. *If CP, CD be conjugate semi-diameters, then*

$$CP^2 \sim CD^2 = CA^2 \sim CB^2.$$

In fig., Prop. XIII., since $HP = 2CA + SP$ (Prop. III., p. 100), the squares of the whole HP and the part SP are equal to $2HP.SP$ together with the square of $2CA$. [Euc. II., 7.

Therefore $HP^2 + SP^2 = 2HP.SP + 4CA^2$.

But $HP^2 + SP^2 = 2CP^2 + 2CS^2$,*

since C is the middle part of SH.

Therefore $HP.SP + 2CA^2 = CP^2 + CS^2$,

or $CD^2 + 2CA^2 = CP^2 + CA^2 + CB^2$.

Therefore $CP^2 \sim CD^2 = CA^2 \sim CB^2$.

---

* Todhunter's *Euclid*, Appendix.

Or thus:

Let the ordinates NP, RD (fig., Prop. VIII.) be produced to meet in Q. Then CQ is an asymptote. [Prop. X.

Hence $\qquad CQ^2 - CP^2 = QN^2 - PN^2$ [Euc. I., 47.

$\qquad\qquad = CB^2.$ [Prop. I.

Therefore $\qquad CP^2 + CB^2 = CQ^2$

$\qquad\qquad = CD^2 + CA^2$, similarly.

Therefore $\qquad CP^2 \sim CD^2 = CA^2 \sim CB^2.$

PROP. XVI. *If the chord Qq meet the asymptotes in R, r, then*

$$QR = qr.$$

Let CV, the diameter bisecting Qq, cut the curve in P. Then the tangent at P is parallel to Qq. [Prop. XII., Cor. 1, p. 16.

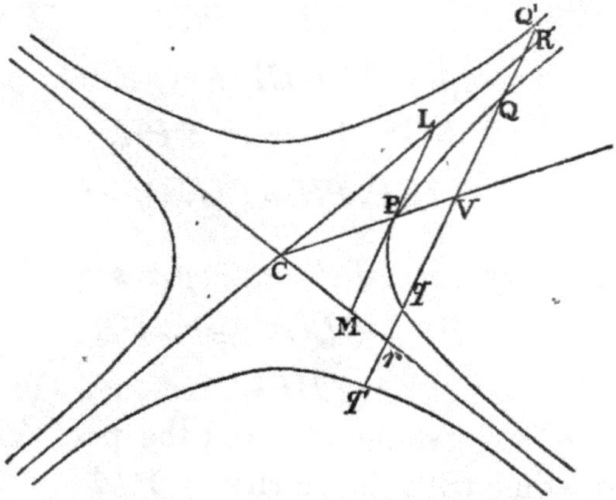

Let the tangent meet the asymptotes in L, M. Then $PL = PM$. [Prop. III., Cor.

Hence, also $\qquad RV = rV.$

But $\qquad QV = qV.$ [Construction.

By subtraction $\qquad QR = qr.$

COR. Let Qq meet the conjugate hyperbola in Q', q'. Then, since $QR = qr$ and $Q'R = q'r$ similarly, therefore

$$QQ' = qq'.$$

PROP. XVII. *If CV be the abscissa of any point Q on the hyperbola, measured along the diameter PP', then*

$$QV^2 : CV^2 - CP^2 = CD^2 : CP^2,$$

and

$$QV^2 : PV.VP' = CD^2 : CP^2,$$

where CD is the conjugate semi-diameter.

The proof of Prop. XVI., p. 109, is applicable. The *letters* only require to be changed.

COR. Let VQ meet the conjugate hyperbola in Q'. Then $Q'V$ is equal to the abscissa and CV to the ordinate of Q', the corresponding semi-diameters being CD and CP.

Hence $\quad CV^2 : Q'V^2 - CD^2 = CP^2 : CD^2.$

Therefore $\quad Q'V^2 - CD^2 : CD^2 = CV^2 : CP^2.$

Componendo $\quad Q'V^2 : CD^2 = CV^2 + CP^2 : CP^2.$

PROP. XVIII. *If Q be one extremity and V the middle point of a chord, which meets the asymptotes in R, r and is parallel to the semi-diameter CD, then*

$$CD^2 = RV^2 - QV^2 = RQ.Qr.$$

By the last proposition, alternando,

$$QV^2 : CD^2 = CV^2 - CP^2 : CP^2.$$

Componendo $\quad QV^2 + CD^2 : CD^2 = CV^2 : CP^2$

$$= RV^2 : PL^2.$$

by similar triangles CVR, CPL.

But $PL^2 = CD^2$, since, by Prop. V., Cor., $PL = CD$.

Therefore $RV^2 = QV^2 + CD^2$.

Hence $\quad CD^2 = RV^2 - QV^2 = RQ.Qr.$ [Euc. II., 5, Cor.

Similarly it may be shown, by means of Prop. XVII., Cor., that

$$CD^2 = Q'V^2 - RV^2 = RQ'.Q'r,$$

Q' being the point in which VQ meets the conjugate hyperbola.

PROP. XIX. *If TPP′ be any diameter and TQ the tangent at a point Q, whose abscissa is CV, then*

$$TC.TV = TP.TP'.$$

When the diameter meets the hyperbola, the method of Prop. x., p. 48, is applicable.

Otherwise, if Prop. xiii., (the proof of which is *general*) be assumed, then

$$TC^2 = TC.TV + TC.CV \qquad \text{[Euc. II., 3,}$$
$$= TC.TV + CP^2.$$

Therefore $$TC.TV = TC^2 - CP^2$$
$$= TP.TP'. \qquad \text{[Euc. II., 5, Cor.}$$

The following propositions may be proved by the methods applied to the ellipse. [p. 84–88.

PROP. XX. *The rectangle contained by the segments of a chord QR which passes through a fixed point O bears a constant ratio to the square on the parallel semi-diameter CD.*

Also the rectangles contained by the segments of any two intersecting chords are to one another as the squares of the parallel semi-diameters.

PROP. XXI. *If a circle and a hyperbola intersect in four points their common chords will be equally inclined to the axis of the hyperbola.*

PROP. XXII. *If the tangent at P meet any diameter in T and the conjugate diameter in t, then*

$$PT.Pt = CD^2,$$

where CD is the conjugate semi-diameter.

PROP. XXIII. *If a chord pass through a fixed point the tangents at its extremities will intersect on a fixed straight line.*

PROP. XXIV. *If from any point t, tpp′ be drawn to meet the hyperbola in p, p′ and the chord of contact of tangents through t in o, then tpop′ will be cut harmonically.*

EXAMPLES.

1. If a directrix and an asymptote of a hyperbola intersect in E, then $CE = CA$.

2. If the tangent at P meet the directrices in K, K', then $PK.PK' = CD^2$, where CD, CP are conjugate semi-diameters.

3. Any two straight lines drawn parallel to conjugate diameters meet the asymptotes in four points which lie on a circle.

4. If the tangent at P cut an asymptote in T, and SP cut the same asymptote in Q, then $SQ = ST$.

5. Perpendiculars from the foci upon the asymptotes meet the asymptotes on the circumference of the circle described upon the axis.

6. The tangents at A, A' meet the circle upon SH in the asymptotes.

7. If from the point P in a hyperbola PK be drawn parallel to the transverse axis cutting the asymptotes in I, K, then $PK.PI = CA^2$.

8. If from a point P in the hyperbola PN be drawn parallel to an asymptote to meet the directrix in N, then $PN = SP$.

9. If from a point P, in the hyperbola, PR be drawn parallel to an asymptote to meet the tangent at the vertex in R, then the difference of SP, PR is equal to half the latus rectum.

10. Prove by means of Examples 2, 8, that the rectangle contained by the focal distances of any point on the hyperbola is equal to the square on the parallel semi-diameter.

11. A hyperbola being defined as the locus of a point whose distance from a fixed point equal to its distance from a fixed straight line, measured parallel to any other given straight line, prove that the second line is parallel to an asymptote of the hyperbola.

12. If PQ be any chord, R the point of contact of the parallel tangent, and PD, RE, QH be drawn parallel to one asymptote to meet the other, then $CD.CH = CE^2$.

13. With two conjugate diameters of an ellipse as asymptotes a pair of conjugate hyperbolas are described. Prove that, if one hyperbola touch the ellipse, the other will do so likewise, and that the diameters through the points of contact are conjugate.

14. If any two tangents be drawn to a hyperbola, and their intersections with the asymptotes be joined, the joining lines will be parallel.

15. The tangent to a hyperbola, terminated by the asymptotes, is bisected where it meets the curve. Assuming this, prove that the tangent forms, with the asymptotes, a triangle of constant area.

16. The tangent at P meets one asymptote in T, and TQ, drawn parallel to the other, meets the curve in Q. Prove that, if PQ meet the asymptotes in R, R', then RR' will be trisected in the points P, Q.

17. If CP, CD be conjugate semi-diameters, and through C a line be drawn parallel to either focal distance of P, the perpendicular from D upon this line is equal to half the minor axis.

18. PM, PN are drawn parallel to the asymptotes CM, CN, and an ellipse is constructed having CN, CM for semi-conjugate diameters. If CP cut the ellipse in Q, the tangents at Q, P to the ellipse and hyperbola are parallel.

19. Any focal chord of a conic is a third proportional to the transverse axis and the diameter parallel to the chord.

20. The difference of two focal chords, which are parallel to the conjugate diameters of a hyperbola, is constant.

21. If straight lines be taken inversely proportional to focal chords of a conic, which include a right angle, the sum or difference of these lines is constant.

22. A chord of a hyperbola which subtends at the focus an angle equal to that between the asymptotes, always touches a fixed parabola.

23. Given two conjugate diameters of a hyperbola; determine the directions of the axes.

24. The radius of a circle which touches a hyperbola and its asymptotes is equal to the part of the latus rectum intercepted between the curve and the asymptote.

25. A line drawn through one vertex of a hyperbola and terminated by two lines drawn through the other, parallel to the asymptotes, will be bisected where it cuts the curve again.

26. If P be a fixed point on a hyperbola and QQ' an ordinate to CP, the circle QPQ' will meet the hyperbola in a fixed point.

27. Tangents are drawn to a hyperbola, and the portion of each tangent intercepted by the asymptotes is divided in a constant ratio; prove that the locus of the point of section is a hyperbola.

28. Given the asymptotes and one point on the curve; find the foci and construct the curve.

29. If a line through the centre of a hyperbola meet in R, T, lines drawn parallel to the asymptotes from any point on the curve, then, the parallelogram $PQRT$ being completed, Q is a point on the hyperbola.

30. If PQ, $P'Q'$, straight lines terminated by the asymptotes, intersect in O, then

$$PO.OQ : CD^2 = P'O.OQ' : CD'^2,$$

where CD, CD' are the semi-diameters parallel to PQ, $P'Q'$ respectively.

This follows from Prop. XVIII., by similar triangles.

Prop. XX. may be deduced from the above result.

31. Straight lines are drawn through a fixed point; show that the locus of the middle points of the portions of them intercepted between two fixed straight lines is a hyperbola, whose asymptotes are parallel to those fixed lines.

32. TP, TQ are tangents to an ellipse at P, Q, and asymptotes of a hyperbola. Show that a pair of their common chords are parallel to PQ. One of these chords being RS, prove that if PR touches the hyperbola at P, then QS touches it at S.

33. Prove also that the straight line drawn from T to the intersection of PS, QR, bisects PQ.

34. A hyperbola, of given eccentricity, always passes through two given points; if one of its asymptotes always pass through a third given point in the same straight line with these, the locus of the centre of the hyperbola will be a circle.

35. If, from any point P in the hyperbola, $RPQS$ be drawn meeting the hyperbola in P, Q, and the asymptotes in R, S, then PK, QL being drawn parallel to one asymptote to meet the other, $LS = PK$.

36. If a chord PQ intersect the asymptotes in R, S, and a tangent RE be drawn to the hyperbola; then, PM, QN, EL being drawn parallel to one asymptote and meeting the other, $2EL$ is equal to $PM + QN$.

37. Tangents through V cut one asymptote in S, T and the other in S', T'; prove that

$$VS : VS' = VT' : VT.$$

38. The area of the sector of a hyperbola made by joining any two points of it to the centre is equal to the area of the segment made by drawing parallels from those points to the asymptotes.

39. Lines drawn parallel to an asymptote from the points P, Q, R, S, on the curve, meet the other asymptote in K, L, M, N. Prove that the areas $PQKL$, $RSMN$, will be equal, if

$$PK : QL = RM : SN.$$

40. The lines PK, QL, RM, drawn parallel to one asymptote, meet the other in K, L, M; P, Q, R are points on the curve. Prove that, if QL bisect the area $PKMR$, it will be a mean proportional between PK and RM.

CHAPTER VIII.

THE RECTANGULAR HYPERBOLA.

In the *Rectangular* or *Equilateral Hyperbola* the asymptotes are at right angles and the axes equal.

In the second proposition of the preceding chapter, if $CB = CA$, then P will be the centre of the circle.

Hence $$CP = PL = CD,$$ [Prop. v., p. 122;

or *conjugate diameters of a rectangular hyperbola are equal to one another.*

Also $$PG = CD = Pg.$$ [Prop. vii., p. 122.

PROP. I. *Conjugate diameters of a rectangular hyperbola are equally inclined to either asymptote.*

Let CP, CD be conjugate semi-diameters (fig., p. 123) and let PD cut the asymptote CO in O.

Then $$OP = OD.$$ [Prop. ix., p. 123.

But $CP = CD$. Hence CO, since it bisects the base of the isosceles triangle PCD, bisects also the vertical angle PCD.

COR. Since CP', CD', any other two conjugate semi-diameters are also equally inclined to CO, therefore

$$\angle PCP' = DCD'.$$

Hence the angle between any two diameters is equal to that between their conjugates.

Prop. II. *In the rectangular hyperbola, diameters at right angles to one another are equal.*

In fig., p. 123, suppose a semi-diameter CP' to be drawn, equally inclined to the axis with CP. Then, since the asymptotes CM', CO are equally inclined to the axis,

$$\angle P'CM' = PCO = DCO. \qquad \text{[Prop. I.}$$

Therefore $$\angle P'CM' + DCM' = DCO + DCM',$$

or $$\angle DCP' = LCM' = \text{a right angle.}$$

Also $$CP' = CP = CD.$$

Cor. The rectangles contained by the segments of chords which intersect at right angles are equal. [Prop. XX., p. 130.

Prop. III. *If a conic, described about a triangle, pass through the point of intersection of the perpendiculars drawn from the angular points upon the opposite sides, it will be a rectangular hyperbola.*

Let ABC be the triangle; AD, BE, CF the perpendiculars, intersecting in O.

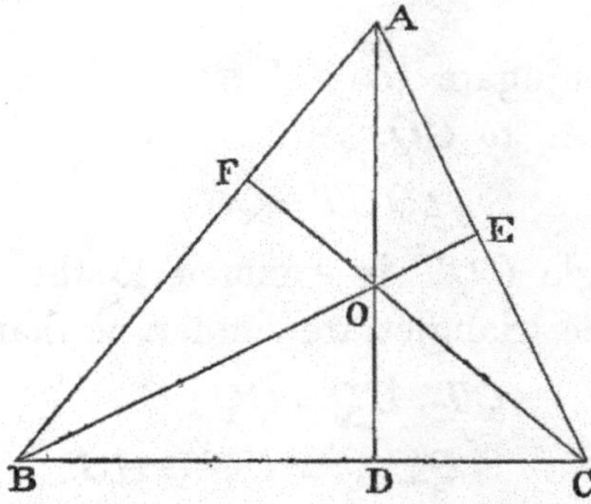

Then, by similar triangles ADC, BDO,

$$AD : CD = BD : OD.$$

Therefore $AD.OD = BD.CD$. Similarly $BE.OE = AE.EC$.

Hence, the conic has *more than one* pair of equal diameters at right angles, viz. those parallel to AD, BC and BE, AC (Prop. XX., p. 130); and, since it cannot be a circle, it must be a rectangular hyperbola. [Prop. II., Cor.

PROP. IV. *If the tangent at any point Q intersect any two conjugate diameters in T, t, then*

$$QT.Qt = CD^2,$$

where CD is the semi-diameter conjugate to CQ.

The angle between any two diameters is equal to that between their conjugates. [Prop. I., Cor.

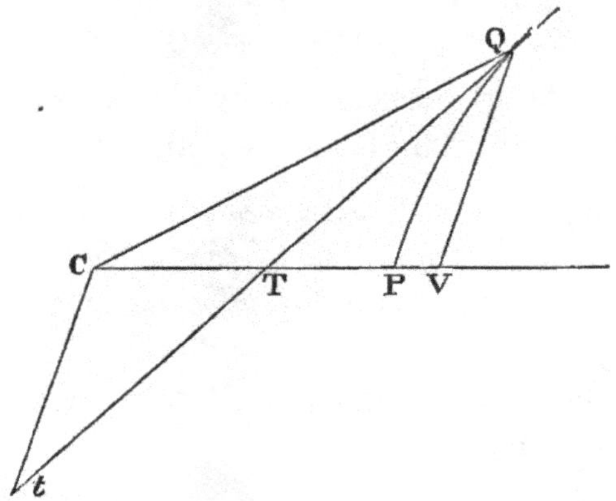

But Ct is conjugate to CT, and QT is parallel to the diameter conjugate to CQ.

Therefore $\angle QCT = QtC.$

Also, the angle CQT is common to the triangles QCT, QtC. Hence, the triangles are similar, so that

$$QT : CQ = CQ : Ct.$$

Therefore $QT.Qt = CQ^2 = CD^2.$

PROP. V. *If the tangent at a point Q, whose abscissa is CV, meet the axis in T, the triangles CVQ, QVT will be similar.*

The angle between the diameters CP, CQ is equal to that between their conjugates (Prop. I., Cor.) and therefore to that between QV, QT, which are parallel to their conjugates.

Hence the triangles CVQ, QVT are similar, since the angles QCV, VQT are equal and the angle CVQ is common.

EXAMPLES.

1. The locus of the centre of an equilateral hyperbola described about a given equilateral triangle is the circle inscribed in the triangle.

2. PG is the normal at P; GE a perpendicular on CP; prove that $PE=PF$, F being the point in which the normal meets the diameter parallel to the tangent at P.

3. The tangent from G to the circle on the axis is equal to PG.

4. In a rectangular hyperbola no pair of tangents can be drawn at right angles to each other.

5. An asymptote of a rectangular hyperbola meets the perpendicular upon it from either focus at a distance from the centre equal to half the axis.

6. The distance of any point from the centre is a geometric mean between its distances from the foci.

7. Straight lines drawn from any point on the curve to the extremities of a diameter are equally inclined to the asymptotes.

8. Q is a point on the conjugate axis of a rectangular hyperbola and QP, drawn parallel to the transverse axis, meets the curve in P; prove that $PQ=AQ$.

9. The locus of the middle point of a line which cuts off a constant area from the corner of a square is a rectangular hyperbola.

10. In a rectangular hyperbola CY is drawn perpendicular to the tangent at P; prove that the triangles PCA, CAY are similar.

11. The foci of an ellipse are situated at the ends of a diameter of a rectangular hyperbola; show that the tangent and normal to the ellipse, at any point where it meets the hyperbola, are parallel to the axes of the latter.

12. If a right-angled triangle be inscribed in a rectangular hyperbola, prove that the hypotenuse is parallel to the normal to the hyperbola at the right angle.

13. If two rectangular hyperbolas touch one another, their common chords through the point of contact will include a right angle and the remaining common chord will be parallel to the common tangent.

14. If a rectangular hyperbola circumscribe a right-angled triangle, the locus of its centre will be a circle passing through one of the angular points.

15. If AA' be any diameter of a circle, PQ any ordinate to it, then the locus of the intersection of AP, $A'Q$ is a rectangular hyperbola.

16. In a rectangular hyperbola, focal chords parallel to conjugate diameters are equal.

17. LL' is any diameter of a rectangular hyperbola, P any point on the curve; prove that the external and internal bisectors of the angle LPL' are parallel to fixed straight lines.

18. Straight lines parallel to conjugate diameters meet the asymptotes in four points which lie on a circle.

19. Assuming Prop. XVIII., p. 129, show how to deduce from Prop. V. that in the rectangular hyperbola

$$CV.CT = CP^2.$$

20. Ellipses are inscribed in a given parallelogram; show that their foci lie on a rectangular hyperbola.

21. If two concentric rectangular hyperbolas be described, the axes of one being asymptotes of the other, they will intersect at right angles.

22. The portion of the tangent intercepted by the asymptotes subtends a right angle at the foot of the normal.

23. If, between a rectangular hyperbola and its asymptotes, any number of concentric elliptic quadrants be inscribed the rectangle contained by their axes will be constant.

24. The base of a triangle ABC remaining fixed, the vertex C moves along an equilateral hyperbola which passes through A and B. If P, Q be the points in which AC, BC meet the circle on AB as diameter, the intersection of AQ, BP is always situated on the hyperbola.

25. Any conic which passes through the four points of intersection of two rectangular hyperbolas, must be itself a rectangular hyperbola.

26. If two concentric rectangular hyperbolas have a common tangent, the lines joining their points of intersection to their respective points of contact with the common tangent, will subtend equal angles at their common centre.

27. If lines be drawn from any point of a rectangular hyperbola to the extremities of a given diameter, the difference between the angles which they make with the diameter will be equal to the angle which it makes with its conjugate.

28. From fixed points A, B straight lines are drawn intersecting in C, such that the difference of the angles CBA, CAB is constant; find the locus of C.

29. Prove that in a rectangular hyperbola the triangle formed by the tangent at any point and its intercepts on the axes, is similar to the triangle formed by the straight line joining that point with the centre, and the abscissa and semi-ordinate of the point.

30. On opposite sides of any chord of a rectangular hyperbola are described equal segments of circles; show that the four points, in which the circles to which the segments belong again meet the hyperbola, are the angular points of a parallelogram.

31. If a conic be described through the centres of the inscribed and exscribed circles of any triangle, its centre will lie on the circle which circumscribes the triangle.

32. The locus of the centre of a rectangular hyperbola described about a triangle is the circle passing through the middle points of the sides of the triangle.

33. If PQR be a triangle inscribed in a rectangular hyperbola, the intersections of pairs of tangents at P, Q, R lie on the lines joining the feet of the perpendiculars from the angular points of the triangle upon the opposite sides.

34. Given a triangle such that any vertex is the pole of the opposite side with respect to an equilateral hyperbola; the circle circumscribing the triangle passes through the centre of the curve.

35. A circle, described through the centre of a rectangular hyperbola and any two points, will also pass through the intersection of lines drawn through each of these points parallel to the polar of the other.

CHAPTER IX.

CORRESPONDING POINTS.

Any fixed straight line being taken as axis, if the ordinate NP of a variable point P to be produced, in a constant ratio, to p, then the points p, P *correspond*, and the locus of either point corresponds to the locus of the other. [fig., Prop. III.

Hence, if any other ordinate MQ be produced to q, so that

$$MQ : Mq = NP : Np,$$

then the points Q, q correspond.

PROP. I. *Straight lines correspond to straight lines.*

Let P, p be corresponding points and let the locus of P be a straight line which meets the axis in T. Join Tp and draw any ordinate MQq, meeting the straight lines TP, Tp in Q, q respectively.

Then $$MQ : Mq = NP : Np,$$

or the points Q, q correspond.

Hence, to any point Q on TP corresponds a point q on Tp. In other words, the straight line Tp corresponds to TP.

COR. Corresponding straight lines intersect on the axis.

PROP. II. *Tangents correspond to tangents.*

Let P, Q be adjacent points on any curve and p, q the corresponding points. Then the straight line pq corresponds to PQ.

Let Q move up to P. Then q, which always lies on the same ordinate as Q, moves up to p, and when PQ becomes the tangent at P to the locus of P, pq becomes the tangent at p to the locus of p.

PROP. III. *Parallel straight lines correspond to parallel straight lines.*

Let P, P' be points on any two parallel straight lines

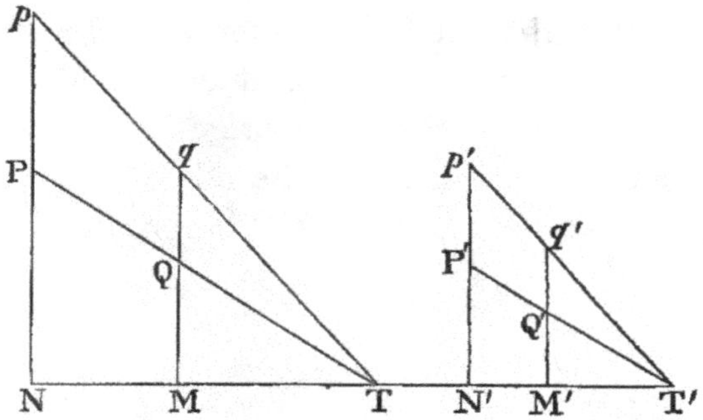

which meet the axis in T, T'. Produce NP, $N'P'$, the ordinates of P, P', to meet the corresponding straight lines in p, p' respectively.

Then, since p corresponds to P and p' to P', the straight lines NPp, $N'P'p'$ are cut in the same ratio. [*Def.*

Hence $$Np : N'p' = NP : N'P',$$
$$= NT : N'T',$$

by similar triangles NPT, $N'P'T'$.

Therefore pT, $p'T'$ are parallel, which proves the proposition.

PROP. IV. *Parallel straight lines are to one another as the parallel straight lines to which they correspond.*

In the last proposition let Q, Q' be any two points on TP, $T'P'$, and let q, q' be the corresponding points.

Then, since TP, $T'P'$ and also Tp, $T'p'$ are parallel, therefore, by similar triangles TPp, $T'P'p'$,

$$TP : Tp = T'P' : T'p'.$$

But TP is to Tp as PQ to pq. [Euc. VI., 2.
Similarly $T'P'$ is to $T'p'$ as $P'Q'$ to $p'q'$.

Therefore $\qquad PQ : pq = P'Q' : p'q'$.

Hence the parallel straight lines PQ, $P'Q'$ are as the parallel straight lines pq, $p'q'$ to which they correspond.

Cor. Let CD, QOP (fig., p. 146) be parallel straight lines, and let the points d, q, o, p correspond respectively to D, Q, O, P.

Then $\qquad OQ : CD = oq : Cd$,

and $\qquad OP : CD = op : Cd$.

Therefore $\qquad OP.OQ : CD^2 = op.oq : Cd^2$.

Prop. V. *Points of intersection correspond to points of intersection.*

Let the straight lines PQ, $P'Q'$ intersect in O and the corresponding straight lines pq, $p'q'$ in o.

Then since O lies on PQ, the point which corresponds to O must lie on pq. For a like reason it must lie also on $p'q'$, and therefore coincides with o, the point of intersection of pq, $p'q'$.

This method is applicable when PQ, $P'Q'$ are curved lines.

Cor. Hence, if any number of lines meet in a point, the corresponding lines will meet in the corresponding point.

Prop. VI. *Corresponding areas are to one another in a constant ratio.*

The method of Prop. XVIII., p. 88, is applicable to *any* two curves whose ordinates are to one another in a constant ratio.

(1) It has been proved (Prop. XVIII., p. 64) that the common ordinates of an ellipse and its auxiliary circle are to one another in a constant ratio. Hence the ellipse and its auxiliary circle correspond.

In consequence of this correspondence many properties of the ellipse may be deduced from properties of the circle, as in the following articles.

(2) *In an ellipse, the rectangle contained by the segments of a chord which passes through a fixed point varies as the square of the parallel semi-diameter.*

Let PQ be the chord, O the fixed point, and CD the parallel semi-diameter.

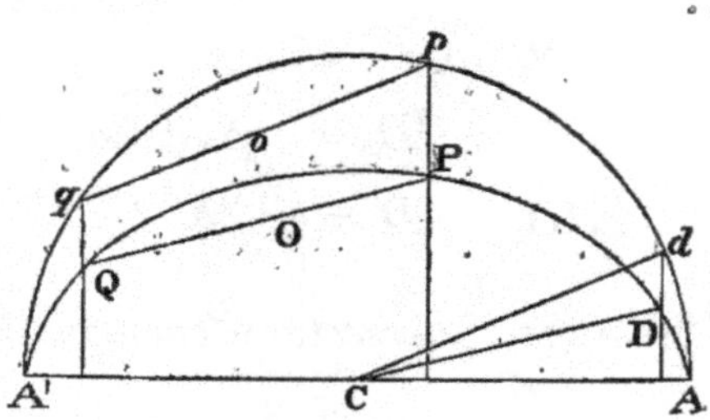

Take corresponding points p, q, o, d in the auxiliary circle. [Prop. XVIII., p. 64.

Then $OP.OQ : CD^2 = op.oq : Cd^2$. [Prop. IV., Cor.

But O is a fixed point. Hence the corresponding point o is fixed and $op.oq$ is constant. [Euc. III., 35.

Also, the radius Cd is constant.

Hence $OP.OQ$ bears to CD^2 a constant ratio.

(3) *The middle points of all parallel chords of an ellipse lie on the same straight line.*

In the last figure, let O be the middle point of PQ. Then o is the middle point of pq. [Prop. IV.

Let pq move parallel to itself. Then PQ moves parallel to itself. [Prop. III.

But Co is a fixed straight line, since in the circle the same diameter bisects all parallel chords. Hence, the locus of o being a straight line, that of O is also a straight line. [Prop. I.

(4) *Tangents to an ellipse at the extremities of any chord intersect on the diameter which bisects the chord.*

If o, O be middle points of pq, PQ, as above, then the diameter CO corresponds to Co. Also, the tangents at P, Q correspond to those at p, q. [Prop. II.

But, in the circle, the diameter Co and the tangents at p, q meet in a point.

Hence, in the ellipse, the diameter CO and the tangents at P, Q meet in a point. [Prop. V., Cor.

(5) *Conjugate diameters in the ellipse correspond to diameters at right angles in the circle.* [Prop. II., p. 76.

(6) The method of corresponding points may also be applied to deduce properties of the hyperbola from those of the rectangular hyperbola. For, it has been shown, Prop. XVII., p. 129, that if Q, Q' be points on a hyperbola and its conjugate, which have a common abscissa CV, then

$$QV^2 : CV^2 - CP^2 = CD^2 : CP^2,$$

and
$$Q'V^2 : CV^2 + CP^2 = CD^2 : CP^2.$$

Now, on the ordinate common to Q, Q', take points q, q', such that

$$QV : qV = CD : CP,$$

and
$$Q'V : q'V = CD : CP.$$

Then q corresponds to Q and q' to Q'.

Also $qV^2 = CV^2 - CP^2$ and $q'V^2 = CV^2 + CP^2$.

Hence the *loci of q, q' are conjugate rectangular hyperbolas.*

(7) The following are examples of corresponding theorems. The left-hand column contains theorems which are true either for the circle or else for the rectangular hyperbola, while to

the right of each theorem is placed the corresponding theorem in the ellipse or hyperbola.

THE CIRCLE.	THE ELLIPSE.
The area of the circumscribing square is constant.	The area of the circumscribing parallelogram whose sides are parallel to conjugate diameters is constant.
If a diameter meet the tangent at Q in T, the circle in P, and the ordinate of Q in V, then $$CV.CT = CP^2,$$ and $QV^2 = CP^2 - CV^2$.	If a diameter meet the tangent at Q in T, the ellipse in P, and the ordinate of Q in V, then $$CV.CT = CP^2,$$ and $QV^2 : CV^2 - CP^2 = CD^2 : CP^2$.
If the tangent at P meet any two diameters at right angles to one another in T, T', then $$PT.PT' = CD^2,$$ where CD is the radius parallel to PT.	If the tangent at P meet any two conjugate diameters in T, T', then $$PT.PT' = CD^2,$$ where CP, CD are conjugate semi-diameters.

THE RECTANGULAR HYPERBOLA.	THE HYPERBOLA.
The area of the circumscribing parallelogram whose sides are parallel to conjugate diameters is constant.	The area of the circumscribing parallelogram whose sides are parallel to conjugate diameters is constant.
If a diameter meet the tangent at Q in T, the curve in P, and the ordinate of Q in V, then $$CV.CT = CP^2,$$ and $QV^2 = CV^2 - CP^2$.	If a diameter meet the tangent at Q in T, the curve in P, and the ordinate of Q in V, then $$CV.CT = CP^2,$$ and $QV^2 : CV^2 - CP^2 = CD^2 : CP^2$.
If the tangent at P meet any two conjugate diameters in T, T', then $$PT.PT' = CD^2,$$ where CD is the semi-diameter conjugate to CP.	If the tangent at P meet any two conjugate diameters in T, T', then $$PT.PT' = CD^2,$$ where CD is the semi-diameter conjugate to CP.

EXAMPLES.

1. If CP be a semi-diameter of an ellipse, and AQQ' be drawn parallel to CP, meeting the curve and CB in Q, Q', then $2CP^2 = AQ'.AQ$.

2. What parallelogram circumscribing an ellipse has the least area?

3. If straight lines drawn through any point of an ellipse to the extremities of a diameter meet the conjugate CD in M, N, then $CM.CN = CD^2$.

4. If two tangents to an ellipse and the chord of contact include a constant area, the area included between the chord of contact and the ellipse is constant.

5. Prove also that the chord of contact always touches a concentric similar ellipse, and that the intersection of the tangents lies on another concentric similar ellipse.

6. If CP, CD be conjugate and AD, $A'P$ meet in O, then $BDOP$ is a parallelogram. When is its area greatest?

7. From the ends, P, D, of conjugate diameters in an ellipse draw lines parallel to any tangent line, and from the centre C draw any line cutting these lines and the tangent in points p, d, t; then will $Cp^2 + Cd^2 = Ct^2$.

8. The least triangle circumscribing a given ellipse has its sides bisected at the points of contact.

9. If an ellipse be inscribed in a given parallelogram its area will be greatest when the sides are bisected at the points of contact.

10. A polygon of a given number of sides is described about an ellipse and has its sides bisected at the points of contact. Prove that its area is constant.

11. Prove also that if the adjacent points of contact be joined the area of polygon thus formed will be constant.

12. If a triangle be inscribed in an ellipse, the straight lines drawn through the angular points parallel to the diameters bisecting the opposite side meet in a point.

13. The greatest triangle which can be inscribed in an ellipse has one of its sides bisected by a diameter of the ellipse and the others cut in points of bisection by the conjugate diameter.

14. The tangent and ordinate, at any point of an ellipse, meet the axis in T, N. Prove that

$$AN.A'N : AT.A'T = CN : CT.$$

15. Circles correspond to similar and similarly situated ellipses.

16. Parallel straight lines which pass through the extremities of conjugate diameters meet the ellipse again at the extremities of conjugate diameters.

17. Two ellipses of equal eccentricity and whose major axes are equal can only have two points in common. Prove this, and show that if three such ellipses intersect, two and two, in the points P, P'; Q', Q'; R, R', the lines PP', QQ', RR' meet in a point.

18. The locus of the middle points of all focal chords in an ellipse is a similar ellipse.

19. The locus of the middle points of all chords of an ellipse which pass through a fixed point is a similar ellipse.

20. The greatest triangle that can be inscribed in an ellipse has its sides parallel to the tangents at the opposite vertices.

21. P, Q, R are any three points on an ellipse; the diameter ACA' bisects PQ and meets RP, RQ in N, T. Prove that $CN.CT = CA^2$.

22. From an external point two tangents are drawn to an ellipse; show that an ellipse, similar and similarly situated, will pass through the external point, the points of contact, and the centre of the given ellipse.

23. A and B are two similar, similarly situated, and concentric ellipses; C is a third ellipse similar to A and B, its centre being on the circumference of B, and its axes parallel to those of A or B. Show that the common chord of A and C is parallel to the tangent to B at the centre of C.

24. Any chord of a conic which touches a similar, similarly situated and concentric conic is bisected at the point of contact.

25. The two portions of any straight line intercepted between two similar, similarly situated, and concentric conics, are equal.

26. A tangent to the interior of two similar, similarly situated, and concentric ellipses, cuts off a constant area from the exterior.

27. Through a given point draw a straight line cutting off a minimum area from a given ellipse.

28. If a chord of an ellipse pass through a fixed point, pairs of tangents at its extremities will intersect on a fixed straight line.

29. A chord of an ellipse, drawn through any point, is cut harmonically by the point, the curve, and the polar of the point.

30. If a tangent drawn at V the vertex of the inner of two concentric, similar, and similarly situated ellipses, meet the outer in the points T, T', then any chord of the inner, drawn through V, is half the sum, or half the difference of the parallel chords of the outer through T, T'.

CHAPTER X.

CURVATURE.

Let a circle be described touching a conic at P and cutting it in an adjacent point Q. Then, when Q moves up and ultimately coincides with P, the circle becomes the *Circle of Curvature* at the point P.

The chord of this circle drawn in any direction from P, is said to be the *Chord of Curvature* at P in that direction.

The radius, diameter, and centre of the circle of curvature are called respectively the *Radius*, *Diameter* and *Centre of Curvature.*

PROP. I. *The focal chord of curvature at any point of a conic is equal to the focal chord of the conic parallel to the tangent at that point.*

Let PSP' be any focal chord of the conic; and RR' the focal chord parallel to the tangent PT.

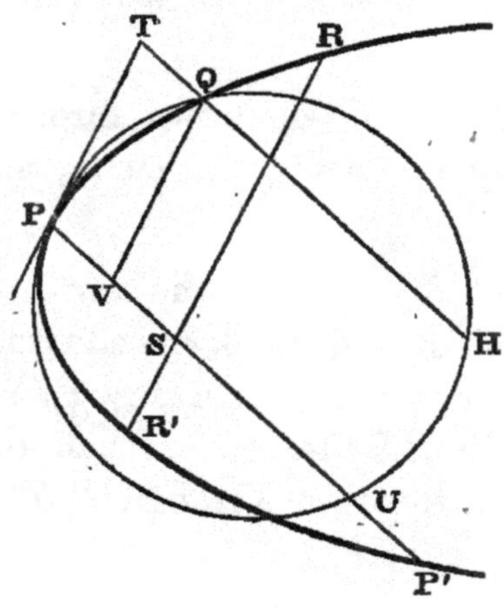

Let a circle be described touching the conic at P and cutting it in Q. Also let QH, a chord of this circle, parallel to PP', meet PT in T.

Then, if TQ meet the conic again in Q',

$$TP^2 : TQ.TQ' = RR' : PP'. \quad \text{[Cor. 3, p. 85.}$$

But $$TP^2 = TQ.TH. \quad \text{[Euc. III., 36.}$$

Hence $$TH : TQ' = RR' : PP'.$$

Let Q move up to P. Then TQ' becomes equal to PP', and the circle becomes the circle of curvature at P.

Hence the focal chord of curvature PU, to which TH becomes equal, is equal to RR'.

Cor. 1. Hence $PU.SE = 2PG^2$, [Ex. 21, p. 21.
where PG is the normal at P, SE the semi-latus rectum, and PU the focal chord of curvature as in the proposition.

Cor. 2. In a central conic

$$PU.CA = 2CD^2. \quad \text{[Ex. 26, p. 92.}$$

Prop. II. *To determine the length of the chord of curvature of a parabola drawn in any direction.*

Let PSU be the focal chord of curvature at P, and PV a chord of curvature drawn in any other direction. [fig., Prop. III.

Join UV, and draw SY parallel to VP to meet the tangent at P in Y. Then the triangles UPV, PSY are similar, since the alternate angles UPV, PSY are equal and SPY is equal to PVU in the alternate segment.

Therefore $$PV : PU = SP : SY.$$

But PU is equal to the focal chord of the parabola parallel to the tangent at P (Prop. I.) that is, to $4SP$. [Prop. VIII., p. 29.

Hence $$PV : 4SP = SP : SY,$$

or $$PV.SY = 4SP^2.$$

COR. 1. Let PV be the diameter of curvature.

Then $$PV.SY = 4SP^2,$$

where SY is the *focal perpendicular* upon the tangent at P.

COR. 2. The chord of curvature parallel to the axis of the parabola is equal to $4SP$, since, in this case, SY is measured along the axis and is equal to ST (fig., p. 27), that is, to SP. [See Appendix, § 12.

PROP. III. *To determine the length of the chord of curvature of a central conic drawn in any direction.*

Let PSU be the focal chord of curvature at P, and PV a chord of curvature drawn in any other direction.

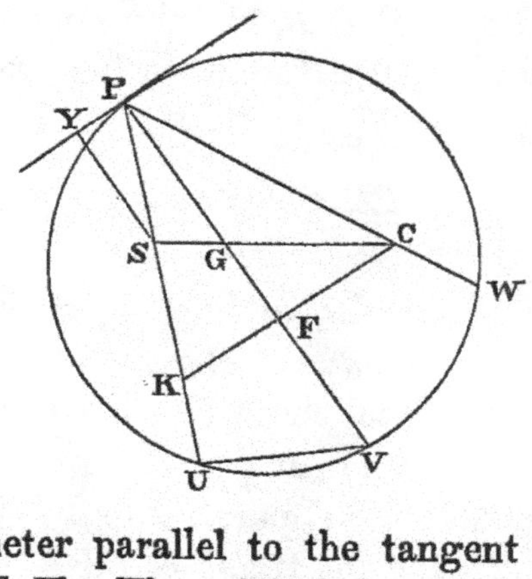

Let the diameter parallel to the tangent at P meet PV and PU in F and K. Then, PY being the tangent at P,

$$\angle PVU = SPY = \text{alternate angle } FKP.$$

Hence the triangles PVU, FKP, having the angle at P common, are similar, so that

$$PV : PU = PK : PF$$
$$= CA : PF.$$ [Cor., p. 58.

Hence $$PV.PF = PU.CA$$
$$= 2CD^2.$$ [Prop. I., Cor. 2.

COR. 1. Let PV be the diameter of curvature. Then

$$PV.PF = 2\,CD^2,$$

F being the point in which the *normal* meets the diameter conjugate to CP.

COR. 2. Let PW be the central chord of curvature.

Then F coincides with C the centre of the conic and

$$PW.CP = 2\,CD^2.$$

The following is a *direct* investigation of a general expression for the chord of curvature.

The figure is drawn to suit the case of the ellipse, and a knowledge of Newton is assumed. If however TH be parallel to PP', the central chord may be determined without this assumption, the proof being *word for word the same* as in Prop. B.

PROP. A. *To determine an expression for the chord of curvature of an ellipse drawn in any direction.*

Describe a circle touching the ellipse at P and cutting it

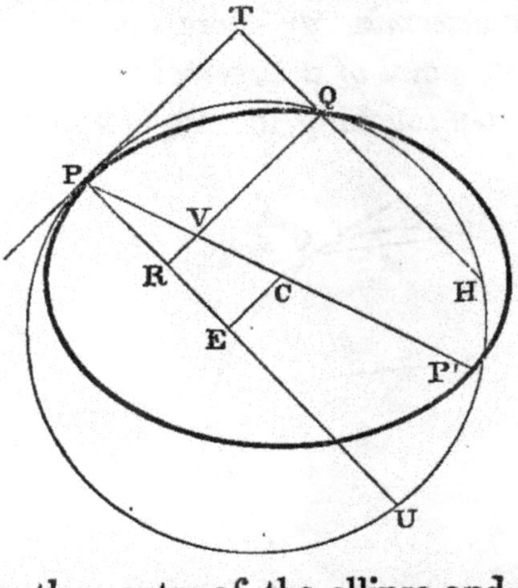

in Q. Let C be the centre of the ellipse and CV the abscissa of Q measured along the diameter PP'.

Draw QH, PU, any two parallel chords of the circle, and let the former meet the tangent at P in T.

Produce QV to meet PU in R, and draw CE, parallel to QV or TP, to meet PU in E.

Then $\qquad QV^2 : PV.VP' = CD^2 : CP^2.$ [*Note*, p. 83.

Let Q move up to P. Then the circle becomes the circle of curvature at P. Also QV^2 is ultimately equal to QR^2* or TP^2, that is (Euc. III., 36) to $TQ.TH$ or $PR.TH$.

Therefore $\quad PR.TH : PV.VP' = CD^2 : CP^2.$

Now TH is ultimately equal to the chord of curvature PU, and VP' to PP' or $2CP$.

Hence $\qquad PU : 2CP = TH : VP'.$

Also $\qquad PE : CP = PR : PV.$ [Euc. VI. 2.

By compounding,

$$PU.PE : 2CP^2 = PR.TH : VP.PV'$$
$$= CD^2 \quad : CP^2, \text{ from above.}$$

Therefore $\qquad PU.PE = 2CD^2.$

PROP. B. *To determine an expression for the central chord of curvature at any point of a hyperbola.*

Describe a circle touching the hyperbola at P and cutting

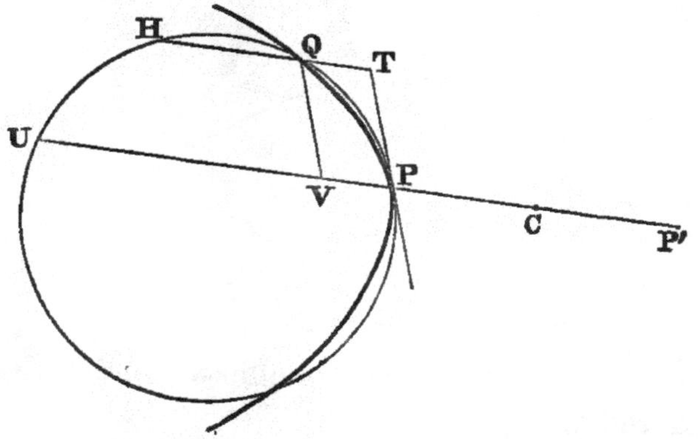

* Newton, Lemma VII., Cor. 2.

it in the adjacent point Q. Let C be the centre of the hyperbola and CV the abscissa of Q, measured along the diameter PP'.

Draw QH parallel to CP, and let it meet the circle in H and the tangent at P in T.

Then $\quad QV^2 : PV.VP' = CD^2 : CP^2$. [Prop. XVII., p. 129.

But QV^2 is equal to TP^2, and therefore to $TQ.TH$ (Euc. III., 36), or $PV.TH$.

Hence $\quad TH : VP' = CD^2 : CP^2$.

Let Q move up to P. Then the circle becomes the circle of curvature at P.

Also VP' becomes equal to PP' or $2CP$, and TH to PU, the central chord of curvature.

Therefore $\quad PU : 2CP = CD^2 : CP^2$.

Hence $\quad PU.CP = 2CD^2$.

EXAMPLES.

1. The radius of curvature at any point of a conic is to the normal at that point in the duplicate ratio of the normal to the semi-latus rectum.

For, with the notation of Prop. X., p. 12, the diameter of curvature at P is to the focal chord of curvature as PG to PK. The required result follows by Prop. I., Cor. 1.

2. Hence deduce the following construction for determining the centre of curvature at any point of a conic. From the foot of the normal at P draw GL perpendicular to the normal to meet SP, and draw LO perpendicular to SP to meet the normal in O. Then O is the centre of curvature at P.

3. The radius of curvature at the extremity of the latus rectum of a parabola is equal to twice the normal.

4. The circle of curvature at P, in a parabola, cuts off from the diameter through P a portion equal to the parameter of that diameter.

5. If SY be perpendicular to the tangent at P in a parabola, then $2PY$ is a mean proportional between the distance of any point on the curve from the vertex, and the chord of curvature, at that point, through the vertex.

6. In the parabola, $2SP$ is a mean proportional between SA and the portion of the axis cut off by the circle of curvature at P.

7. The circle of curvature at P, in any conic, meets the curve again in V; prove that PV and the tangent at P are equally inclined to the axis of the conic.

Let a circle be described intersecting any conic in the points Q, Q', R, R'. [fig., Prop. XV., p. 34.

Then QR, $Q'R'$ are equally inclined to the axis of the conic. [Props. XV., p. 34, and XIV., p. 85.

Let Q' move up to and coincide with Q, then the circle touches the conic at Q.

Again, let R move up to coincidence with Q. Then the circle becomes the circle of curvature at Q, and the *tangent* QR is equally inclined with QR' to the axis of the conic.

8. Assuming this result, show how to deduce the chord of curvature through the focus of a parabola.

9. The circles of curvature at the extremities P, D of two conjugate diameters of an ellipse meet the curve again in Q, R respectively; show that PR is parallel to DQ.

10. Find the points at which the radius of curvature of a central conic is a mean proportional between the major and minor axes.

11. The circle of curvature at an extremity of one of the equi-conjugate diameters passes through the other extremity of that diameter.

12. The circle of curvature at a point P of an ellipse meets the curve again in U; the ordinates of P, U meet the auxiliary circle in p, u; prove that pu and the tangent at p are equally inclined to the axis of the ellipse.

13. There are three points P, Q, R, on an ellipse, whose osculating circles* pass through a given point on the curve; these lie on a circle passing through the point, and form a triangle of which the centre of the ellipse is the intersection of the bisectors of the sides.

14. If the ordinates of the points P, Q, R meet the auxiliary circle in p, q, r, the triangle pqr is equilateral.

15. Prove also that the normals at P, Q, R meet in a point.

16. The sum of the focal chord of curvature, at any point of an ellipse, and the focal chord of the ellipse parallel to the diameter through the point is constant.

17. The circle round SBH, in an ellipse, cuts the minor axis in the centre of curvature at B.

18. The tangent at P, in an ellipse, meets the axes in T, t; CP is produced to meet in L the circle described about the triangle TCt. Prove that PL is half the central chord of curvature at P, and that $CL.CP$ is constant.

19. With conjugate diameters of an ellipse as asymptotes a hyperbola is described touching the ellipse. Prove that the curvatures of the two curves at the point of contact are equal.

Curvature is measured by the reciprocal of the radius of curvature.

---

* That is, *Circles of Curvature.*

20. The tangent at any point P, in an ellipse of which S, H are foci, meets the axis in T; TQR bisects HP in Q, and meets SP in R. Prove that PR is one-fourth of the chord of curvature at P through S.

21. In an ellipse the circle of curvature cannot pass through the focus if CA is greater than SH.

22. If a straight line CN be drawn from the centre of an ellipse to bisect that chord of the circle of curvature at P which is common to the ellipse and circle, and if, being produced, it cut the ellipse in Q and the tangent in T, then CP, CQ are equal, and each of them is a mean proportional between CN and CT.

23. Normals to a conic at P, P' meet in O; prove that when P' moves up to and ultimately coincides with P, the point O becomes the centre of curvature at P.

24. The central chord of curvature at any point of a rectangular hyperbola is equal to that diameter of the curve which passes through the point.

25. The radius of curvature at any point P of a rectangular hyperbola is to CP in the duplicate ratio of CP to CA.

CHAPTER XI.

CONES.

From the centre of a circle draw a straight line at right angles to the plane of the circle, and in this line take a fixed point O. Then the surface generated by an indefinite straight line OP (fig., Props. V., VIII.), which moves so as always to pass through the fixed point and through some point P on the circumference of the circle, is said to be a *Right Circular Cone*, or simply a *Cone*. The point O is called the *Vertex*, and the line in which it is taken is called the *Axis*.

Any straight line passing through the vertex and lying upon the surface of the cone is said to be a *Generating Line*.

If N (fig., p. 166) be the centre of the circle, so that ON is the axis, the right-angled triangle ONP will have its sides and angles constant. All generating lines being therefore inclined at the same angle to the axis, it follows that a plane through the axis intersects the cone in two straight lines which include a constant angle. This angle is termed the *Vertical Angle*.

It is evident that any section of a cone by a plane drawn perpendicular to the axis is a circle.

Also:

I. If a generating line cut two sections, which are perpendicular to the axis, in the points Q, R (fig., Props. VII., VIII.), then since OQ and OR are constant for all positions of the generating line, therefore $OQ \pm OR$ is constant. Hence, in either case, QR is constant.

II. Let the plane of the paper, in fig., Prop. V., contain the axis of the cone and the generating lines OL, OM.

Draw any plane $APA'P'$, perpendicular to the plane of the paper (AA' being the axis of the section), and any plane $LPMP'$ perpendicular to the axis of the cone.

Let these planes intersect in the straight line PP', and let LM, which is a diameter of the *circular* section, cut PP' in N. Then PP' is perpendicular to the plane of the paper, and therefore to LM, which is a diameter of the circle. Also

$$P'N = PN.$$

Hence $$PN^2 = LN.NM,$$ [Euc. III., 35.

Also PN is perpendicular to the axis AA'. Hence, *the ordinate of any point P on the section APA', is a mean proportional between LN and NM.*

A CONIC SECTION is the curve of intersection of a plane with a cone, and will, in general, be a Parabola, an Ellipse, or a Hyperbola.

In the following figure one-half only of the section is represented.

PROP. I. *To determine the nature of any given section of a right circular cone.*

Let $OE'L$, $OEAR$ be two generating lines lying in the plane of the paper, which is perpendicular to ANP the plane of the section.

In the cone inscribe a sphere touching the plane of the section in S, and let the plane of contact EE' cut the plane of section in the line MX.

Let LPR be a circular section, and PN perpendicular to LR. Draw PM perpendicular to MX, and let OP touch the sphere in Q.

Then, since PS, PQ are tangents to the same sphere,

$$PS = PQ = RE.$$ [§ I., p. 161.

Therefore $$SP : NX = RE : NX$$
$$= AE : AX.$$ [Euc. VI., 2.

Also AE, AS, being tangents to the same sphere, are equal; and $NX = PM$.

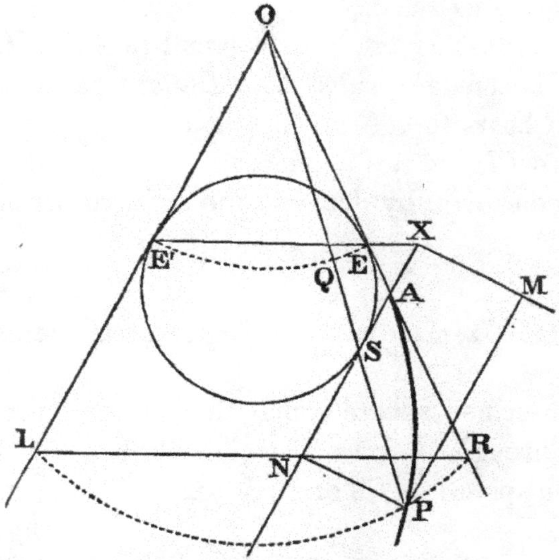

Therefore $SP : PM = SA : AX$.

Hence the locus of P is a conic, having S for focus and MX for directrix.

(i) Let the plane of section be parallel to a generating line, as OL. Then the section will consist of one infinite branch, and will therefore be a *Parabola*. [§ 5, p. 4.

(ii) Let the plane of section cut all generating lines on the same side of the vertex (fig., Prop. V.). Then the curve consists of one oval branch, and is an *Ellipse*.

(iii) Let the plane of section cut the cone on both sides of the vertex (fig., Prop. VIII.). Then the curve consists of two infinite branches, and is a *Hyperbola*.

The last part of the proposition may be thus proved:

(i) If XN, OL be parallel, the triangle AEX will be isosceles. Therefore $SP = NX = PM$, or the curve is a parabola.

(ii) Let the angle EAS diminish, so that XN, OL meet if produced. Then the angle EXA, and therefore the ratio $AE : AX$, diminishes, &c.

PROP. II. *If PN be the ordinate of any point on a section whose plane is parallel to a generating line OL, then PN^2 varies as the abscissa AN.*

For, in the last figure, PN^2 is equal to $LN.NR$.

But LN is constant, since NX, LO are parallel.

Also NR bears to AN a constant ratio.

Therefore PN^2 varies as AN.

It may be shown, by drawing the ordinate through S, that

$$PN^2 = 4AS.AN.$$

PROP. III. *To determine the length of the latus rectum of any section.*

Let an inscribed sphere touch the plane of section in the focus S. Through S draw a straight line meeting the cone in D, D', the sphere in S', and the axis of the cone, at right angles, in L. [fig., Prop. IV.

Draw DO to the vertex O and let it touch the sphere in Y.

Then $$DY^2 = DS.DS' \quad \text{[Euc. III., 36,}$$
$$= DS.SD'.$$

Hence the ordinate through S, that is *the semi-latus rectum*, is equal to DY, since it is a mean proportional between DS and SD'.

PROP. IV. *The perpendicular from the vertex of the cone upon the plane of section varies as the parameter* of the section.*

Let C be the centre of the sphere, in Prop. III., and let YC meet DD' in E. Draw OM perpendicular to the plane of section, and CN perpendicular to OM. Join CS.

Then the angle NCS is a right angle, and

$$\angle LCS = \text{complement of } OCN = CON.$$

---

* The latus rectum is sometimes called the *Parameter* of a section.

Hence, by similar right-angled triangles CLS, CNO,

$$CL : CS = ON : OC,$$

or
$$ON.CS = CL.CO$$
$$= CE.CY, \quad \text{[Euc. III., 35,}$$

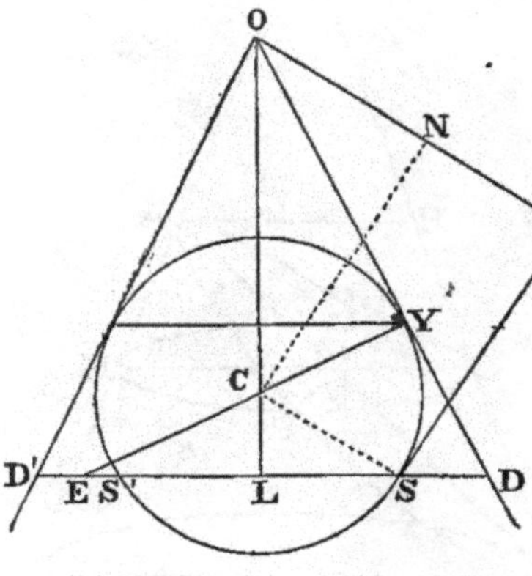

since a circle goes round $OYLE$, the angles at Y, L being right angles.

But $CS = CY$; therefore $ON = CE$.

By addition, $ON + CS = CE + CY$,

or $OM = EY$.

But EY varies as DY, since the angle at D is constant. Therefore OM varies as DY, or as the parameter of the section. [Prop. III.

PROP. V. *The semi-minor axis of any section, whose plane is not parallel to a generating line, is a mean proportional between the perpendiculars drawn from the vertices of the section upon the axis of the cone.*

Let A, A' be the vertices of the section; AH, $A'K$, straight lines, perpendicular to the axis of the cone and meeting the generating lines through A', A in H, K respectively. Through N, the middle point of AA', draw LNM parallel to $A'K$ and terminated by OA', OK, and let PN be the semi-minor axis or ordinate through N.

Then, since $AN = \frac{1}{2}AA'$ and NM is parallel to $A'K$, therefore $NM = \frac{1}{2}A'K$.

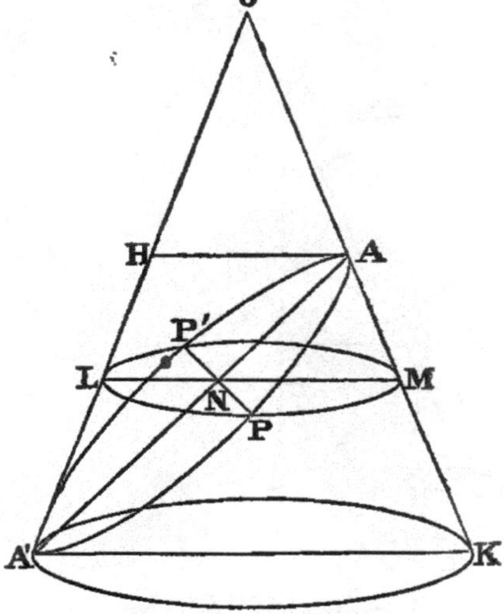

Similarly $$LN = \tfrac{1}{2}AH.$$
Therefore $$PN^2 = LN.NM = \tfrac{1}{4}A'K.AH,$$
or the semi-minor axis is a mean proportional between $\frac{1}{2}A'K$ and $\frac{1}{2}AH$, that is, between the perpendiculars from A', A upon the axis of the cone.

Prop. VI. *To prove that*

$$PN^2 : AN.NA' = CB^2 : CA^2,$$

where PN is the ordinate of any point P on the section, and CA, CB are the semi-axes.

In the last figure, let N be *any* point upon AA'.

Then, by similar triangles,

$$NM : AN = A'K : AA',$$
and $$LN : NA' = AH : A'A'.$$
By compounding, since $PN^2 = LN.NM$,
therefore $$PN^2 : AN.NA' = A'K.AH : AA'^2$$
$$= CB^2 : CA^2.$$ [Prop. v.

PROP. VII. *If two spheres be inscribed in the cone, so as to touch the plane of section upon opposite sides, in the points S, H, then will $SP+PH$ be constant, where P is any point on the curve.*

Let O be the vertex of the cone, and let the generating line through P touch the spheres in Q, R.

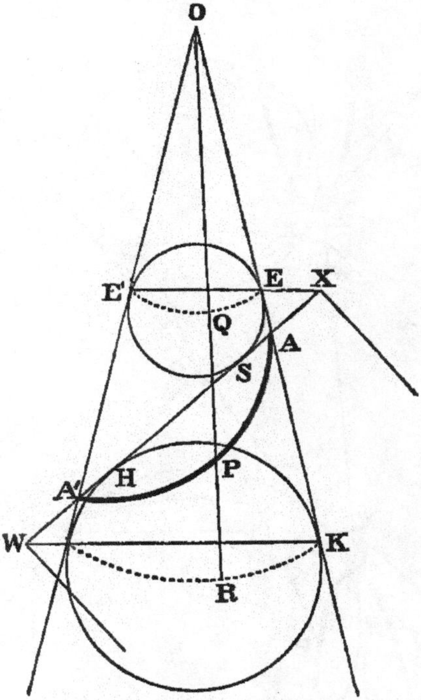

Then PS, PQ, being tangents to the same sphere, are equal. Similarly PH, PR are equal.

By addition, $$SP+PH=QR,$$
which is constant for all positions of P on the curve.

Lines are drawn through X and W, in the figure, to represent the directrices of the section. The directrices being the lines in which the planes of contact EQE', KR cut the plane of section. See Prop. I.

PROP. VIII. *If two spheres be inscribed in the cone, so as to touch the plane of section upon the same side, in the points* S, H, *then will* $HP \sim SP$ *be constant, where* P *is any point on the curve.*

As in Prop. VIII., $SP = PQ$ and $HP = PR$.

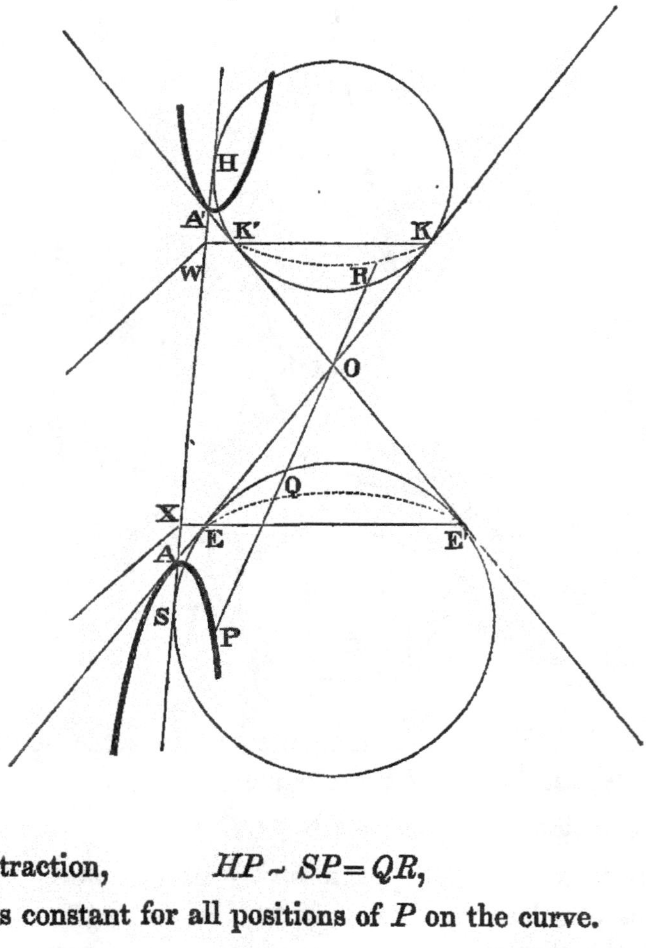

By subtraction, $HP \sim SP = QR$,

which is constant for all positions of P on the curve.

EXAMPLES.

1. The latus rectum of a parabola cut from a given cone varies as the distance between the vertices of the cone and the parabola.

2. The foci of all parabolic sections, which can be cut from a given right cone, lie upon a right cone.

3. The distance between the foci of an elliptic section is equal to the difference of the distances of its vertices from the vertex of the cone.

4. The foci of all elliptical sections of the same eccentricity lie on two cones.

5. The eccentricity of any section is a ratio of greater or less inequality according as the acute angle between the axes of the cone and of the section is less or greater than the semi-vertical angle of the cone.

6. If two plane sections have the same directrix the corresponding foci lie on a straight line which passes through the vertex.

7. The extremities of the minor axes of the elliptical sections of a right cone made by parallel planes, lie on two generating lines.

8. Show how to cut a right cone so that the section may be an ellipse whose axes are of given lengths.

9. Give a geometrical construction by which a cone may be cut so that the section may be an ellipse of given eccentricity.

10. Given a right cone and a point within it, there are but two sections which have this point for focus; and the planes of these sections make equal angles with the straight line joining the given point and the vertex of the cone.

11. If the curve formed by the intersection of any plane with a cone be projected upon a plane perpendicular to the axis, prove that the focus of the curve of projection will lie on the axis of the cone.

12. Show how to cut from a cone a section of given latus rectum.

13. The latus rectum being constant, the envelope of the plane of section is a sphere.

14. The vertical angle of a cone being a right angle, prove that the perpendicular from the vertex upon any plane is equal to the semi-latus rectum of its curve of intersection with the cone.

15. In any section, the latus rectum is a mean proportional between the axes.

16. Show how to cut from a given cone a hyperbola whose asymptotes shall contain the greatest possible angle.

17. Under what conditions is it possible to cut a rectangular hyperbola from a given right cone?

18. The angle between the asymptotes of a section being given, determine the locus of either focus.

19. Prove that the plane of the hyperbola of greatest eccentricity, which can be cut from a given cone, is parallel to the axis of the cone.

20. A plane through the vertex, parallel to the plane of a hyperbolic section, intersects the cone in generating lines which are parallel to the asymptotes of the section.

CHAPTER XII.

MISCELLANEOUS PROPOSITIONS.

1. *To prove*, Prop. IX., p. 30, *the definition only being assumed.*

Having made the same construction as in Prop. I., p. 25,

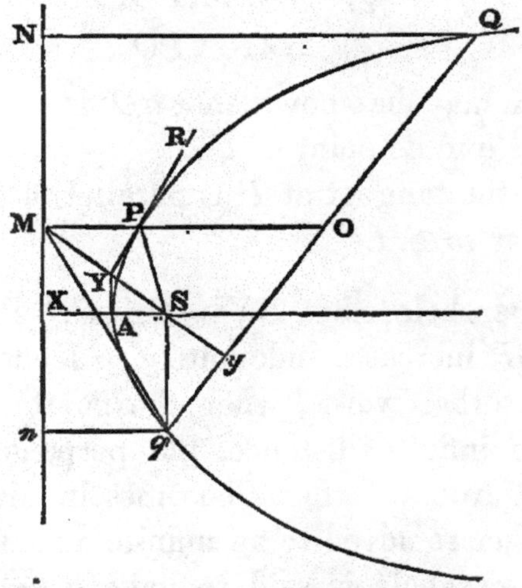

draw QD perpendicular to MO. Also draw PY perpendicular to yM and therefore parallel to Qq.

Then, by similar triangles, QD is to QO as MY to PM, and therefore as Yy to PO. [Euc. VI., 2.

By compounding,

$$QD^2 : QO^2 = MY.Yy : PM.PO.$$

But the triangle SPM is isosceles and PY is the perpendicular upon the base. Therefore $MY = SY$.

Hence S divides Yy so that $Yy + SY = My$.

Therefore $My^2 = Sy^2 + 4SY.Yy$, [Euc. II., 8.

or $My^2 - Sy^2 = 4MY.Yy$.

Also DM is equal to QN, or to SQ. [*Def.*

Therefore $QD^2 = QM^2 - DM^2$ [Euc. I., 47.

$$= QM^2 - SQ^2.$$

But QM^2 is equal to $Qy^2 + My^2$, and SQ^2 to $Qy^2 + Sy^2$ (Euc. I., 47).

Therefore QD^2, being equal to $QM^2 - SQ^2$, is equal to $My^2 - Sy^2$, or to $4MY.Yy$.

Hence $QO^2 = 4PM.PO$, from above,

$$= 4SP.PO.$$

Similarly it may be shown that qO^2 is equal to $4SP.PO$. Hence O is the middle point of Qq.

Hence also the tangent at P is parallel to Qq (Cor., p. 15) or perpendicular to SM.

2. In the parabola, since $SY^2 = SA.SP$ (Prop. XI., p. 32), therefore, as SP increases indefinitely, SY also increases indefinitely. In other words, when the point of contact P is removed to an infinite distance, the perpendicular distance of the tangent from the focus becomes infinite, and the tangent is altogether removed to an infinite distance.

Hence the parabola is said to have *a tangent at infinity.* Conversely, it may be shown that a conic which has a tangent at infinity is a parabola.

3. Let the tangents to a curve at the adjacent points P, Q intersect in R. [fig., p. 27.

Let the point Q move up to P, the latter point remaining stationary. Then R moves up to P, and ultimately coincides with it when Q coincides with P. Hence *the point P may be regarded as the point of intersection of two tangents whose points of contact are indefinitely near to one another.*

4. *The asymptotes of a hyperbola may be regarded as tangents whose points of contact are at an infinite distance.*

For, in Prop. XIII., p. 108, if CN be indefinitely increased, CT vanishes and the tangent passes through the centre.

Also, in Prop. XVI., p. 109, NT becomes equal to CN, so that

$$PN^2 : NT^2 = CB^2 : CA^2.$$

Hence, the tangent becomes parallel to an asymptote and therefore coincides with it, since both pass through the centre.

5. The points of contact of the asymptotes being at an infinite distance, their chord of contact lies altogether at infinity.

Conversely, it may be shown that if the chord of contact of any pair of tangents to a conic lies at infinity, the conic is a hyperbola.

6. *The asymptotes of a hyperbola are themselves a conic of the same eccentricity.*

For the distances of all points upon them from the centre are in the ratio $CS : CA$ to their perpendicular distances from the minor axis.

The asymptotes of a hyperbola are the limiting form which the curve assumes when the axes are indefinitely diminished, their ratio remaining unaltered.

7. *The parabola is the limiting form of the ellipse or hyperbola when the centre is removed to an infinite distance.*

For, let CS be increased indefinitely (fig., p. 55), the latus rectum remaining constant and the point S being fixed. Then the ratio $CS : CA$, that is, the eccentricity, becomes a ratio of equality.

In this case, the focus H is removed to an infinite distance and TH (fig., p. 56) becomes parallel to the axis.

Compare Prop. XIII., p. 33.

8. *The circle is the limiting form of the ellipse when the distance between the foci is indefinitely diminished.*

For, in this case, S and H coincide with C.

Therefore $$CP = \tfrac{1}{2}(SP + HP) = CA.$$

9. *If a chord of a circle pass through a fixed point, the tangents at its extremities will intersect on a fixed straight line.*

In fig., p. 87, supposing the curve a circle, let T be the intersection of tangents at the extremities of that chord which is bisected in *the fixed point* O.

Let o be the middle point of any other chord through O, and t the intersection of tangents at its extremities.

Then $$CO.CT = (\text{radius})^2 = Co.Ct.$$

Hence a circle goes round $OotT$. [Euc. III., 36, Cor.

Therefore $\angle OTt + Oot =$ two right angles. [Euc. III., 22.

But $\angle Oot$ = a right angle. [Euc. III., 3.

Therefore OTt is a right angle, and Tt *a fixed straight line*, since T is by construction a fixed point.

10. *A chord of a circle, drawn from any point, is cut harmonically by the point, the curve, and the polar of the point.*

Using the construction of Prop. XVII., p. 88, and remembering that chords of a circle are perpendicular to the diameters which bisect them, we have

$$tp.tp' = (\text{tangent from } t)^2 \quad \text{[Euc. III., 36.}$$
$$= tO.tC,$$

by similar right-angled triangles.

Also, since the angles at O and c are right angles, a circle goes round $OCco$.

Therefore $$tc.to = tO.tC \quad \text{[Euc. III., 36.}$$
$$= tp.tp', \text{ from above.}$$

Hence $$2tp.tp' = to\,(tp + tp').$$

11. *To construct an equilateral triangle* corresponding *to a given triangle.*

In the definition on p. 143, the ordinates may be parallel to any fixed straight line and the ratio may be any given ratio.

Let SPH be the given triangle. [fig., p. 102.

Describe the equilateral triangle SgH and let gP meet HS in G.

Let *the ordinates* be parallel to PG, and let $PG : gG$ be *the constant ratio.*

Then the straight line gH corresponds to PH. [Prop. I., p. 143.

Similarly, gS corresponds to PS.

Hence the equilateral triangle gHS corresponds to the given triangle.

12. *To construct a square* corresponding *to a given parallelogram.*

Let $ABCD$ be the given parallelogram.

Describe the square $ABC'D'$ and let $D'D$ meet AB in N. Then, if *the ordinates* be parallel to $D'D$ and *the constant ratio* be that of ND to ND', the square $ABC'D'$ will correspond to the given parallelogram, for AD' corresponds to AD and BC' to BC. [Prop. I., p. 143.

13. *Corresponding Points applied to circles of curvature.*

It has been shown that parallel straight lines correspond to parallel straight lines. [Prop. III., p. 144.

By a very similar process it may be proved that, if two straight lines PV, PT be equally inclined to the axis in *opposite* directions, the corresponding lines will be equally inclined to the axis in opposite directions.

Let the circle of curvature at P, in an ellipse, cut the ellipse in V, and let the tangent at P meet the axis in T. Take points p, v (on the auxiliary circle), corresponding to P, V. Then pv and the tangent pT are equally inclined to the axis of the ellipse, since they correspond to lines which are equally inclined to the axis. [Ex. 7, p. 158.

Ex. 1. If the circles of curvature at the extremities P, D of two conjugate diameters of an ellipse meet the curve again in Q, R respectively, then PR is parallel to DQ.

This theorem may be reduced to the following:

If from the extremities p, d of two diameters at right angles, in a circle, the chords pq, dr be drawn equally inclined with the tangents at p, d respectively to a fixed diameter, then pr is parallel to dq.

Ex. 2. Any point O on a circle being given, it may be shown that there are three points P, Q, R on the circumference, situated at the vertices of an equilateral triangle, such that OP, OQ, OR are equally inclined with the tangents at P, Q, R to a given diameter.

It follows that there are three points P, Q, R on an ellipse, the circles of curvature at which pass through a given point on the curve, &c. [Ex. 13, p. 159.

Def. If the opposite sides of any quadrilateral ($ABCD$) be produced to meet (in O, P) the figure thus formed is called a *Complete Quadrilateral.*

The straight lines AC, BD, OP are the *Diagonals* of the complete quadrilateral.

14. *The middle points of the diagonals of a complete quadrilateral lie on the same straight line.*

Complete the quadrilateral $ABCD$ and let OP be the exterior diagonal.

Complete the parallelograms $BODR$, $AOCQ$, and let BR AQ cut PD in V, T respectively.

Then, since AQ is parallel to OC,

$$PC : CT = PB : BA \qquad \text{[Euc. VI., 2.}$$

$$= PV : VD, \text{ similarly.}$$

Alternando $PC : PV = CT : VD$

$$= CQ : VR,$$

by similar triangles CTQ, VDR.

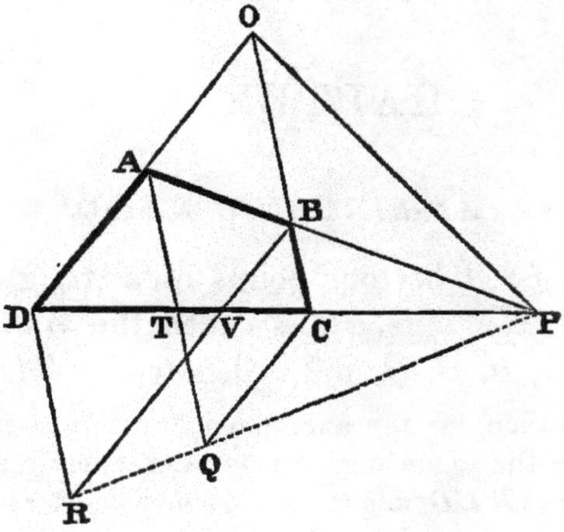

Hence, PQR is a straight line and the middle points of OP, OQ, OR lie upon a straight line parallel to PQR. [Euc. VI., 2.

But the middle point of OQ is also the middle point of AC, since the diagonals of parallelograms bisect one another. Similarly, the middle point of OR is also the middle point of BD.

Therefore the middle points of AC, BD, and OP lie on a straight line parallel to PQR.

CHAPTER XIII.

ANHARMONIC RATIO.

Let A, B, C, D be four points on a straight line. Then the ratio $AB.CD : AD.BC$ is called the *Anharmonic Ratio* of the range A, B, C, D, and is denoted by $\{ABCD\}$.

In the expression for the anharmonic ratio of a range the letters which constitute the range might have been taken in a different order. Thus $AD.BC : AB.CD$ might have been defined as the anharmonic ratio of the above range. It is of course necessary to retain throughout any investigation the particular order adopted at its commencement.

1. *If four fixed straight lines which meet in O be cut by any transversal in the points A, B, C, D, then will* $\{ABCD\}$ *be constant.*

Draw the straight line aBb, parallel to OD, and meeting OA, OB in a, b.

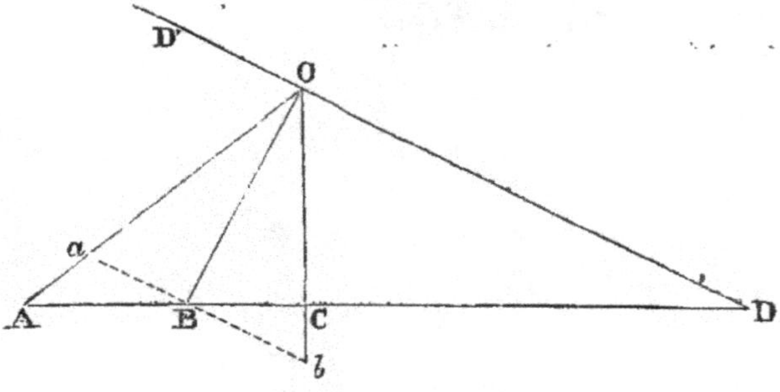

Then $$AB : AD = aB : DO,$$

by similar triangles ADO, ABa.

Similarly, $CD : BC = DO : Bb$.

Therefore $AB.CD : AD.BC = aB : Bb$,

which is a constant ratio for all positions of ab parallel to OD.

Thus $\{ABCD\}$ is constant.

Def. The *Anharmonic Ratio of a Pencil* is the anharmonic ratio of the range in which its rays are intersected by any transversal.

Pencils and ranges are said to be *equal* when their anharmonic ratios are equal.

Let P be the vertex (fig., p. 184) and PA, PB, PC, PD the rays of any pencil. Then the anharmonic ratio of the pencil P is denoted by $P\{ABCD\}$.

2. *The transversal may cut the rays of the pencil on either side of the vertex.*

For if, in the preceding article a transversal had been drawn through B, cutting OA, OB, OC, OD', where D' lies in DO produced, then it would have appeared, by a precisely similar proof that $O\{ABCD'\}$ is equal to the same constant ratio $aB : Bb$.

Ex. Consider the pencil O (fig., p. 183), one of whose ranges is $\{DMAQ\}$. The rays of the pencil are here taken in the order OD, OM, OA, OQ. These rays, *taken in the same order*, meet the straight line CQ in the range B, R, C, Q.

Hence $\{DMAQ\} = \{BRCQ\}$.

A pencil whose rays are produced through the vertex may be distinguished as a *Complete Pencil.*

3. *Equiangular pencils are equal to one another.*

This is proved in Arts. 1, 2, where it is shown that, the angles of a pencil being fixed, its ranges are all equal.

Ex. 1. Let the variable straight line TR (fig., p. 11) subtend a right angle, or any constant angle, at the fixed point

S, and let T_1, T_2, T_3, T_4 denote any four positions of the variable point T. Also let R_1, R_2, R_3, R_4 denote the corresponding positions of R.

Then $$S\{T_1T_2T_3T_4\} = S\{R_1R_2R_3R_4\},$$
since these pencils are equiangular.

Ex. 2. Let TP, TQ (fig., p. 56) be fixed straight lines, and TS, TH variable lines such that $\angle STQ = HTP$.

Then, if suffixes be employed as in Ex. 1,
$$T\{S_1S_2S_3S_4\} = T\{H_1H_2H_3H_4\},$$
since these pencils are also equiangular.

4. *Condition that a variable straight line may pass through a fixed point.*

Take any two fixed straight lines intersecting in A, and

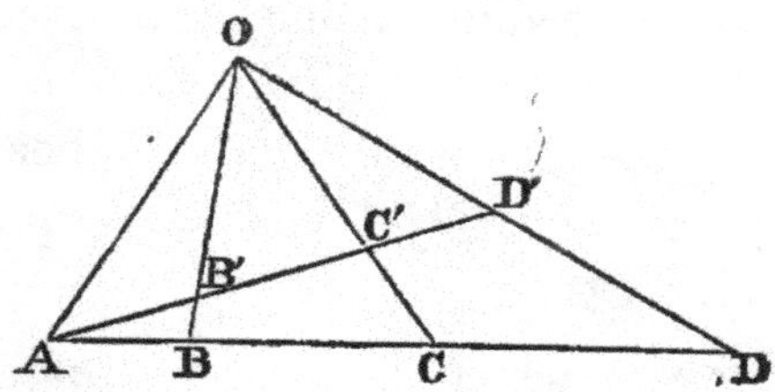

let the variable line, in any three of its positions, intersect one of the fixed lines in B, C, D, and the other in B', C', D'.

Let BB', CC' intersect in O. Join AO, DO, and let
$$\{AB'C'D'\} = \{ABCD\}.$$

Then will DO cut AD' in a point which forms with A, B', C' a range equal to $\{ABCD\}$, that is, in the point D'.

Hence, *if* $\{AB'C'D'\} = \{ABCD\}$, *the straight lines* BB', CC', DD' *meet in a point.*

Now let BB', CC' be fixed positions of the variable line. Then, the above condition being satisfied, DD' passes through the fixed point O.

5. *Condition that a variable point may lie on a fixed straight line.*

Let O, O' be fixed points and B, C, D any three positions of the variable point.

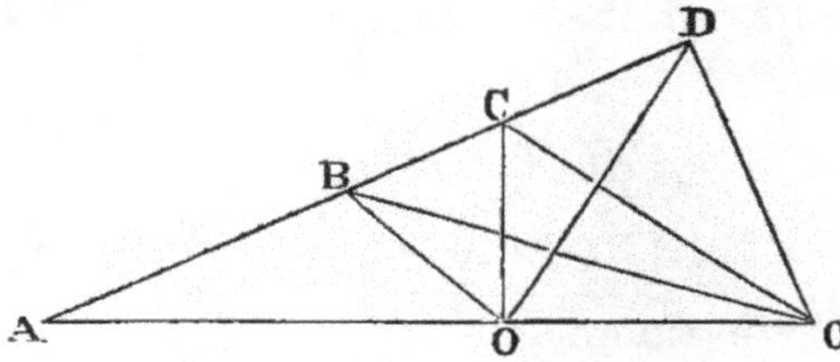

Join CB; produce it to meet $O'O$ in A; construct the pencils O, O', as in the figure; and let

$$O\{ABCD\} = O'\{ABCD\}.$$

Then the pencils O, O' being equal, the rays OD, $O'D$ will meet the straight line ABC in points which form with A, B, C equal ranges. This is to say, they will both meet it in the same point. Therefore D lies on the straight line ABC.

Now let B, C be fixed positions of the variable point. Then D lies on the fixed straight line BC.

Hence, also *if two pencils have one ray* (OO') *in common their remaining rays will intersect two and two in three points which lie on a straight line.*

The notation (AA', BB') will be used to express the point of intersection of the straight lines AA', BB'.*

HARMONIC PENCILS AND RANGES.

6. Pencils and ranges are said to be harmonic when their anharmonic ratios are ratios of equality.

Let $\{ABCD\}$ be a ratio of equality.

Then $$AB.CD = AD.BC.$$

Therefore $$AB : AD = BC : CD,$$

or AB, AC, AD are in harmonical progression.

* Smith's Prize Examination, 1852.

7. *Condition that a range* $\{ABCD\}$ *may be harmonic.*

If the ratio $AB.CD : AD.BC$ be equal to its reciprocal $AD.CB : AB.DC$ it must be a ratio of equality. This follows by a reductio ad absurdum.

But the former of these ratios is equal to $\{ABCD\}$, and the latter to $\{ADCB\}$. [*Def.*

Therefore, if $\{ABCD\} = \{ADCB\}$,

or if $\{ABCD\} = \{CBAD\}$, similarly,

the range will be harmonic.

Hence, a range will be harmonic if in the expression for its anharmonic ratio, the second and fourth, or the first and third, letters of the range can be interchanged without altering the value of the expression.

Conversely, both of these changes will be possible if the range be harmonic.

8. *Conditions that a pencil may be harmonic.*

(i) Let OB, OD (fig., p. 178) be the internal and external bisectors of the angle AOC. Then will the pencil O be harmonic.

For, if $ABCD$ be any transversal, then

$$AB : BC = AO : CO \qquad \text{[Euc. VI., 2,}$$
$$= AD : CD.$$

Therefore $AB.CD = AD.BC$,

or $O\{ABCD\}$ is a ratio of equality.

(ii) A pencil will also be harmonic when a transversal aBb, drawn parallel to one of its rays OD, is divided into equal segments aB, Bb, by the points in which it intersects the other three rays. [fig., § 1.

For $O\{ABCD\}$ being equal, as in the first article, to $aB : Bb$, becomes in this case a ratio of equality.

9. *Harmonic properties of a complete quadrilateral.*

Let the opposite sides of the quadrilateral $ABCD$ intersect in P, Q, as in the figure.

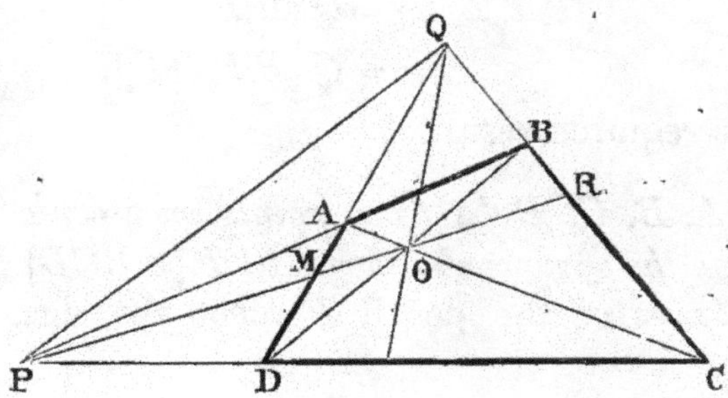

Let AC, BD intersect in O, through which draw $PMOR$, cutting AD, BC in M, R respectively. Draw QO.

Then $\{DMAQ\} = \{BRCQ\}$, [Ex., p. 179,

since all ranges of the pencil O are equal.

Similarly $\{DMAQ\} = \{CRBQ\}$, in the pencil P.

Therefore $\{CRBQ\} = \{BRCQ\}$,

or the pencils O, P are harmonic. [§ 7.

So too is the pencil Q.

ANHARMONIC PROPERTIES OF CONICS.

10. *The range in which four tangents to a conic are intersected by any fifth tangent is equal to the pencil formed by joining the points of contact of the four tangents to the point of contact of the fifth.*

Let the chord PQ (fig., p. 11) meet the directrix in R, and let the tangents at its extremities intersect in T. Then TR subtends a right angle at the focus S.

Take any four positions of the points R, T, and let Q

remain fixed. Then, the same letters being used, with suffixes as in Ex. 1, p. 180,

$$S\{T_1T_2T_3T_4\} = S\{R_1R_2R_3R_4\}.$$

Hence
$$\{T_1T_2T_3T_4\} = Q\{R_1R_2R_3R_4\}$$
$$= Q\{P_1P_2P_3P_4\}.$$

which is the required result.

11. *If A, B, C, D be fixed points on a conic and P any other point on the same conic, then will $P\{ABCD\}$ be constant.*

Let the rays of the pencil P meet the directrix in the

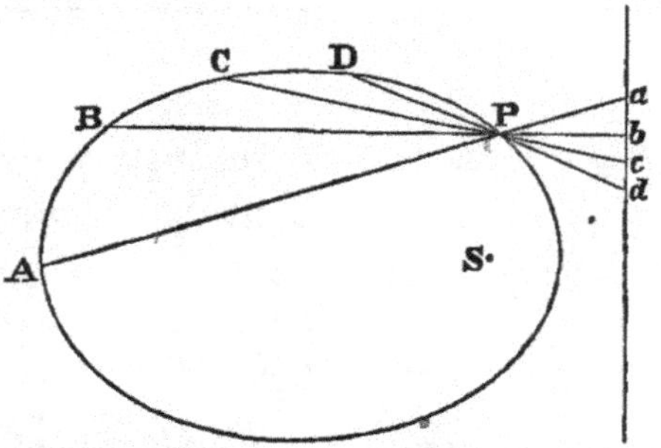

points a, b, c, d. Then the angle aSb is constant, since it is equal to half the angle ASB. [Prop. VII., p. 10.

Similarly it may be shown that each of the angles bSc, cSd is constant.

Hence $\{abcd\} = S\{abcd\} =$ a constant.

Therefore $P\{ABCD\}$, being equal to $\{abcd\}$, is constant.

Conversely, *if $P\{ABCD\}$ be constant, the points A, B, C, D being fixed, then the locus of P is a conic passing through the four fixed points.*

12. *If the tangents to a conic at four fixed points A, B, C, D intersect the tangent at P in the points a, b, c, d respectively, then will $\{abcd\}$ be constant.*

For, if S be the focus, the angle aSb is constant, since it equal to half the angle ASB. [Prop. VII., p. 10.

Similarly it may be shown that the angles bSc, cSd are constant.

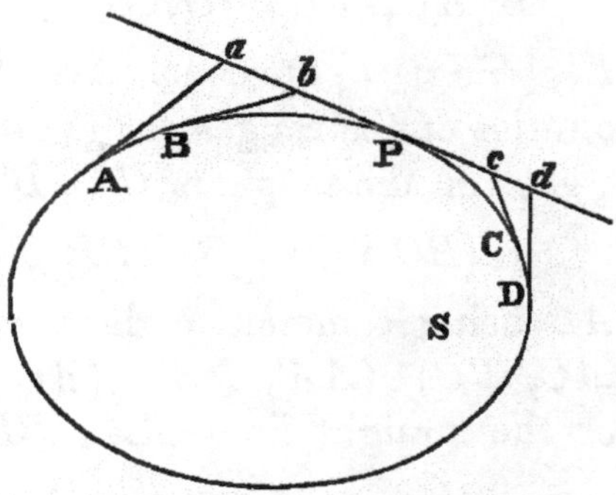

Hence $S\{abcd\}$, and therefore $\{abcd\}$, is constant.

Conversely, *if a variable straight line be intersected by four fixed straight lines in a range of constant anharmonic ratio, the envelope of the variable line will be a conic touching the four fixed lines.*

BRIANCHON'S THEOREM.

13. *If $ABCA'B'C'$ be a hexagon circumscribing a conic, then will the straight lines AA', BB', CC' meet in a point.*

Let AB, AC' meet $A'C$ in the points E, F.

Then $$A\{BCA'C'\} = \{ECA'F\}.$$

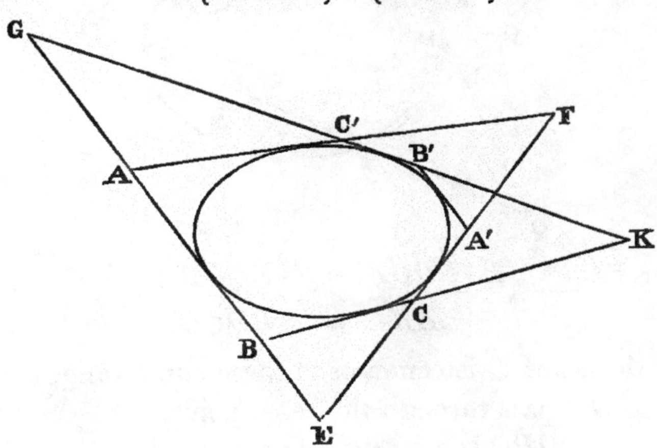

Again, let BA, BC meet $B'C'$ in the points G, K.

Then $$B\{ACB'C'\} = \{GKB'C'\}.$$

But $\{ECA'F\}$, $\{GKB'C'\}$ are equal (Art. 12), since they are the anharmonic ratios of the ranges of the same four tangents AB, BC, $B'A'$, AC' on the tangents CA', $B'C'$ respectively.

Therefore $$A\{BCA'C'\} = B\{ACB'C'\},$$

and, the ray AB being common to these equal pencils, the three points (AC, BC), (AA', BB'), (AC', BC') lie on a straight line, or the straight lines AA', BB', CC' meet in a point.

PASCAL'S THEOREM.

14. *If ABCDEF be a hexagon inscribed in a conic, then will the points of intersection of the three pairs of opposite sides AB, ED; BC, FE: CD, AF lie in a straight line.*

Let O, P, Q be the three points of intersection, and let PB, PF cut OE, QC respectively in the points K, L.

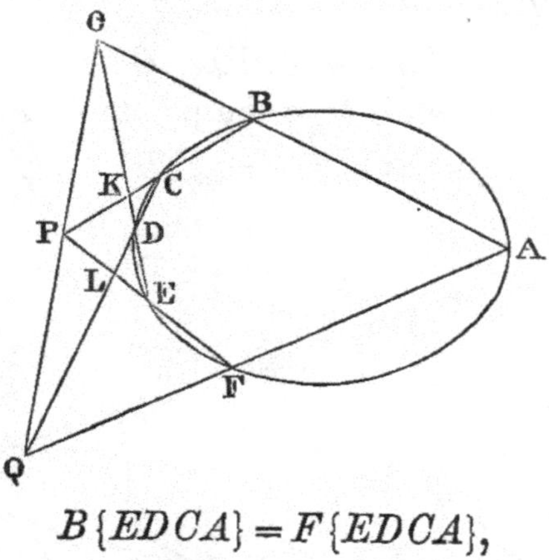

Therefore $$B\{EDCA\} = F\{EDCA\},$$

or $$\{EDKO\} = \{LDCQ\}.$$

But the point D is common to these equal ranges. Hence EL, KC, OQ pass through the same point.

Therefore OPQ is a straight line.

15. Let D coincide with C. Then the straight line which joins the points (AB, EC), (BC, FE) passes through the point in which the tangent at C meets AF.

Conversely, when five points on a conic are given, the tangents at those points may be drawn.

INVOLUTION.

Def. Let A, A'; B, B'; ... be any number of pairs of points lying in a straight line, and let

$$OA.OA' = OB.OB' = ...,$$

where O is a point in the same straight line.

Then the points A, A', ... are said to form a system *in Involution* of which O is the *Centre*.

Two points as A, A' are said to be *conjugate*, and a point at which two conjugate points coincide is said to be a *Focus*.

When conjugate points lie on opposite sides of the centre, it follows from this definition that the system has no foci.

When conjugate points as A, B (fig., p. 189) lie on the same side of the centre, then the point F, whose distance from O is a mean proportional between OA and OB, is a focus. There will also be a second focus (at an equal distance from O) in FO produced.

16. *Any two points which form with two fixed points a harmonic range belong to a system in involution, of which the fixed points are foci.*

The construction of the Lemma, p. 14, being used, let SN produced meet PQ in R'. Then SR, SR', being the external and internal bisectors of the angle PSQ, the range $PR'QR$ is harmonic.

Now, since NQ, SR are parallel,

$$OQ : OR = ON : OM \qquad \text{[Euc. VI., 2,}$$
$$= OR' : OQ, \text{ similarly.}$$

Therefore $OR.OR' = OQ^2$,

which proves that R, R' are involution with the foci P, Q.

Any two conjugate points, as R, R', are hence said to be *Harmonic Conjugates* with respect to the foci.

Conversely, *any two conjugate points of a system in involution form with the foci a harmonic range.*

17. *The range formed by any four points of a system in involution is equal to the range formed by their four conjugates.*

Let A, B, C, D be four points of a system in involution, and A', B', C', D' their conjugates. Then $OA.OA' = OB.OB'$, where O is the centre of the system. [*Def.*

Therefore $OA' : OB' = OB : OA$.

Dividendo $A'B' : OB' = AB : OA$.

Similarly, $C'D' : OD' = CD : OC$.

Hence, by compounding, the rectangle $A'B'.C'D'$ is to $OB'.OD'$ as $AB.CD$ to $OA.OC$; also, if the *letters* B, D be interchanged throughout, the antecedents of this proportion become $A'D'.B'C'$ and $AD.BC$, the consequents remaining unaltered.

Therefore $A'B'.C'D' : A'D'.B'C' = AB.CD : AD.BC$,

or $\{A'B'C'D'\} = \{ABCD\}$.

18. *A system in involution is determinate when, any point being given, its conjugate may be found.*

This is evidently the case when the centre is given, and also the rectangle contained by its distances from any two conjugate points.

Hence a system is determinate:

(i) If the foci be given. For, in this case, the centre is the middle point of the line joining them, and *the rectangle* is equal to the square on half the line.

(ii) If two pairs of conjugate points be given. For, through the points A, A' draw parallel straight lines AP,

$A'Q$; and through the conjugate points B, B' draw parallel

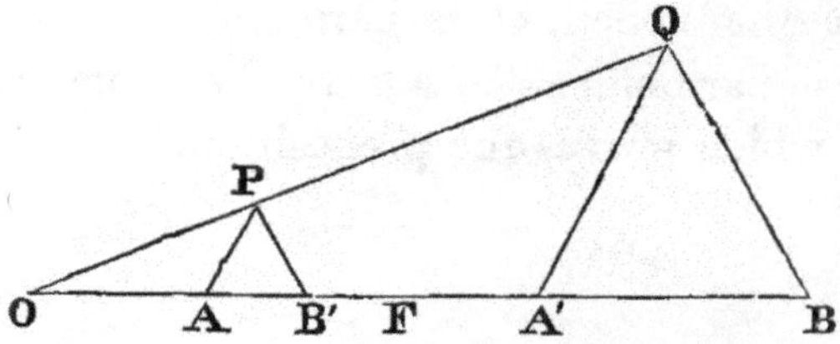

straight lines meeting the former in P, Q respectively. Then, if QP, $A'A$ meet in O,

$$OA : OA' = OP : OQ \qquad \text{[Euc. VI., 2,}$$
$$= OB' : OB, \text{ similarly.}$$

Therefore $$OA.OB = OA'.OB'.$$

Hence the centre O and *the rectangle* are determined.

19. The following are examples of two general methods by which it may be proved that a system of points is in involution.

Ex. 1. Let any number of circles be described passing through the same two points A, A', and let any straight line cut these circles in the pairs of points P, P'; Q, Q'; ....

Let the two straight lines intersect in O.

Then, $$OP.OP' = OQ.OQ' = ...,$$

since each of these rectangles is equal to $OA.OA'$. [Euc. III., 36.

Hence P, P'; Q, Q'; ... are conjugate points of a system in involution, O being the centre.

Ex. 2. Through O, the intersection of the interior diagonals of the complete quadrilateral in fig., p. 183, draw any straight line, cutting the third diagonal in O'. Let this straight line also cut the sides DA, CB in M, M', and the sides AB, DC in N, N'. Then will M, M'; N, N' be conjugate points in a system in involution which has O, O' for foci.

For, since the pencil Q is harmonic, Art. 9, the range O', M, O, M' is harmonic. Similarly the range O', N, O, N' is harmonic; which proves the proposition.

EXAMPLES.

1. If a pencil cut two transversals, neither of which is parallel to one of its rays, in the points A, B, C, D; A', B', C', D', prove by a direct method that

$$\{A'B'C'D'\} = \{ABCD\}.$$

2. If a straight line passing through a fixed point cut two fixed straight lines, the straight lines which join the points of section to two fixed points intersect on a fixed conic.

3. A straight line having one extremity on a fixed straight line moves so as to subtend constant angles at two fixed points. Prove that its other extremity traces out a conic section.

4. The sides of a triangle pass through fixed points and two of its vertices move on fixed straight lines: determine the locus of the third.

5. Given three points of a harmonic range, show how to determine the fourth by a geometrical construction.

6. If an ellipse be inscribed in a triangle and one focus move along a fixed straight line, the locus of the other focus will be a conic passing through the angular points of the triangle.

7. If the sides of a triangle pass through fixed points lying in a straight line, and if two of its vertices lie on given straight lines, the locus of the third will be a pair of straight lines passing through the intersection of the given straight lines.

8. If two triangles circumscribe a conic their angular points will lie on another conic.

9. Two triangles are constructed, such that two sides of each are tangents to a conic, the chords of contact being the third sides, prove that the six angular points lie on a conic.

10. Assuming that the pencil which joins four fixed points on a conic to a variable point on the curve is constant, prove that, if from any point on a conic pairs of perpendiculars be drawn to the opposite sides of a given inscribed quadrilateral, the rectangle contained by one pair varies at that contained by the other.

11. The square of the perpendicular from a point on a conic upon any chord varies as the rectangle contained by the perpendiculars from that point upon the tangents at the extremities of the chord.

12. Hence prove that a chord of a conic is divided harmonically by any point in its length and the point in which it intersects the chord of contact of tangents through that point.

13. If normals be drawn to a parabola from any point on the curve, the chord joining their extremities will meet the axis in a fixed point.

14. PG is a chord of an ellipse normal at P, and QR any chord which subtends a right angle at P. Prove that the opposite sides of the quadrilateral $PQGR$ intersect on a fixed straight line.

15. If A, B, C; A', B', C' be fixed points on two straight lines, and $\{A'B'C'D'\} = \{ABCD\}$, determine the envelope of DD'.

16. Find the envelope of the base of a triangle inscribed in a conic, two of its sides passing through fixed points.

17. Three pairs of conjugate diameters of a conic form a pencil in involution.

18. A straight line is cut in involution by the sides and diagonals of a quadrilateral.

19. Straight lines drawn from any point to the extremities of the diagonals of a complete quadrilateral form a pencil in involution.

20. A straight line is cut in involution by any conic and the sides of an inscribed quadrilateral.

CHAPTER XIV.

POLES AND POLARS.

The *Polar* of a fixed point with respect to a conic is the straight line which is the locus of intersection of tangents at the extremities of a chord which passes through the fixed point. See p. 87.

Conversely, if pairs of tangents be drawn to a conic from points on a fixed straight line, the fixed point through which their chords of contact pass is said to be the *Pole* of the fixed straight line.

A triangle is said to be self-conjugate with respect to a conic when each vertex is the pole of the opposite side.

1. *If a chord of a conic pass through a fixed point, the tangents at its extremities will intersect on a fixed straight line.*

Let LN be the chord of contact of tangents drawn from

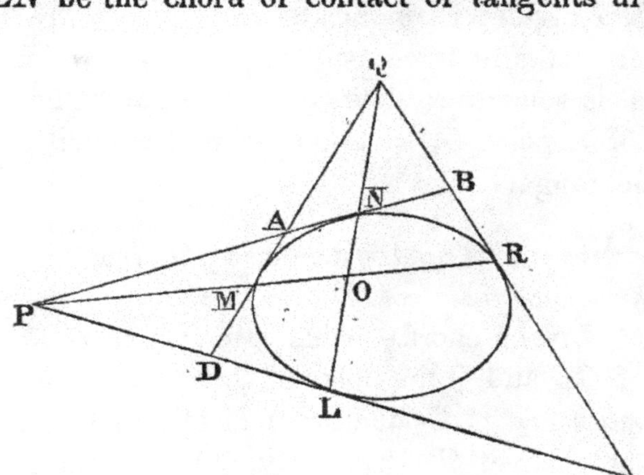

the fixed point P, and MR any chord through P, cutting LN in O. Let the tangents at M, R intersect in Q, and form with those at L, N the quadrilateral $ABCD$, as in the figure. Then P, A, N, B is the range in which the tangents at L, M, N, R cut the tangent at N. [§ 3, p. 173.

Therefore $\{PANB\} = N\{LMNR\}$ [§ 10, p. 183,

$= L\{LMNR\}$, [§ 11, p. 183,

or $\{PANB\} = \{PMOR\}$.

Since these equal ranges have the point P common, the straight lines MA, ON, RB meet in a point. [§ 4, p. 180.

Hence the tangents at M, R intersect on the fixed straight line LN.

The fixed point may lie *within* the curve, as on p. 87, or *without* it, as in the present article.

2. *A chord of a conic, drawn through any point, is cut harmonically by the point, the curve and the polar of the point.*

In the last figure QL is the polar of P.

Also $L\{LMNR\} = N\{LMNR\}$, [§ 11, p. 183,

or $\{PMOR\} = \{OMPR\}$.

Hence MR is divided harmonically in O, P. [§ 7, p. 182.

The polar of any fixed point P, through which a chord RM passes, is sometimes defined as the straight line which is the locus of a point O, so taken as to form with P, M, R a harmonic range.

3. *The intersection of any two straight lines is the pole of the line which joins their poles.*

Let RM, LN be chords which intersect in O. Let P be the polar of OQ and Q the polar of OP.

Then, since MR is divided harmonically in O, P, therefore P lies on the polar of O. Similarly, Q lies on the polar of O.

Therefore PQ is the polar of O.

4. *If a quadrilateral circumscribe a conic the intersections of its opposite sides and of its diagonals will be the vertices of a self-conjugate triangle.*

Let BA, CD and DA, CB, opposite sides of the circumscribing quadrilateral, intersect in P, Q respectively. Also let the polars of P, Q intersect in O. Then O is the pole of PQ, and the triangle OPQ is self-conjugate. Join PQ.

Then the pencil P is harmonic, since PR is the polar of Q. Hence, by the harmonic properties of a complete quadrilateral the intersection of AC, BD must lie upon PR.

For a like reason it lies also upon QL, and therefore coincides with O; which proves the proposition.

5. *If a quadrilateral be inscribed in a conic the intersections of its opposite sides and of its diagonals will be the vertices of a self-conjugate triangle.*

Let BA, CD and DA, CB, opposite sides of the inscribed

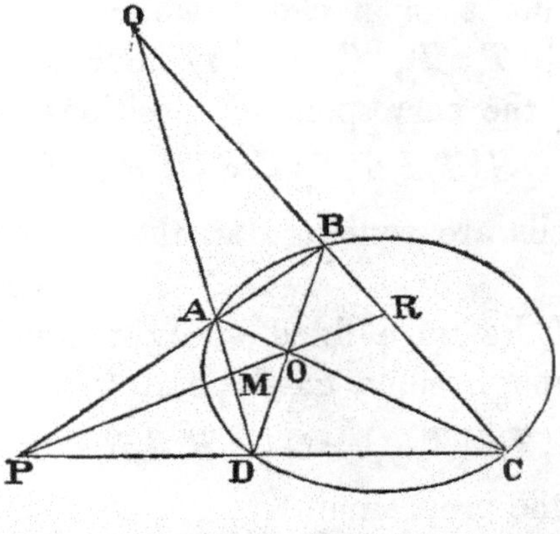

quadrilateral, intersect in P, Q respectively. Let AC, BD intersect in O, and draw $PMOR$ cutting AD, BC in M, R.

Join PQ. Then, by the harmonic properties of a complete quadrilateral, the pencil P is harmonic.

Hence, AD being cut harmonically in M and Q, the point M lies on the polar of Q. So too does R.

Therefore OP is the polar of Q, and similarly OQ is the polar of P. It follows that O is the polar of PQ and that the triangle OPQ is self-conjugate.

6. *If a quadrilateral be described about a conic and an inscribed quadrilateral be formed by joining the points of contact, then will the diagonals of the two intersect in the same point.*

Also, if the quadrilaterals be completed, they will have a common third diagonal.

The first part of the proposition was proved in Art. 4, where it was shown that the diagonals of the quadrilaterals $ABCD$, $LMNR$ intersect in O.

Also, by Arts. 4, 5, the third diagonal is in each case the polar of O, and is therefore common.

7. *The range formed by four points which lie in a straight line is equal to the pencil formed by their polars.*

Let T be the intersection of tangents to a conic (fig., p. 11) at the extremities of a chord which meets the directrix in R. Let T_1, T_2, T_3, T_4 be any four positions of T, and R_1, R_2, R_3, R_4 the corresponding positions of R.

Then $$S\{T_1T_2T_3T_4\} = S\{R_1R_2R_3R_4\},$$

for these pencils are equiangular, the angle TSR being constant. [Prop. VIII., p. 11.

Now let T lie on a fixed straight line. Then will its polar pass through some fixed point O.

Therefore $\{T_1T_2T_3T_4\} = O\{R_1R_2R_3R_4\}$, from above, which proves the proposition.

RECIPROCAL THEOREMS.

8. In consequence of the properties of polars already proved, many theorems are reciprocally related in such a manner that, when one is given, another may be immediately deduced.

Ex. 1. The theorems of Arts. 4, p. 180 and 5, p. 181 are reciprocal.

In the figure of the former article, to avoid confusion, suppose the letters A, B, ... changed into a, b, ...

In fig., p. 181, let O, O' be any two pencils which have the ray OO' common, and B, C, D the intersections of their remaining rays, taken two together in the same order.

Let a, b, c, d be the poles of the rays of the pencil O, and a, b', c', d' the poles of the rays of the pencil O'.

Then $$\{abcd\} = O\{ABCD\}.$$

Similarly $$\{ab'c'd'\} = O'\{ABCD\}.$$

Also bb', cc', dd' are the polars of B, C, D respectively. [§ 3.

Now if B, C, D lie on a straight line, then will their polars bb', cc', dd' pass through the same point.

The condition for the former is

$$O\{ABCD\} = O'\{ABCD\}.$$

Therefore the condition for the latter is

$$\{abcd\} = \{ab'c'd'\}.$$

Conversely, the latter condition being assumed, the former may be deduced.

Ex. 2. If four chords be drawn from a point P on a conic (fig., p. 184) to meet the curve again in A, B, C, D, and, if the tangents at these four points meet the tangent at P in a, b, c, d respectively, then will a, b, c, d be the poles of the four chords.

Therefore $$\{abcd\} = P\{ABCD\}.$$ [§ 7.

Now, if it be assumed that $\{abcd\}$ is constant, it follows that $P\{ABCD\}$ is constant, and conversely.

Hence the theorems in question are reciprocal.

9. *If the locus of a point be a conic the envelope of its polar will be a conic.*

Let A, B, C, D be fixed points and P any variable point. Let the polars of the fixed points, with respect to any given conic, cut the polar of P in the points a, b, c, d, which are therefore the poles of PA, PB, PC, PD. [§ 3.

Then $$\{abcd\} = P\{ABCD\}.$$ [§ 7.

Now let the locus of P be a conic passing through A, B, C, D. Then $P\{ABCD\}$ is constant. [§ 10, p. 183.

Hence, $\{abcd\}$ being constant, the polar of P touches a fixed conic. [§ 11, p. 183.

Ex. The theorems of Pascal and Brianchon are reciprocal.

For, if $ABCDEF$ (fig., p. 186) be a hexagon inscribed in a conic, the polars of its angular points will form a hexagon $abca'b'c'$ enveloping a conic, and the vertices of the latter hexagon will be the poles of the sides of the former.

Hence, if AB, ED intersect in P, then will P be the pole of one of the lines, as aa', which join opposite vertices of the enveloping hexagon. Similarly P, Q will be the poles of bb', cc'.

It follows that, if O, P, Q lie in a straight line, aa', bb', cc' will meet in a point; and conversely.

It will be found that the *proofs* of these theorems already given in Chapter XIII. are reciprocal throughout.

10. *General method of reciprocation.*

It has been proved that, if any number of points lie on a conic, their polars will envelop another conic. Hence, in reciprocating theorems which relate to conics, the words *locus* and *envelope* must be interchanged.

Similarly, *point* must be written for *line; point on a conic* for *tangent to a conic; inscribed* for *circumscribed;* &c. and conversely.

The method by which theorems are deduced from their reciprocals is called the method of *Reciprocal Polars.*

The following are examples of reciprocal theorems:

If a conic be inscribed in a triangle, the straight lines joining the points of contact to the opposite vertices meet in a point.

If a conic be circumscribed to a triangle, the tangents at the vertices meet the opposite sides in three points lying on a straight line.

If a quadrilateral circumscribe a conic, the intersections of its opposite sides and of its diagonals will be the vertices of a self-conjugate triangle.

If a quadrilateral be inscribed in a conic, the intersections of its opposite sides and of its diagonals will be the vertices of a self-conjugate triangle.

The pole of a fixed straight line, with respect to a conic inscribed in a given quadrilateral, lies on a fixed right line.

The polar of a fixed point, with respect to a conic circumscribing a given quadrilateral, passes through a fixed point.

If two triangles be polar reciprocals with respect to any conic, the intersections of their corresponding sides lie on a straight line.

If two triangles be polar reciprocals with respect to any conic, the straight lines which join their corresponding vertices meet in a point.

EXAMPLES.

1. OA, OB are tangents to a conic and CD a chord which subtends a right angle at A. Prove that, if AC bisect the angle OAB, then CD passes through O.

2. Apply the method of the present chapter to draw tangents from a given point to a conic with the help of the ruler only.

Compare Ex. 24, p. 22.

3. Four straight lines, drawn from the same point, meet a conic in A, B, C, D; A', B', C', D'. Prove that

$$P\{ABCD\}=P\{A'B'C'D'\},$$

where P is any point on the curve.

4. AB, CD are parallel chords of a conic, and DE a chord which bisects AB. Prove that the tangents at C, E intersect on AB.

5. If the tangents to a parabola and their chords of contact be produced, two and two, show that each tangent is cut harmonically.

6. A quadrilateral being inscribed in a circle, a triangle is formed by joining the points of intersection of its diagonals and opposite sides. Prove that the perpendiculars from the angular points of this triangle upon the opposite sides pass through the centre of the circle.

7. A chord of a conic which subtends a right angle at a fixed point on the curve passes through a fixed point on the normal.

8. The anharmonic ratio of the pencil formed by any four diameters of a conic is equal to that of the pencil formed by the conjugate diameters.

9. Hence deduce that the anharmonic ratio of any range is equal to that of the pencil formed by the polars of the points which constitute the range.

10. Any number of points which lie on a straight line are in involution with the points in which their polars cut the straight line. Hence deduce the result of the last example.

11. The sum of a pair of supplemental chords equally inclined to the normal at their point of intersection is equal to the diameter of the circle which is the locus of intersection of tangents at right angles.

12. PQ is a chord of a circle whose pole lies on RS. The chord QT being parallel to RS, prove that PT bisects RS.

13. The envelope of the polar of a point on the circumference of a circle, with respect to a circle whose centre is S, is a conic having S for focus.

14. Prove that the eccentricity of the conic varies directly as the distance between the centres of the circles, and inversely as the radius of the former. Hence determine in what cases the conic will be an ellipse, a hyperbola, or a parabola respectively.

15. OA, OB are tangents to a conic; C any point on the curve. Prove that if P, Q be points in AC, BC, such that OPQ is a straight line, then BP, AQ intersect on the curve.

16. A conic is inscribed in a triangle ABC, the points of contact being A', B', C'. If P be any point on $B'C'$, the straight line joining the points in which BP, CP meet AC, AB respectively touches the conic.

17. If two triangles be so related that the sides of each are the polars of the vertices of the other, their six angular points will lie on a conic.

18. If two triangles be self-conjugate with respect to the same conic, their angular points will lie on a conic.

19. If two triangles be polar reciprocals with respect to a conic, the straight lines joining their corresponding vertices meet in a point, and the intersections of corresponding sides lie in a straight line.

20. Pp, Qq are chords of a conic parallel to the tangents QT, PT respectively. Prove that the tangents at p, q intersect on the diameter through T.

CHAPTER XV.

PROJECTION.

If all points of a plane figure be joined to a point not in the same plane, the joining lines form a *Cone* of which the fixed point is vertex, and the figure in which this cone is cut by any plane is said to be the *Conical Projection*, or simply the *Projection*, of the original figure.

The plane of the original figure will be called the *Primitive Plane*, and the cutting plane the *Plane of Projection*.

1. In the figure, let the large curve represent the projection of the small curve, V being the vertex. Then the two curves are so related that a straight line drawn from V to any point on the latter curve will pass through some point on the former. The second of these points is the projection of the first.

2. The projection of a straight line, as BO, is determined by the intersection of the plane BOV, drawn through that line and the vertex, with the plane of projection. Thus the projection of BO is the *straight line* BO'.

It is evident that if a straight line pass through a fixed point, its projection will pass through a fixed point, and if the locus of a point be a straight line, that of its projection will be a straight line.

In what follows, the primitive plane and the plane of projection are supposed to be fixed. The vertex has, in each case, to be determined.

3. *To project an angle into any given angle.*

Let AOB be any angle in the primitive plane; a, b points in AO, BO respectively. On ab describe a segment of a circle (in a plane parallel to the plane of projection) containing an angle equal to that into which it is required to project AOB, and let V be any point on the segment.

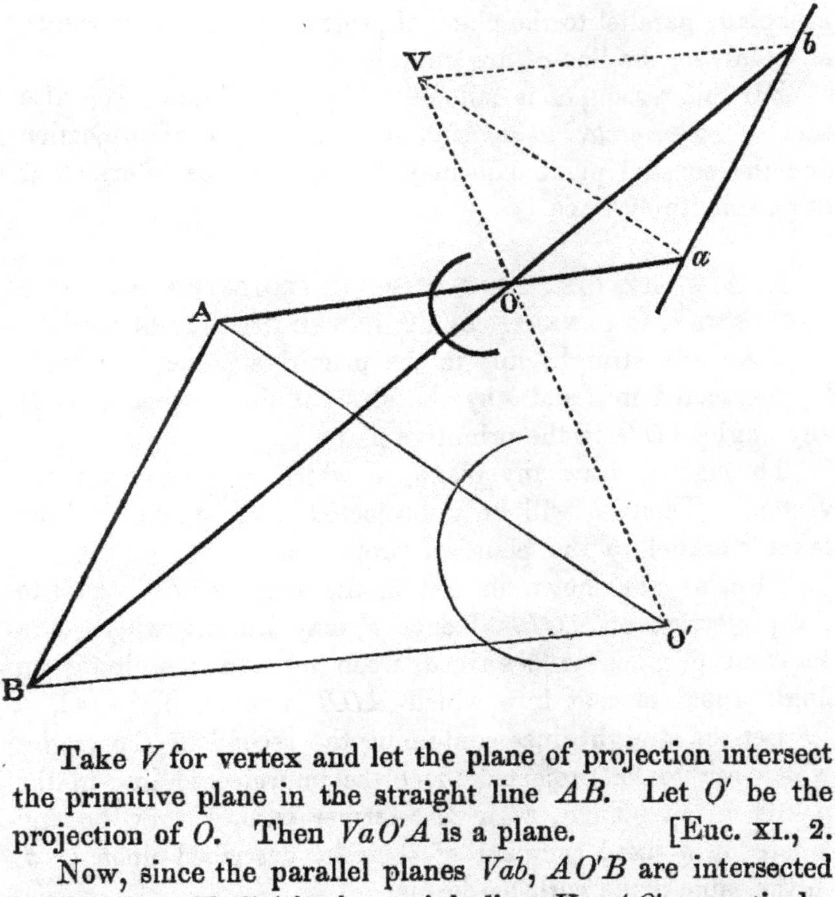

Take V for vertex and let the plane of projection intersect the primitive plane in the straight line AB. Let O' be the projection of O. Then $VaO'A$ is a plane. [Euc. XI., 2.

Now, since the parallel planes Vab, $AO'B$ are intersected by the plane $VaO'A$ in the straight lines Va, AO' respectively, therefore Va and AO' are parallel (Euc. XI., 16). Similarly Vb, BO' are parallel. Hence $\angle AO'B = aVb$. [Euc. XI., 10.

But AO' is the projection of AO, and BO' that of BO.

Hence $AO'B$ is the projection of AOB, and it is equal to aVb or to the given angle.

4. Let a plane through the vertex, parallel to the plane of projection, cut the primitive plane in the line ab. Then a straight line drawn through the vertex and any point on ab will not meet the plane of projection, since it lies wholly in a plane parallel to the plane of projection. In other words, all points on the line ab are unprojected.

For this reason, ab is called the *Unprojected* line. It is also said to be *projected to infinity*, since the plane of projection and the parallel plane Vab may be regarded as intersecting at an infinite distance.

5. ANY STRAIGHT LINE BEING UNPROJECTED, ANY TWO ANGLES MAY, IN GENERAL, BE PROJECTED INTO GIVEN ANGLES.

Take any straight line in the primitive plane, and let it be intersected in a and b by the straight lines which contain any angle AOB, in the primitive plane.

Through ab draw any plane, in which take a point V for vertex. Then ab will be unprojected if the plane Vab be taken parallel to the plane of projection.

Also, as was shown in Art. 3, the angle aVb is equal to the projection of AOB. Hence V may lie any where on a segment of a circle described upon ab and containing an angle equal to that into which AOB is to be projected.

Let the straight lines containing the second of the angles which are to be projected meet the unprojected line in the points a_1, b_1. Then, as in the former case, V may lie any where on a fixed segment of a circle, described upon a_1, b_1 in the same plane with the former.

Hence, if the intersection of the two segments be taken as vertex, the original figure will be projected as required.

The segments will not always intersect. In such cases the conditions cannot be all satisfied.

The straight line in which the plane of projection cuts the primitive plane is sometimes called the *Intersection*.

The plane through the vertex parallel to the plane of projection may be called the *Vertex Plane.*

6. *To project any quadrilateral into a square.*

Complete the quadrilateral and let the exterior diagonal be unprojected. Then the projection is a parallelogram, since the points of intersection of its opposite sides are removed to an infinite distance.

Project an angle of the quadrilateral into a right angle. The projection is then a rectangle.

Project the angle between the interior diagonals into a right angle. Thus the projection becomes a square.

7. *The anharmonic ratios of ranges and pencils are equal to those of their projections.*

Let O be any point and O' its projection; A, B, C, D

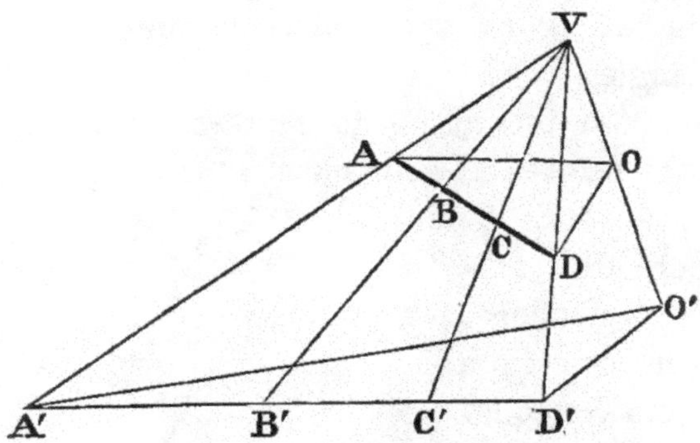

any range of a pencil whose vertex is O, and A', B', C', D' its projection; V the vertex.

Then, since all ranges of the pencil V are equal,

$$\{ABCD\} = \{A'B'C'D'\};$$

which proves the first part of the proposition.

Hence also $\quad O\{ABCD\} = O'\{A'B'C'D'\};$

which proves the second part.

8. *Conics project into conics.*

Let A, B, C, D be four fixed points on a conic; A', B', C', D' their projections: P any other point on the conic; P' its projection.

Then $$P\{ABCD\} = P'\{A'B'C'D'\}. \qquad [\S\ 7.$$

But $P\{ABCD\}$ is constant. [§ 11, p. 184.

Therefore, $P'\{A'B'C'D'\}$ being constant, the locus of P' is a conic, passing through the fixed points A', B', C', D'. [§11, p.184.

9. *To project a conic into a circle having the projection of a given point for centre.*

Take any point C and let its polar be unprojected. Then the projection of C will be the centre of the projection, the centre being that point in a conic whose polar is at infinity, since tangents at the extremities of any diameter are parallel.

Draw any chord ACA', take any two points P, Q on the conic, as in the figure, and project the angles APA', AQA' into right angles.

Now suppose the figure to represent the projection, so that C is the centre. Then, since $CA = CA'$, and P, Q are right angles, therefore $CA = CP = CQ$. Hence the projection is a circle, since it is a conic in which three real diameters are equal.

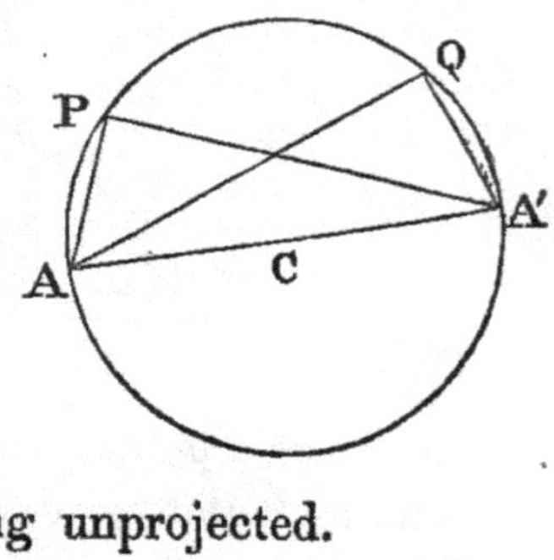

It follows that a conic may be projected into a circle, any arbitrary straight line in its plane being unprojected.

10. *Tangents project into tangents.*

For, let P, Q be adjacent points on any curve, and P', Q' their projections. Then, when Q moves up to coincidence with P, Q' moves up to coincidence with P'; and, when PQ becomes the tangent at P to the locus of P, $P'Q'$ becomes the tangent at P' to the locus of P'.

11. *The relations of pole and polar are unaltered by projection.*

For, if a chord pass through a fixed point, its projection will pass through a fixed point; and if the tangents at the extremities of the chord meet on a fixed straight line, the projections of these tangents will be tangents which intersect on a fixed straight line.

12. *To project a given conic into a parabola.*

Let any tangent be unprojected. Then the projection is a parabola, since it is a conic which has a tangent at infinity. [§ 2, p. 172.

13. *To project a conic into a conic having the projections of given points for focus and centre.*

Let C, S be the given points, and let the polar of C be unprojected. Then the projection of C is the centre of the projection.

Let CS meet RX, the polar of S, in X. Project the angle SXR into a right angle. Then the projection of S lies on an axis of the projection.

Draw any tangent RP and project the angle PSR into a right angle. Thus the projection of S becomes a focus (Prop. I., p. 6), its polar being the corresponding directrix. See Prop. II., p. 7.

14. *To project a conic into a hyperbola, of given eccentricity, and having a given point for centre.*

Let PQ, the chord of contact of tangents through any point C, be unprojected. Then, the projection of C is the centre and CP, CQ project into tangents whose chord of contact is at infinity, that is, into the asymptotes of a hyperbola. [§, p. 173.

Again, if the eccentricity of the projection be given, the angle between its asymptotes is given. Hence, if the angle

PCQ be projected into the given angle, the thing required is done.

15. *Straight lines which intersect in a point may be projected into parallel straight lines.*

Conversely, parallel straight lines project into straight lines which intersect in a point.

A system of intersecting straight lines being given, let any straight line through their point of intersection be unprojected. The point of intersection being therefore projected to infinity, the projected lines will be parallel.

Conversely, if a system of straight lines in the plane of projection be parallel, the straight lines in the primitive plane to which they correspond will meet upon the unprojected line.

16. If three pairs of lines, in the plane of projection, be parallel, the corresponding pairs of lines in the primitive plane will, by the last article, intersect upon the unprojected line.

Hence in order to prove that the intersections of three pairs of lines lie in a straight line, it will be sufficient to show that the three pairs of lines may be projected into parallels.

The same is true of any number of systems of intersecting lines.

17. Projective Properties are those which, if true for any figure, are true for any other figure into which it can be projected. The use of projection, in such cases, is to simplify the figure without diminishing the generality of the proof.

It follows from Art. 7 that anharmonic and harmonic properties are, in general, projective. Properties which relate to poles and polars are also included in this class. [§ 11.

Ex. 1. *To prove the harmonic properties of a complete quadrilateral.* [§ 9, p. 183.

Project the quadrilateral into a square. Then the diagonals form a harmonic pencil with the straight lines drawn through their intersection parallel to the sides. [§ 8, p. 182.

Hence the pencil O is harmonic, &c. [fig., p. 183.

Ex. 2. *To prove Pascal's Theorem.* [p. 186.

Let the conic be projected into a circle, the straight line which joins the intersections of two pairs of opposite sides of the inscribed hexagon being unprojected. Then the proposition is reduced (§ 16) to the following, which is easily proved.

A hexagon inscribed in a circle has two pairs of opposite sides parallel; prove that the remaining sides are parallel.

Ex. 3. *Two sides of a triangle inscribed in a conic pass through fixed points; prove that the envelope of the third is a conic.*

Let the conic be projected into a circle, the line which joins the fixed points being unprojected. Then two sides of the projected triangle are parallel to fixed lines.

Hence the third side, subtending a constant angle at the circumference and therefore at the centre, envelops a concentric circle.

ORTHOGONAL PROJECTION.

18. If from all points of any plane figure perpendiculars be drawn to a given plane, the feet of the perpendiculars trace out what is called the *Orthogonal Projection* of the original figure.

Orthogonal projection is a particular case of conical projection, since, when the vertex of the cone is removed to infinity, the generating lines become parallel.

19. *Parallel straight lines project orthogonally into parallel straight lines.*

For planes drawn through the lines perpendicular to the plane of projection are parallel, and therefore cut the plane of projection in parallel lines.

20. *Parallel straight lines are to their projections in a constant ratio.*

For if PQ be any straight line (fig., p. 144) and NM its orthogonal projection, then, the inclination of PQ, MN being constant, their ratio is also constant.

21. In general, all theorems which are true of Corresponding Points hold also in Orthogonal Projection. The connection between the methods may be exhibited as follows:

Let a circle be supposed to be orthogonally projected into an ellipse. Let the planes of the curves first move parallel to themselves until the axis of the ellipse coincides with a diameter of the circle, and then revolve about that diameter until they coincide. The distance of any point on the ellipse from the axis will then bear a constant ratio to the distance from the axis of the point of which it is the projection. Hence points and their projections are thus made to *Correspond*.

EXAMPLES.

1. The projection of a conic will be a hyperbola or an ellipse according as the unprojected line cuts or does not cut the conic.

2. Project two conics into concentric conics.

3. Project a quadrilateral inscribed in a conic into a rectangle inscribed in a circle.

4. Hence prove that the intersection of the diagonals of a quadrilateral inscribed in a conic is the pole of the line joining the intersections of its opposite sides; and that, if a second quadrilateral be formed by drawing tangents at the vertices of the first, the diagonals of the two will meet in a point.

5. Project a conic inscribed in a quadrilateral into a parabola inscribed in an equilateral triangle.

6. Project a conic circumscribing a triangle into a parabola circumscribing an equilateral triangle.

7. Project any conic into a parabola having a given focus.

8. If two triangles be such that the intersections of their corresponding sides lie on a straight line, the straight lines which join their corresponding vertices meet in a point.

9. If a quadrilateral be divided by any straight line, the diagonals of the original and the component quadrilaterals intersect in three points which lie on a straight line.

10. If a triangle be inscribed in a conic, the tangents at the vertices will intersect the opposite sides in three points which lie on a straight line.

11. Show how to project two conics into similar conics.

12. Under what circumstances is it possible to project any number of conics into similar and concentric conics?

13. Project any two conics into conics whose axes are parallel.

14. In a given conic inscribe a triangle whose sides shall pass through fixed points.

15. If through a fixed point O a line be drawn meeting a conic in P, Q, and if $\{OPQR\}$ be constant, the locus of R will be a conic having double contact with the former.

Project the fixed point to infinity and the conic into a circle. What is the result when $\{OPQR\} = 1$?

16. If a tangent to a conic meet two fixed tangents in P, Q, and a fixed straight line in R, the locus of a point S, so taken that $\{PQRS\}$ is constant, will be a conic passing through the intersections of the fixed tangents with the fixed straight line. What does this theorem become when the fixed line is projected to infinity?

17. POP', QOQ', ROR', SOS' being chords of a conic, the conics which pass through O, P, Q, R, S; O, P', Q', R', S' respectively have a common tangent at O.

18. If Pp, Qq, Rr be intersecting chords of a conic, another conic can be described touching the six lines PQ, QR, Rp, pq, qr, rP.

19. Show that there are two solutions of the problem of projecting a conic into a circle having a given centre.

20. Given a cone described upon a conic as base; determine the planes of circular section, and show that they are parallel to one of two fixed planes.

Many of the examples of previous chapters will serve also as examples on projection.

APPENDIX.

In the following articles an *Ellipse* is considered to be defined as the locus of a point, the sum of whose distances from two fixed points is constant; and a *Hyperbola* as the locus of a point the difference of whose distances from two fixed points is constant. In either case it is easily seen that the constant length is equal to AA' or $2CA$, with the usual notation.

The fixed points are called *Foci*, and will be denoted by S, H.

I. *The straight line which bisects the exterior angle between the focal distances of any point P on the ellipse is the tangent at that point.*

Draw YPZ (fig., p. 58) bisecting the angle between HP produced and SP, and let SY, drawn perpendicular to PY, meet HP in R. Then $PR = SP$.

Therefore $\qquad HR = HP + SP = AA'$.

Also, if Z be any point on the line PY, then $SZ = RZ$.

Therefore $\qquad HZ + SZ = HZ + RZ$.

Therefore $HZ + SZ$ is greater than HR or AA', except when Z coincides with P. Hence the line PY meets the ellipse in one point only, and therefore touches it.

II. It follows that *the bisector of the angle SPH, being at right angles to PY, is the normal at P.*

III. *If the normal at P, in the ellipse, meet the axis in G, then*

$$SG : SP = CS : CA.$$

Since PG bisects the angle SPH,

$$SG : HG = SP : HP. \qquad \text{[Euc. III., 2.}$$

Therefore $\quad SG : SG + HG = SP : SP + HP.$

But $\quad SG + HG = 2CS$ and $SP + HP = 2CA.$

Hence $\quad SG : SP = CS : CA.$

IV. The circle which passes through the foci of a central conic and any point P on the curve may be called the *Focal Circle* of the point P, so that Props. VI., p. 55 and VII., p. 103 may be thus enunciated:

The focal circle meets the tangent and normal in the minor axis.

V. *The distance of a point on the ellipse from either focus bears a constant ratio to its perpendicular distance from a fixed straight line.*

Let the normal at P meet the axes in G, g. Describe the circle $SPHg$.

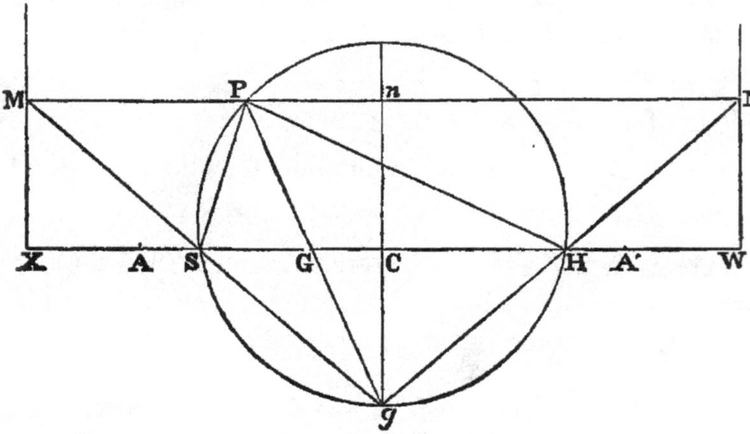

Through P draw a straight line parallel to the axis, and let it meet gS, gC, gH in M, n, N respectively. Draw MX, NW perpendicular to the axis.

Then, since angles in the same segment are equal, and the triangle gSH is isosceles,

$$\angle SPG = gHS = gSH.$$

Hence $\qquad \angle SMP = gSH \qquad$ [Euc. I. 29,

$$= SPG, \text{ from above.}$$

Also $\qquad \angle SPM = PSG. \qquad$ [Euc. I., 29.

Hence, the triangles SMP, SPG being similar, SP is to PM as SG to SP.

But $\qquad SG : SP = CS : CA. \qquad$ [§ III.

Therefore $\qquad SP : PM = CS : CA,$

or SP bears to PM the *constant ratio* of CS to CA ...... (i).

Also $\qquad SG : PM = CS^2 : CA^2.$

But, by similar triangles, the ratio $SG : PM$ is equal to $gS : gM$, which is equal, similarly, to $CS : nM$. Also $nM = CX$.

Therefore $\qquad CS : CX = CS^2 : CA^2,$

which proves that X is a fixed point, and therefore MX *a fixed straight line* .... (ii).

Similarly, NW is a fixed straight line, and

$$HP : PN = CS : CA.$$

VI. *The straight line which bisects the angle between the focal distances of any point P on the hyperbola is the tangent at that point.*

Draw SY (fig., p. 105) perpendicular to the bisector of the angle SPH and meeting HP in k. Then $Pk = SP$.

Therefore $\qquad Hk = HP - SP = AA'.$

Let Z be any point on PY. Then $SZ = kZ$.

Therefore $\qquad HZ \sim SZ = HZ \sim Zk.$

Therefore, $HZ - SZ$ being less than Hk or AA', the point Z lies on the convex side of the curve, except when it coincides with P. Hence PY is the tangent at P.

VII. Hence *the straight line which bisects the angle between HP produced and SP, being at right angles to PY, is the normal at P.*

VIII. *If the normal at P meet the axis in G, then*

$$SG : SP = CS : CA.$$

Since PG bisects the angle between HP produced and SP,

$$SG : HG = SP : HP. \qquad \text{[Euc. VI., A.}$$

Therefore $$SG : HG - SG = SP : HP - SP.$$

But $$HG - SG = 2CS \text{ and } HP - SP = 2CA.$$

Therefore $$SG : SP = CS : CA.$$

IX. *The distance of a point on the hyperbola from either focus bears a constant ratio to its perpendicular distance from a fixed straight line.*

Let the normal at P meet the axes in G, g. Describe the

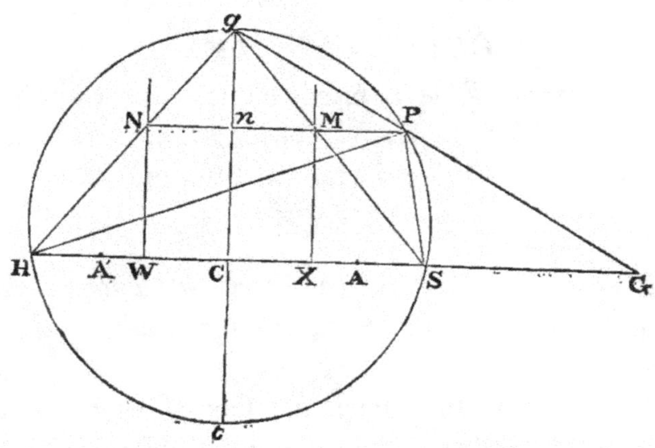

circle $SPgH$. Through P draw a straight line parallel to the axis, and let it meet gS, gC, gH in M, n, N respectively. Draw MX, NW perpendicular to the axis.

Then $\angle SPG =$ supplement of $SPg = SHg$. [Euc. III., 22.

Also $\angle SMP =$ alternate angle $HSg = SHg$.

Hence, the angles SMP, SPG being equal and also the alternate angles SPM, PSG, the triangles SMP, SPG are similar and SP is to PM as SG to SP. [Euc. VI., 7.

But $$SG : SP = CS : CA. \quad [\S\ \text{VIII.}$$

Therefore $$SP : PM = CS : CA,$$

or SP bears to PM *a constant ratio* .... (i).

Also $$SG : PM = CS^2 : CA^2.$$

But, by similar triangles, the ratio $SG : PM$ is equal to $gS : gM$, which is equal, similarly, to $CS : nM$. Also $nM = CX$.

Therefore $$CS : CX = CS^2 : CA^2,$$

which proves that X is a fixed point, and therefore *MX a fixed straight line* .... (ii).

Similarly, NW is a fixed straight line and

$$HP : PN = CS : CA.$$

X. *All diameters of an ellipse or a hyperbola pass through the centre.*

(i) Let a straight line drawn parallel to the major axis of an ellipse meet the curve in P and the minor axis in O. [fig. 1, p. 17.

In PO produced take a point Q such that $OQ = OP$.

Then $$HQ = SP \text{ and } SQ = HP.$$

Therefore $$SQ + HQ = SP + HP,$$

which proves that Q lies on the curve.

Hence the minor axis divides the curve into equal and similar parts, for, corresponding to any point P on the curve, there is a point Q, lying on the curve, equidistant with P from the minor axis.

But the major axis also divides the curve into equal and similar parts. Hence AA' and BB' (fig., p. 64) divide the curve into four equal and similar parts.

It follows that all chords through C are bisected in that point, and hence that all diameters pass through C, a diameter being a straight line which bisects a system of parallel chords. [Prop. XII., p. 15.

(ii) In the case of the hyperbola it may be shown (fig. 2, p. 17) that

$$HP - SP = SQ - HQ,$$

where P, Q are equidistant from the minor axis.

Hence it may be shown, as in the case of the ellipse, that all diameters pass through C.

XI. With the construction of the Lemma, p. 14, OC is equal to $\frac{1}{2}SP$, and the radius of the circle to $\frac{1}{2}SQ$.

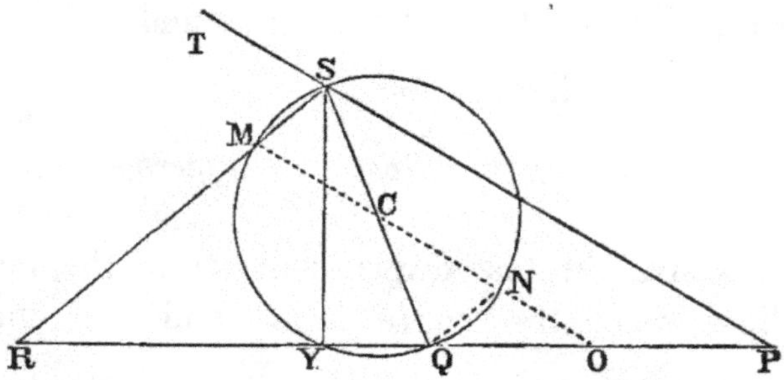

Therefore $OM = OC + CM = \frac{1}{2}(SP + SQ)$ ....(i),

and $ON = OC - CN = \frac{1}{2}(SP - SQ)$.........(ii).

Again, $ON.OM = OQ.OY$. [Euc. III., 36, Cor.

Therefore $OY : OM = ON : OQ$

$= OM : OR$, [Euc. VI., 2,

or $OY.OR = OM^2$ .... (iii).

Similarly $OY.OR' = ON^2$ .... (iv),

R' being the point in which SN, the internal bisector of the angle PSQ, meets PQ.

It has also been shown (p. 188) that

$$OR.OR' = OQ^2 \text{.....................(v)},$$

and (p. 14) $$OY : OR = SP^2 : PR^2 \text{............(vi)}.$$

Let an ellipse and a hyperbola be described, having P, Q for foci and passing through S. Then SR touches the former, and SR' the latter. Also QM, QN are perpendicular to SR, SR'.

Hence the results (i)—(iv) correspond respectively to Props. IX., p. 57; IX., p. 104; XV., p. 62; XIII., p. 108.

Also (v) and (vi) may be written, with the more usual notation,

$$CG.CT = CS^2,$$

and $$CN : CG = SP^2 : SG^2$$

$$= CA^2 : CS^2. \text{ [Prop. IX., p. 12.}$$

XII. *The chord of curvature of a parabola, drawn parallel to the axis through any point P, is equal to $4SP$.*

In fig. p. 152 suppose PU to be drawn parallel to the axis, instead of through the focus, and let PV be the abscissa of Q. The rest of the construction being the same as before, denote the focus by S'.

Then $$QV^2 = 4S'P.PV, \quad \text{[Prop. IX., p. 30,}$$

and $$PT^2 = TQ.TH. \quad \text{[Euc. III., 36, Cor.}$$

But QV, PT are equal.

Hence $$TQ.TH = 4S'P.PV.$$

Also $TH = PU$ ultimately; and $TQ = PV$.

Therefore $$PU = 4S'P.$$

XIII. The notation $S\{R\}$ may be used to express the anharmonic ratio of the pencil formed by joining any four positions of a variable point R to the vertex S. If T be a second variable point connected with the former, then $S\{T\}$ expresses the anharmonic ratio of the pencil formed by joining to S the four *corresponding* positions of T. These expressions may be regarded as abbreviations of $S\{R_1R_2R_3R_4\}$, $S\{T_1T_2T_3T_4\}$.

The following article will exemplify the use of the above notation.

XIV. *If a chord of a conic pass through a fixed point, the tangents at its extremities will intersect on a fixed straight line.*

Let a chord drawn through a fixed point O meet the

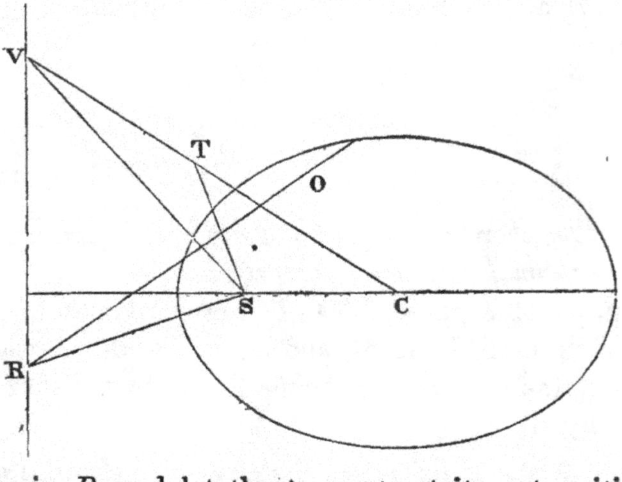

directrix in R, and let the tangents at its extremities intersect in T. Draw CT, from the centre, to meet the directrix in V. Join SV, ST.

Then TSR is a right angle. [Prop. VIII., p. 11.

Therefore $$S\{T\} = S\{R\} = O\{R\}.$$

But SV is perpendicular to OR. [Cor. 2, p. 16.

Therefore $$O\{R\} = S\{V\} = C\{V\}.$$

Hence $$S\{T\} = C\{V\} = C\{T\},$$

or $$S\{T_1T_2T_3T_4\} = C\{T_1T_2T_3T_4\}.$$

Let T_1 lie on the axis. Then the equal pencils S, C have the axis for a common ray.

Hence the locus of T is a straight line. [§ 5, p. 181.

XV. *Any two conjugate points of a system in involution form with the foci a harmonic range.*

The two ranges formed by any four points and their conjugates are equal, and either focus is, by definition, its own conjugate. Hence, if A, A' be conjugate points and F, F' the foci,

$$\{AFA'F'\} = \{A'FAF'\},$$

which proves the proposition. [§ 7, 182.

XVI. The anharmonic ratio of the pencil formed by joining four fixed points on a circle to a variable point on the curve is constant, for its angles are constant since they stand upon fixed arcs.

XVII. Props. III., IV., VIII.—X., Chapter II. are the geometrical equivalents of the following analytical results:

(i) *Polar equation of a conic.*

Let e denote the eccentricity and θ the angle PSX. [fig., p. 12.

Then $$PK = SP - SG\cos(\pi - \theta)$$
$$= SP + e.SP\cos\theta.$$ [Prop. IX., p. 12.

Let $$PK = l \text{ and } SP = r.$$

Therefore $$l = r + e.r\cos\theta,$$

or $$\frac{l}{r} = 1 + e\cos\theta.$$

(ii) *Polar equation of the tangent to a conic.*

Let $$\angle TSX = \theta \text{ and } \angle PSX = \alpha.$$ [fig., p. 7.

Then $$SX = TN + ST\cos\theta.$$

Therefore $$e.SX = SL + e.ST\cos\theta$$ [Prop. III., p. 7,
$$= ST\cos(\alpha - \theta) + e.ST\cos\theta.$$

But $e.SX = l$. Hence, if $ST = r$,

$$l = r\cos(\alpha - \theta) + e.r\cos\theta,$$

or

$$\frac{l}{r} = e\cos\theta + \cos(\alpha - \theta).$$

(iii) *Polar equation of the chord of a conic.*

From any point T' on QR (fig., p. 12) draw $T'N$ perpendicular to the directrix, and $T'L$ parallel to RS or perpendicular to ST. [Prop. VIII., p. 11.

Let $\angle T'SX = \theta$; $\angle TSP = \beta$; $\angle TSX = \alpha$.

Then, if ST, $T'L$ intersect in O,

$$SL\cos\beta = SO = ST'\cos(\alpha - \theta).$$

Also $SX = ST'\cos\theta + T'N$.

Therefore $e.SX = e.ST'\cos\theta + SL$ [Prop. IV., p. 8,

$$= e.ST'\cos\theta + ST'\sec\beta\cos(\alpha - \theta).$$

But $e.SX = l$. Hence, if $ST' = r$,

$$l = e.r\cos\theta + r\sec\beta\cos(\alpha - \theta).$$

Therefore

$$\frac{l}{r} = e\cos\theta + \sec\beta\cos(\alpha - \theta).$$

THE END.

CPSIA information can be obtained
at www.ICGtesting.com
Printed in the USA
LVHW040426110522
718423LV00002B/443

9 783375 006945